CHEATING
DEATH

JOHN DRAKE

For information about the story, contact;

johndrakewriter@gmail.com

@JohnDrakeWriter on Twitter

Credits:

Cheating Death written by John Drake/published by John Drake–
1st edition, 2019

Cheating Death written by John Drake/published by Three Ravens
Publishing – 2nd edition, 2020

Cover art by Colin Brennan

Cover Photo by Phil Drake - Twitter @PhilDrakePhoto

ISBN: 978-1-951768-04-1

With thanks to Peter Nowlan and Catherine Nowlan for editing
assistance.

FOR KIARA

If you can make one heap of all your winnings
And risk it on one turn of pitch-and-toss,
And lose, and start again at your beginnings
And never breathe a word about your loss;

If you can trust yourself when all men doubt you,
But make allowance for their doubting too;
If you can bear to hear the truth you've spoken
Twisted by knaves to make a trap for fools;

If you can wait and not be tired by waiting,
Or being lied about, don't deal in lies,
If you can meet with Triumph and Disaster
And treat those two impostors just the same;

If you can talk with crowds and keep your virtue,
Or walk with Kings – nor lose the common touch,
Yours is the Earth and everything that's in it,
And – which is more – you'll be a Man, my son!

If ~ Rudyard Kipling

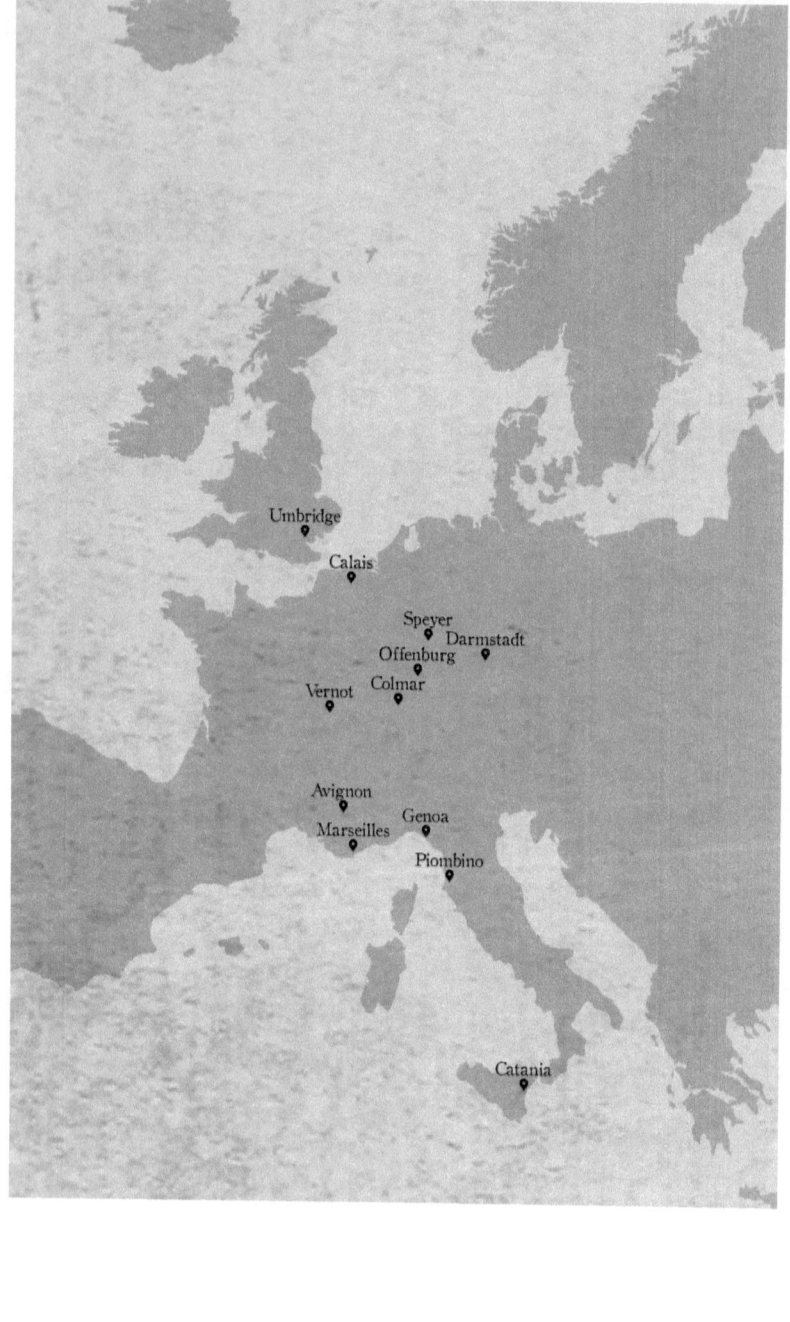

PROLOGUE

CATANIA, SICILY

6th December, 1332

Nicolo Anatra looked again at the ornate wooden door of the Church of St Augustine the Meek. Through those imposing doors lay adventure, he knew. To most it was a place of worship, a sparsely furnished stone building with few distractions from their zealous piety during mass, but Nicolo was a boy whose existence was rarely troubled by such passions. He worked at his family's market stall during the daylight hours of every day, despite his tender age, gutting the fish that his father, Franco, caught before the sun rose each morning. The only typical deviation from this routine were the feast days his father deemed important, or convenient enough to honour. On such days Nicolo would be marched to the church to listen to the myriad ways his soul could be denied its eternal salvation, like merchants convincing a crowd that failure to buy their unique and exotic cloth was an undeniable precursor to them perishing in the upcoming winter. After all, it was said to become the coldest in living memory as any cloth merchant would tell you. Those selling sleeveless tunics would tell you something quite different, of course.

Inside the church was always cooler than the summer heat and warmer than the winter chill, perhaps the only evidence Nicolo could identify for the existence of a higher being. He was not a religious boy, unlike almost everyone else in the town. He was raised on facts, not conjecture, on problem-solving, not self-doubt, and with a distinct focus on how to get to the end of the day with more than he had when he woke, be it financially, physically or emotionally. His father was a pragmatic man, content to pour his efforts into keeping his family away from starvation more than worrying about his soul. Why would he invest in something intangible when he could hold two fish in his hands, from which the subsequent payment could be turned into five loaves? This was the closest he ever got to being philosophical. Any show of faith was done as much to keep his family safe from the tyrannical observations of the religious authorities than to ensure their ticket to the preferred afterlife of the time.

Today was the feast of Saint Nicolo of Undetermined Origin, a day that young Nicolo always looked forward to more than the priests themselves. This was his day, once a year, when he was free to do as he pleased, released from the burden of being an only child in a working family. Such was the dearth of frivolous activities in Catania for a boy of eight summers, he usually found himself retreating to familiar haunts to explore them with more vigour than he could when the shackles of parental conformity kept him away from the exciting parts.

The Church of St Augustine the Meek held a host of hidden alcoves and private corners for him to explore. He had no interest in the few valuable treasures adorning the sills and walls, other than to curse them for giving him a locked door to negotiate. Even at eight years old, however, he was determined enough to find an answer to the problem. He scouted around to the right of the building, stroking the trunks of the apple trees with an outstretched hand as he went. He picked a dull red apple from a low branch and bit into it hungrily. The majority of people in Catania lived on grain, bread, and fish. The population growth of recent years meant that all available land was used to grow enough wheat to maintain the expanding throngs and so there was no space for luxuries like fruit and meat, other than for the noblemen and religious leaders of course. They needed to stay strong and well-nourished to protect the masses from temptation and the perils of greed.

He threw the apple core into the long grass and studied his options. The main windows of the small church were too high for a boy of his size but he knew that, more often than not, outcomes that seemed unattainable at first inspection were often not so when you really studied the situation. *Things often seem impossible, until they are done* was a motto that shaped his imagined life of escapism.

He looked to his right and made his way further into the church grounds. As he rounded the outer wall of the transept he noticed a single, small window that sat lower than the rest, with a hole in the thin pane of dull, translucent glass. It was still too high for him to clamber up himself, and the gap itself was too small even for him. He looked about the churchyard for something to raise him up. The apple trees didn't extend around the corner and were too far from the church walls in any case. Surrounding the building at a distance of about twenty paces was a stone wall that ran continuously around the yard, broken only by the main entrance and a smaller, narrower opening that led to the cemetery. In there was his favourite gravestone, a strange thing to have, but then Nicolo was a strange boy. It read:

"Here lies Giancarlo, killer of bees and warden of the lands of hope. Remember him when you hope for honey, but find a bruise on your elbow."

It was an enigmatic message to leave for all eternity above your bones and had just the right levels of mystery and humour to echo in Nicolo's thoughts for longer than a headstone should. By the time he himself had died, he decided, he would have come up with a similarly perplexing epitaph.

He walked past and on to the last side of the church. About halfway down the wall some of the larger stones had fallen from their places to form a small heap. He hefted one of them from the top of the pile, quickly dropping it as its weight revealed itself. If he could move these boulders over to the window he could raise himself to the level of the broken pane and study how he might crawl into the adventure beyond. He started with the largest, rolling it all the way to the window before returning to repeat the process with the smaller ones. Before too much of his free time was used he had rebuilt the pile of stones against the church and climbed up to the sill, placing his elbows across it to better study the glass. About half of it had gone, leaving a misshapen hole between him and exploration. He would have to smash the remaining glass if he was to get inside and even then it would be a tight squeeze. He had done nothing so far that could get him into trouble with his father, or at least nothing he couldn't talk his way out of with a few well-constructed apologies and his wide, innocent eyes, and he knew he was at a pivotal moment.

Simply being somewhere he should not have been, in this case the church outside of service time, would not cause any financial penalty, just an emotional one. He knew, though, that if he broke the glass then his father would have to pay for it to be replaced, and in turn so would Nicolo. It was all too easy to imagine his father looming over him, his bald pate glistening in the Sicilian sunshine as he meted out some onerous punishment. The only logical course of action then was to remove the glass without breaking it. He may then be able to replace it on his return, like a burglar locking the door on his way out. He used his fingers, strong and sinewy from years of nimble gutting of his father's fish, to work at the hard putty that kept this part of the window intact when the other broke away. He sharpened a twig to get into the tiny gap between the stone and the pane and gradually worked the window loose. After some gentle wobbling back and forth it came free with a sudden jolt, sending his elbow into the hard stone wall and almost bouncing the glass from his hand. He steadied himself, climbed down the rubble and placed the glass a few paces away in the grass.

The opening was tight, but enough. He put his arms through and out to the sides as if swimming and pushed his torso into the sacred space. As he edged his hips through he realised he was past the point of no return with no way to reach the distant floor. The ground around the outside of the church had built up over time and the floor there was much higher than on the inside. His eyes widened as his muscles strained against the cold stone. He was also aware that he was pointing head first at the soon-to-be unyielding tiles.

The only option available to him was to fall in such a way as to not land on his rather important head. He pushed off with his hands, curling his body as it came free from the snug fit of the window, and fell. He was hoping to land on his feet, which he didn't. He also failed to crack his head on the floor, however, and so was satisfied with his efforts as he landed with a painful thud on his coccyx.

He raised himself to a crouch, rubbing his lower back as he did so, and felt a rush of adrenalin. This was far and away the most exciting and dangerous thing he had ever done, more daring even than stealing a loaf of black bread from the table at Signore Bonetti's birthday party. Above him were the new wooden beams, paid for by the tithes the poor gave so generously to keep the devil at bay and made from the trees the lords cut down to build more houses for their profitable tenants. In every way the priests grew their share of spoils beyond that which could reasonably be described as complimentary to their vows of poverty. The grey stone walls towered over him on either side, their coloured windows casting rainbow shadows across the floor. Far ahead was the transept that had captured his imagination from the moment he saw it. It ran across the front of the altar, creating the building's cross shape and hiding parts of the church from his view in the nave during mass. The strict discipline of the services meant that he had never seen their secrets, despite the frequency of his visits with his father and mother. He got to his feet and made his way through the kneeling pews until the alcove came into view.

He paused for a moment, savouring the moment that was to come. He was sure he would finally be creating his own adventure, his first anecdote of any value to retell to his friends. Once he made some.

His shoulders sagged as he took in the full view of the transept. To his right was a small tapestry of a lamb, made smaller by the mass of dull grey wall that surrounded it. Light from the coloured windows splashed across the floor in front of him and onto the wall to his left. The rest of the transept was disappointingly empty. He trudged around the space despondently, as much to be able to say he had been there than to do any meaningful exploration. He kicked out absent-mindedly at a small stone on the floor and was surprised to hear a metal clang a second later. He peered into a shadowy corner and could just make out a break in the grey uniformity of the wall. There was a gate here, small but inviting. The rusted bolt holding it together gave way almost imperceptibly as he rocked the cylinder back and forth. After a minute or so it came free and he heaved the metal gate open, releasing a loud and ancient creak to bounce off the old walls. Inside was as black as the heart of a mountain. Without pausing to consider the perils, Nicolo stretched a foot into the low doorway, finding a step and passing his full weight onto it. Down it went, a pathway to hell.

His eyes were useless here, like a lobster pot in the hills. The air became noticeably dank and in parts the stairs were slippy with a green film of slime. After perhaps a dozen steps he was stopped in his tracks by a wall directly in front of him. What a disappointing result it would be if this was simply a dead end, he thought. He felt to his right and found a wall, so searched to his left with his fingers, slowly stepping in that direction as it became clear there was a longer tunnel there. The steps soon began again before ending at an enjoyably flat floor of undeterminable size. He crept into the presumed space before stumbling into something hard at chest height, cold stone that knocked him backwards in shock. Had he been able to see, it would have been merely a surprise, but everything is accentuated in pitch blackness, including a boy's imagination. He felt in front of him again, fumbling in the air until his fingers gripped around what might have been a rounded edge of a shelf. He allowed it to lead him along in the dark, turning to the right occasionally until he guessed he was back where he started. He tried to imagine what it could be, but all he could come up with was that it was an altar of sorts, though he couldn't understand why it would be down here in this cold, damp place. He crouched down to feel below the shelf, playing his fingers across the bumps and depressions of the stone. Most of it was impossible to identify by touch alone, but he was able to make out a cross in the centre and on either side was a raised, rounded feature with a square protrusion at its base. In the same moment that he realised these were skulls a clanging noise far above him froze him to the spot. The unmistakable jangle of keys became louder as a petrified Nicolo continued to remain motionless.

'Santo scassinatore! What has happened?' came a panicked voice from the top of the steps.

Nicolo was trapped. Deacon Lorenzo was above him, doubtless neutralising his only escape route. He had heard of a boy who was hanged for stealing a candle from the cathedral in Palermo, although he wasn't sure how true that was. He was surely going to be in serious trouble now, not least from his father. He may not have been a religious man by local standards but his livelihood depended on an appearance of godliness and news of a blasphemous thief in the family would ruin him. Nicolo's feeling of terror mingled nauseously with guilt and self-deprecating admonishment at not having planned this adventure thoroughly enough. In that moment he vowed to never again be left without an escape route, whether physically or verbally.

He considered his options. He was now sure he had burrowed into a catacomb, which meant there was a dead body within the sarcophagus he was now leaning on. He listened again to the keys clinking outside the stairwell and headed to the far side of the room, hiding behind the tomb despite the darkness. He distilled his thoughts and formulated an escape.

Lorenzo stared at the open gate. He knew the church had been locked, he himself had done so after the dawn service and he had also just unlocked it himself to get in. Perhaps the gate had been open for days, the transept was used so infrequently that little attention was paid to it. Given the choice, he would have preferred to simply lock the small gate again and forget all about it rather than venture into the blackness. As it happened, he did have a choice and so rummaged through the heavy iron keys for the right one. He crouched down beside the opening and began to creak the gate shut. He had closed it to about halfway when he heard an ethereal noise from below, shaking him to his core and toppling him backwards. Nicolo had lowered his voice as much as he could. The effect of this on his eight year old voice was to produce an uncommon noise somewhere between a child's and an adult's tone, one that is normally skipped entirely as a boy's voice breaks. He had listened to enough of Padre Filippo's sermons to know the vague language he should use, and had a sense that any contrition he ordered should be completed within a very specific timeframe.

'Lorenzo Di Cassio! I have seen you and I have heard you from the other side. I know the secrets you dare not tell. Go now and do not return for ten days and ten nights!' he bellowed. *'And you should eat only fish too, I hear Signore Anatra sells a lovely skate'* he added. Some good may come of this yet, he thought.

Lorenzo dropped the keys and ran through the main door of the church, his black and white cassock flapping behind him as he went. A few minutes later Nicolo climbed the stairs and stepped out into the brightness of the transept. He picked up the keys, locked the small gate behind him and walked out through the large ornate wooden doors at the front of the church. He left the heavy ring of keys in the large, sturdy lock and scampered clear of the church.

CHAPTER ONE

GENOA
November, 1347

Nicolo's wobbling reflection looked back at him from the basin as he ran his hands through his dark hair, ruffling it just enough to remove any lingering evidence of money, but not so much as to allow an inference that he lived without a roof. His job required him to exude several traits at once in perfect harmony. Some he did not possess but could engineer, such as honesty and integrity, and some he held in glorious abundance, like persuasiveness and confidence. He had an ability unique among those he had encountered on his travels to blend these together to form a *talent*. He was like a chef on a tightrope.

He pulled a grey tunic over his head and patted it down before sitting on last night's bed of straw and wool to put on his shoes. As was his habit, he checked the collection of gold rings on the necklace at his chest and contented himself that they were hidden. He had a routine of sorts, as much as a wanderer can have such a thing, although he wouldn't have called himself a wanderer of course, had he been asked. He considered himself more of a mobile tradesman. His particular trade of choice required frequent changes of location on the grounds of personal safety and his penchant for living. One minute he was entertaining a crowd, the next he was hurtling down the cobble stones of a nameless town to escape the clutches of a recently disgruntled customer.

This morning he felt at home, however. His latest residence was on Banchina del Mercante in the heart of the bustling noise of the Genoese docks, as vibrant and eclectic a place as there was in the world. From his view through the small, narrow slit in the wall of his rented room he could see ships of all sizes being loaded and emptied. The unmistakable waft of seafood filled his thin nostrils and his memories sent him back to his father's stall in Catania all those years ago. He had left there at a rather brisk pace five years earlier, an exit for which he was utterly unprepared, following a *misunderstanding* with a local carpenter. Nicolo had been very clear about the rules of engagement in his street-side game of chance but the wood worker with arms the size of a bullock's thigh and a temper to match mustn't have been listening, a quality that Nicolo usually hoped for in his customers but that could just as easily be his downfall and the catalyst for him to find fresh crowds further up the road.

He had caught a boat to Salerno and never looked back. There was nothing left for him in Catania, he had convinced himself. His mother had left this world when he was just fourteen after an overly-exuberant discussion with Mortina the Urn Maker concerning the benefits of burial over cremation, the upshot of which was a fulfilled promise by the urn maker to allow her to find out for herself. For all Nicolo knew, his father still ran the fish stall in the market, although he had had no contact with him since the incident with the carpenter. His father had never approved of Nicolo's choice of profession; there was too much risk involved and not enough repeat business for his liking. Franco was a patient man, but not infinitely so. They had gradually grown apart until Nicolo moved out of the family home aged fifteen, and the times when they would meet to catch up on each other's news diminished almost out of existence.

Now he was twenty three and living in Genoa, for the moment at least. He had fallen in love with the city as soon as its maze of buildings and masses of hurried people came into view on his approach from the south. The city had welcomed him with open pockets and he had accrued a sizable wealth for a man of his lowly position. He could afford a private room above a bakery and ate red meat at least once a month while the rest of the population fed themselves to the limit of their finances, mostly with bread and thin soups. Nicolo was experienced enough to know that this was likely to be an exception in a rather volatile career. For a while he had hoarded his coin in a heavy and securely locked wooden box, one that had cost him a month's earnings some years before, and he had made sure to add something to it every day, even if that was to the detriment of his meals. His father's practicality was an unusual trait for someone in his line of work, though, and it helped him to the realisation that holding his wealth in such a weighty way was impractical for someone who often needed to be able to exit a scene quickly. He began to exchange his coins for small, light, expensive items that could be carried covertly on his person. Under his tunic were the gold rings, of course, but there was also the small tapestry of the crucifixion sewn onto the inside of his trousers and the band of Roman leather keeping his underwear up.

It was in this way that Nicolo's appearance remained poor – but not too poor – as his wealth grew. A street entertainer dressed in gold and asking for money rarely received any. A charismatic and honest man, however, trying to scratch out a meagre living for his four daughters and sick wife, none of whom existed but whose likenesses sat on the floor in front of him, was a sure fire way to increase the generosity of the passing trade.

He only used games he himself had created to avoid the chance, however slim, of a customer having seen the ruse beforehand. His current game of choice was *Simple Stones*. He insisted on naming each of his games too; a name is part of something's identity and if he could sway perception even slightly towards his favour then he would take advantage of the opportunity. This was the art of the entertainer, as he saw it. To him there was no magic arrow, no golden rule by which to practise your art. The art was in the compacted layers of tiny things, of giving the game a prejudiced name, of wearing simple clothes but not too simple, of the images of his four daughters, of the deliberate loss of small coins every so often. When all of these were included in the recipe, then his deceitful kitchen usually produced a cake that smelled of money.

He would show his customer two small, flat stones; one jet black and one of purest white. The stones around Genoa were mostly middling shades of grey but on his journey up from the south he had found these two small stones and kept them in the hope that they would seem exotic to somebody, somewhere. It is the differences that mark something out as special, not the similarities, and tradesmen of his ilk needed to have *special things* by the cartload. He would place one in each hand, with his upturned palms open and flat. In one smooth action he would then turn them over, slamming his hands onto the floor as he did so. The key to this game was to allow your hands to descend as slowly as possible so as to give the illusion of transparency, yet not so slow that the stones fell from your hands. To the sceptical viewer the skill lay in flicking the white stone over to the left without it being noticed. Nicolo's talent, however, manifested itself in a different way. The sleight of hand was easy, where the skill really lay was in reading the customer. For those he deemed innocent he would indeed move the stone across, to the amazement of the onlooker, but he was usually able to spot when a customer suspected foul play and for those he would simply slam his hands down without changing the positions of the stones. They too would widen their eyes in surprise when the stone was not where they knew it would be. Over the years he had mastered this perceptive skill until all that was left for him to decide was when to lose.

Today was different, though. Today was going to be memorable. He hoped it was also going to be profitable, but either way he would be recanting the tale of it to the friends he would surely make soon until they were bored enough to go and listen to a padre's sermon rather than hear the tale again. His travels up from Sicily to Genoa along the trade-filled edges of the kingdom of Naples, the Papal States and the Holy Roman Empire, had honed his skills to the point of boredom. When he docked at Salerno he was a boy with an idea. Now he was a man with a talent so perfected and so compatible with transient populations that its complexities had long since ceased to be a challenge for him. After so long in Genoa the lustre of its vibrancy had begun to diminish and he found himself hungry for something less predictable. He had played his last game of Simple Stones and for that reason alone he was already feeling energised. His next step was to be more of a running leap between tall buildings.

He had toyed with the idea of risking slightly more to gain slightly more but surmised that he would eventually become bored of whatever new game he designed as time went by. With this in mind he turned his attention to the other end of the spectrum. He had identified the most powerful man in all of Genoa, its doge Giovanni di Murta, and set himself to conjuring a scheme that would see him reallocate a sizable portion of his wealth into Nicolo's welcoming pockets. If he failed, then at least he would have finally found a limit to his talent.

Nicolo knew he must be meticulous with his planning; the only real problem he faced was in knowing how much forethought was enough. There were few precedents when it came to stealing from the leader of a republic and so he applied the same logic that initially inspired this grand escapade. When he became bored of the planning he would begin the doing.

The time had come.

CHAPTER TWO

Nicolo felt the cloth of his tunic absent-mindedly. Realising that today his gold rings need not be hidden he looped the necklace back over his head, untied the knot and slipped the shiny metal hoops over several of his fingers. On the ring finger of his left hand he placed the dullest of them all, one he had been working on for days. It had been a simple silver ring with a large white stone set into it when he bought it a year ago in Lucca. Nicolo had paid more for the paint he used to add the crimson cross and gold stripes on either side than he did for the ring itself, and had been careful to add a rough patina to its surface. To an untrained eye it would look like the crest of some important institution. To a trained one it could be anything.

A lesser conman would have this one ring as the only one on show, but Nicolo knew that subtlety was what set him apart from his peers, and was as vital to him as the ring itself. The addition of the others, more valuable than the silver one, showed him to be a man of money, a dignitary perhaps, as well as underplaying the value of the crucial ring.

He had applied the same logic when choosing his outfit. He would dress in the same clothes he wore on the streets, with one subtle exception. A rich man may disguise his wealth when walking the streets, so as not to be relieved of some of it, but not to the point of discomfort. With this in mind he had procured a fine pair of leather shoes, as new as he could afford, and kept them for today. When the time came he would ensure they poked out from below his clothing, just enough to be seen by those who needed to be convinced.

He was ready.

He stood up from his bed, took one last look in the reflective water of the basin and, after a minor adjustment to his hair, stepped over the threshold of his room and down the stairwell to the bakery.

It occurred to him that he may never see this place again. He wasn't upset about it, he had no emotional attachment to it, but the feeling of finality was an intriguing perspective. He stepped into the bustle of the docks and was almost knocked over by an old woman with a basket of heavy black bread so large that Nicolo himself would have struggled to lift it. He zigzagged through the crowds of Banchina del Mercante and onto Viale dei Soldi, the 'avenue of money'. From here it was an almost straight line up to the Palazzo Pubblico and the realisation of his grand plan, for good or ill.

Whether by design or convenient chance, the façade of the Palazzo loomed over anyone walking in the piazza that led to the main entrance. The great high walls spoke of wealth and power, but the walls were not the greatest problem for Nicolo; it was the two guards at the front of the enormous wooden door. As a small boy the doors of Saint Augustine the Meek had seemed overbearing but they were a fraction of the size and complexity of those hinged to the Palazzo of Genoa. He planned to stride through them confidently, for the lack of any other clear option. There seemed to be no obvious weakness elsewhere, and certainly no low windows to climb through as he had all those years ago in Catania. He had spent many days curled into an alcove in the piazza, feigning homelessness to better study the movements of the staff within and without the palace. Timing was critical, and the subtlety of his plan was in the reliance on human nature to seek out the path of least resistance when one's goal is almost in sight. In this case, he relied on his premise that the guards were at their most vulnerable just before the shift change after hours in the hot Genoese sun. They wore a striking dark green and bright red uniform of thick, sweltering cloth with more frills than were quite necessary. There were always two stationed at the door at all times, each with a long spear resting against the other to form an 'X'. Ostensibly these were for show, a display of strength and a warning against transgression, but a spear is a spear. Ornamental or not, it would still pass through Nicolo with more ease than he would prefer should they take a dislike to him. After all, it was surely quite a dull job to be a guard at the Palazzo Pubblico and a good impaling could do wonders for a bored spirit.

Deceit came naturally to Nicolo and he was rarely anxious before a show. Today was different. Today the stakes were higher than ever before, and possibly alight in flames under his bound arms and feet too if he wasn't careful. Taking a long, deep breath he puffed out his chest, making himself seem as confident and important as he could manage, and strode up to the protectors of the palace.

'Come on man!' he bellowed with a wave of his arms. 'I haven't got all day.'

Mattimeo and Chiasmo were veteran door-guarders and could remain motionless in the teeth of a gale with a riot exploding across the piazza in front of them and a dog chewing at their ankles. A single man dressed like a common merchant held no fears for them.

'What on earth are you playing at? Let me pass at once, I have vital news for the doge from the House of Fortalino. If Master Sigliano hears of this insubordination you will wish you had been less obstructive to the work of the Lord.'

The House of Fortalino and Master Sigliano were entirely fictional, of course, but information travelled slowly down the chain of command and Nicolo was confident they wouldn't question his assertions once he had played his hand. He had added a suggestion of religious work to cement his ruse. Nobody would dare to use the word of the Lord for ill work, the threat of eternal damnation being a rather good axe to hold over the necks of the downtrodden. Nicolo's actions were not stunted by religion, however, and he was happy to use this to his advantage. Before the guards reached the decision that Nicolo was nudging them towards he stretched his hands from his sleeves, being sure to place his fingers in such a way as to put his shoes in their line of sight.

He paused briefly, long enough to allow the men to begin evaluating the inconvenience but not so long as to give them an opportunity to deduce anything that differed from the outcome Nicolo had planned for them.

'Do I have to spell it out for you?' he said with feigned impatience.

Nicolo raised the ring finger on his left hand slightly, showing the silver ring with the red cross.

'Now, out of my way gentlemen before my patience finds another outlet.'

The two guards looked at each other, each hoping his partner knew the significance of the silver band.

'I am sure the doge would be most... *curious* as to why two of his guards delayed a nobleman with the Sign of the Merciful Apostle on his person. I need not remind you of the irony of its name, I am sure' he said, with just the right balance of mystery and threat.

Mattimeo was the first to break.

'I will put it to the Master of the Keys. Wait here' he said, adding a half-hearted 'please', just in case.

Nicolo knew that the doge of Genoa was the laziest man in the city; that was the only logical conclusion to be drawn. Nicolo was, by nature and necessity, an analytical man and saw the world as a series of puzzles just waiting to be solved. It was one of the reasons he was a man of little faith in a world ruled by it.

As he saw it, the man who empties the latrines is accountable to someone higher up the power chain and must let them know the loathsome job is done. That person wouldn't be seen dead cleaning a latrine and is paid more for the pleasure. Yet he, in turn, reports to a higher power and must tell them that the latrines and the gutters and all the other infested places have been dealt with appropriately. That person is paid even more and doesn't have to be within twenty paces of a foul smelling gutter scraper. And so it goes on, with each layer better paid than the last and, crucially, further removed from the real work. It follows then, that those at the very top of the pile do the least work and have the most money. Ipso facto, the doge was lazy. This was one of the chinks he planned to prise open with his word play and instinct, but first he had to get past the guards.

'He has the Sign of the Merciful Apostle, sir' said Mattimeo, trying not to give away his thoughts on what the correct course of action should be. He did not, in fact, have any thoughts on the matter; decisions were best left to those with wages to warrant them.

'The Sign of the Merciful Apostle, you say?' said the Master of the Keys, his eyebrows contorting in a simultaneous display of scepticism and intrigue. He had never heard of the sign before, but then there were a lot of things he hadn't heard of and he was damned if he was going to let one of his guards know it. 'Tell me, Mattimeo, what did it look like, this *sign*?'

'It was a silver band with a white stone set into it and a red cross in its centre. I think there were gold stripes too.'

'Think? *Think*?' said the Master of the Keys with genuine despair. He needed irrefutable facts if he was to delegate his way out of this. 'I need more than *think*. You are a guard of the Pubblico Palazzo, you do not think, you *know*. Now tell me, were there gold stripes or not?'

Mattimeo wracked his memory. He was never any good at remembering. The most effort his brain ever had to exert involved daydreaming to keep him sane while his day stretched out endlessly in front of the palazzo. He decided to remember that the gold stripes were there.

'Yes sir! Gold stripes sir!' he affirmed, with as much certainty as he could fake.

'Right then, get back to your station' said the Master of the Keys as he turned away to head deeper into the palace. 'Signore Giudice must be told of this turn of events.'

'That's what he said. *A turn of events*. I told you it was important' said Mattimeo, nodding knowingly at his colleague.

'You didn't say a word, I remember that on account of me not hearing anything at the time' said Chiasmo.

'It doesn't matter now anyway, he's gone to see Signore Giudice so we're off the hook.'

The two guards slipped back into their familiar statuesque positions and comforted themselves with the knowledge they had escaped whatever it would turn out to be that they nearly hadn't.

'That's right sir, the Sign of the Merciful Apostle. That's why I came straight to you' said the Master of the Keys confidently.

'Bring him to me immediately' said Signore Giudice, a man to whom decision making was something others did while he got on with the job of calculating how he could make the most of a decision he had just made on instinct.

'Of course, Signore Giudice' said the Master of the Keys, bowing low and offering a silent prayer of thanks for not having to involve himself in palace intrigue.

'The doge will see you now' said Chiasmo in a gently surprised tone. 'Apologies for delaying you, but I'm sure you can understand the need for security in these troubling times' he added. He didn't think they were troubling times at all, but when strangers with mysterious rings are granted access to the doge himself it can be reasonably assumed that times are troubled for those with access to certain information, and Chiasmo could read that sign, at least.

Nicolo climbed the wide staircase to the top of the palace. He had expected to work his way through several layers of security before negotiating a meeting with the doge. He was disappointed to have sculpted so many rehearsed conversations, some of his best work too, that would never see the light of day. Still, he was almost at the doge's rooms and that was more than he could have hoped for so soon into his day.

'Wait here' ordered Giudice, and passed through the simple doorway that marked the entrance to the inner sanctum of Giovanni di Murta, doge of all Genoa.

Inside, the doge was sitting at his desk on a chair of fine, carved mahogany. He wore his usual dark green and black doublet and there was a large silver dish in front of him, overflowing with fruit. To his right was a plate of bones waiting to be removed and a goblet waiting to be refilled. He stared out of the large window despite the arrival of Giudice, who knew better than to think that the doge's mind was as blank as his expression. He waited until Giovanni di Murta acknowledged him with a small flinch of his head.

'Ah, Giudice' he said at last, 'please, invite this stranger in. We wouldn't want to be seen as unwelcoming.'

'As you wish.'

Nicolo successfully failed to appear in awe of his surroundings as he entered the most decorated and luxurious room he had ever experienced. He had to rein in his natural tendency to find opportunity through theft. One covetous look at an elegant table leg would be as terminal as the truth.

'Signore...?' asked the doge.

'My name is Carlo Sigliano of the House of Fortalino, your Serenity.'

'Is it, indeed?'

Giovanni di Murta let the questioning tone hang in the air for longer than Nicolo would have liked. Silence can break a dishonest man, their anxiety to complete the charade winning out over the etiquette to which an honest man would remain loyal. Nicolo was no amateur, though.

'So tell me *Signore* Sigliano, what brings you to the very seat of Giovanni di Murta, doge of the great Genoese empire?'

Nicolo wondered at the emphasis the doge had placed on the word *signore*. His instincts were on full alert and they told him there was a hidden message there if he could only find it. Should he thank the doge for seeing him, or would that seem too crass for the nobleman he was purporting to be? He decided against it, despite his natural desire to stroke the man's ego.

'I come with a simple message from Signore Sigliano. He has sent me, his eldest son, to convey to you the gravest of news. There is a pestilence rising in the south. All who are touched by it pass on to the house of our Lord within a few days and none can cure it.'

The doge listened and calculated. This stranger was not a nobleman, of that he was certain. Aside from the information he already had, no real nobleman would introduce himself without a title, even if that title was of a lowly *signore*. The doge wondered what had brought him to the palace. His message did not, thus far, implore a gift in exchange for the warning of pestilence. He would need more information before casting his judgment upon his soul.

'A conman may enter the house of a nobleman with a story of ill winds and impending doom to better help his agenda. Tell me, Signore Sigliano, what makes you so different from a deceptive street man?'

'A conman is always a storyteller, but a storyteller is not always a conman, your Serenity' said Nicolo with what he hoped was an enigmatic air.

'Indeed.'

The two players sat in a stalemate of secrecy for a time, neither wanting to reveal their cards before the other. Nicolo could legitimately claim to be waiting for his superior to direct the conversation, and so waited in silence to react to the doge's next move.

'You bring news of a pestilence without news of your house, Signore Sigliano. Please, sit and tell me of the latest gossip from the House of Fortalino, it is so long since I saw its walls of ivy and stone.'

The doge had showed his hand, feigning knowledge of a house that did not exist. He either suspected Nicolo for what he was, or was covering for his poor knowledge of the noble houses of the region. Either way, Nicolo had only one option available to him. He could not admit to being a charlatan, and even if the doge had an unmatched knowledge of the region's nobility it was still possible to convince him that one had evaded his awareness, however unlikely that may be.

'It must have been long indeed, your Serenity, for there has not been ivy on the House of Fortalino for many years, not since that unfortunate incident with the bard and his lute, as I'm sure you must have heard. He was a good and pious man, taken from us too soon. May his soul rest in peace.'

'Indeed.'

Giovanni di Murta picked up his empty goblet and ran his finger around the lip thoughtfully.

'Tell me, Signore Sigliano, why would your father send an emissary to me, the doge of Genoa, who has eyes in all lands and ears in all places? Does he think I am not so well informed as to know of the great pestilence of Catania?'

Nicolo's heart froze. He couldn't know of his past, nobody did bar Nicolo himself. Could there really be a plague rising in the south? He tried to control his emotion but knew he had betrayed his ignorance.

'Then you are better informed than I, your Serenity, for I know only of its arrival in Benevento and know not where it came from. Please, forgive me for bringing old news to your door.'

'Very good, signore, very good' said the doge, clapping his hands together mockingly. 'You make a fine spy, but tell me this – why does your espionage reach my door?'

'My Most Serene Prince' replied Nicolo, now on the verge of failure under the crystal glare of the most powerful man in Genoa, but determined to at least make one attempt at getting what he came for. 'I am not what you believe me to be. I bring this news in good faith and with purity of heart. For my part, I am to go from here to the land of my father's ancestors in Avignon and I hope to reach them before the pestilence. It is a righteous and virtuous mission, with many perils along its path. At your bidding I will leave you with the news that came too late, and offer my prayers for your good health and long life during this troubled time.'

Giovanni stood up for the first time and walked to the door. Nicolo turned to face him, taking the doge's movement as a dismissal. The doge turned the key in the lock and walked back past Nicolo to a bookcase in a dark corner of his chamber. It held one of the great collections of the region, almost twenty tomes in all, bound in varying shades of leather. He pulled one seemingly at random and took a small parchment from near the front before settling back down at his desk. He dipped a heavy quill into a dark glass jar and scratched it onto the parchment, finishing with a flamboyant swish. He replaced the quill and reached for a bowl of sand, pouring a liberal measure onto the ink and blowing it onto the floor. He rolled the parchment tightly until it was as small as a chicken bone and sealed it with an elaborate stamp of dark green wax. Nicolo watched in nervous excitement. He had never seen a spectacle so removed from his daily life.

'Signore Sigliano' said Giovanni di Murta in such a way as to prepare Nicolo for an impending order and the closure of their meeting. 'I have a friend in Avignon and would wish for him to be warned of this pestilence at the earliest opportunity. It seems you are that opportunity. My messengers have been gone a week already with a different... directive, before I learned of it. I would be grateful if you could deliver a message on my behalf. This seal will allow safe passage to the city wall. When you are there you should seek out The Cutler. This scroll is to pass into his hands only, with an unbroken seal, on pain of death to you and your family in Catania. I bid you good day, and may the pestilence spare your deceitful soul.'

CHAPTER THREE

UMBRIDGE, ENGLAND
December, 1347

The parish of Umbridge was small, a distant satellite village of the bustling cultural epicentre of Canterbury. The village was far enough away from the city as to be largely untroubled by it, but close enough to be within its reach, should Canterbury decide to swat at it. It was as though the village was spawned by a group of travellers who, on setting off southward from Canterbury with the intention of resettling in some far off land, gave up after a couple of days as they realised they may have eaten their last of Mrs Cabbage's special apple buns. There were no more than a hundred souls there, and most were rambunctious in their piety.

Cuthbert stood in the icy chill of the church of Our Lady of Ostensive Pity. He was a simple young man, with simple priorities, but was beginning to finding modern life confusing more frequently these days and often pined for the time when he could make sense of the world simply by listening to the parish priest and his dictatorial ruminations on the state of his soul. The doubt that Father Joinson sold from the pulpit was growing in him and he wondered how he would ever live a life worthy of salvation. As a younger boy Father Joinson was his barometer and his calibrator. If Father Joinson said he must bathe in pig swill to cleanse the soul of his misdeeds, then bathing in pig swill is what he did. It worked too, he hadn't been sent to hell just yet, although he may be closer to it now than heaven. He had begun to make jokes to his friends that skirted a little too close to blasphemy for his liking. There was a new type of peer pressure surrounding him, one that all young men experience as their childhood ends and their evolution into an adult takes hold. Cuthbert had a tendency to find the good in everyone, to his detriment. In trying to fit in with less pious parishioners he had become more brazen in his behaviour.

Two days earlier he had been talking to his friend, Peter, outside the privvies and had referred to Father Joinson as Father *Johnson*, something all in the parish knew was a shortcut to a beating should he overhear it. Despite being a man of the cloth, or perhaps because of it, Father Joinson held no regard to those who could not pronounce the name of their most holy resident correctly. This was his most sinful act yet, and a perfect example of how Cuthbert's perspective of sin was far removed from those of his friends. They would sometimes even sneak out of mass early, something Cuthbert considered a most certain way to extend your time in purgatory.

'May the mortal shell that holds your soul be cast aside in a triumph of flame and virtue as you pass from this sinful world and into the eternal joy of our father's home in the heavens.' Father Joinson lowered his arms as he stepped from the pulpit and strode purposefully to the simple wooden altar. As he bade them to leave, the faithful flock slowly straightened their backs before bending them again as they genuflected and filed out of the weather beaten church.

Cuthbert crossed over to the front of the pews, stood nervously outside the sacristy and waited for the heavy wooden door to open. Father Joinson had sent word to Cuthbert's parents the day before that he wanted to talk to him on a matter of grave importance for his soul. Cuthbert had not been able to sleep the night before. He had spent it going over all of the sinful deeds he had committed recently. There were so many to choose from, he thought, and any one of them could be the reason the priest wanted to speak with him so urgently. He vowed never to say anything unworthy of a good Christian again. Quite aside from an increased stay in purgatory, it simply wasn't worth all the worry.

After an impossibly long minute the overwhelming presence of Father Joinson strode out, sending dust flying through the multicoloured sunbeams around him and up towards the high ceiling. He loomed over Cuthbert, causing the young man to press himself further into the stone wall behind him.

'Little Cuthbert. *Poor little Cuthbert.* Hear this. God has spoken to me. He has touched me with his spirit and knows you are straying from the righteous path of the good. I am here to help you find your way back to the truth.'

This was precisely as ominous as Cuthbert was expecting. His life had been spent surrounded by devoutly religious sheep, a collection he had considered himself a part of until the last few weeks. He knew that he would have to fall into line and accept whatever course of action Father Joinson deemed appropriate for such an unthinkable deviation, whichever one it was.

'I have noticed a change in you recently, Cuthbert, one that God has told me is not of His making. I have seen you daydreaming during my sermons and smiling during the consecration.'

'Forgive me, father, but I was thinking of the gospel, and it made me lose control of my respect. I will not let it happen again.'

'The gospel?' said Father Joinson, with unrestrained incredulity in his voice. 'The gospel it not a place for humour, my poor little Cuthbert. What was it you found so amusing, dare one ask?'

Cuthbert hesitated. It pays to remain quiet when a decree is hanging over your head. Any words, no matter how well intended, have a way of exaggerating the punishment. Unfortunately for Cuthbert, his nervousness was in full control of his actions and it ploughed a deeper furrow in his field of sin. 'I'm sorry, Father Joinson. It was just the part about the wood. You know, the bit that says '*how can you remove the splinter from a friend's eye when you cannot see the plank in your own?*'It struck me as funny, but I see now the true message and I will be penitent until my soul has been cleansed of my sins.'

'You are not yourself,' continued the priest, squirreling Cuthbert's lines away for use in his final assessment while outwardly ignoring them. 'The devil has taken hold and we must cast him out. I will prepare myself and come to your home; these demons have ways of penetrating even the most ardent of Christian souls. We must protect your parents and your sisters as well as saving you from the fires of hell.'

Cuthbert relaxed. He had expected Father Joinson to sentence him to some interminable penance, most likely involving the cleaning of the sheep pits that bordered the presbytery. He could handle an exorcism, enjoy it even. It was always good to wipe the slate clean of any unintended ill deeds. A fresh start might even return him to a righteous path.

Cuthbert lived with his devout parents, Edmund and Catherine, and three obedient sisters in a small, simple home that sat too close to the animal quarters for anyone's liking, but close enough to make their rent affordable. His father was a baker's hand, for which they were eternally grateful. The family often staved off their hunger with the stale bread that the baker would have thrown out were it not for the desperation in his father's eyes. They lived in a single downstairs room, serving as both the kitchen and the living quarters, and two smaller upstairs rooms. Cuthbert shared one of these cramped rooms with his three sisters but, even so, they were lucky to have so few of them living there; some of Cuthbert's friends had to survive in similar homes with twice the occupants, not all of whom were as particular about the separation of eating and depositing as his family were.

Father Joinson strode up the few stairs in Cuthbert's home with the confidence of a man with the answer to a riddle nobody understands. He threw Cuthbert to the floor without preamble and demanded he kneel before the Lord. There was a rough cross on the floor beside his bed and Cuthbert stared at it, sending his mind to another place, any place but here. He had seen an exorcism once before, but he didn't remember it involving the flinging of the victim to the ground. If this was just the beginning, how violently would it end?

The priest loomed over him, stomping his feet on the bending floor as he began the theatrical performance. He flailed his arms, shouting zealously as he ordered the demons to leave. After several minutes of increasingly unintelligible pronouncements the show grew to its grand crescendo as Father Joinson stepped onto the bed with arms outstretched, leapt upwards in delirious fervour before falling back onto and through the floor with a loud crack, sending him down into the room below and an impromptu meeting of his head with an iron bar protruding stubbornly from the wall.

Cuthbert's father called out in distress. 'Jesus Christ!'

It said a lot about the piety of Edmund that Cuthbert was more shocked by this than the death of the parish priest on his coat hook.

'I mean, Jesus Christ save us and his soul, dear Lord!' said Edmund, trying to recover his wits a little. It wasn't every day a priest fell into your kitchen and he wasn't quite sure what the appropriate course of action was. 'Cuthbert, what have you done?'

'What do you mean? He jumped off my bed like a crazed animal and you're asking me what have *I* done?'

This was, by some considerable distance, the greatest affront he had ever shown to his father. He knew instantly he was in real trouble. Anything could happen, new ground was being broken by the second.

Edmund was panicking. He had a dead priest in an ever increasing pool of dark red liquid at his feet and a son who was losing the run of himself. In a moment of fear-induced lucidity he went for a sledgehammer approach in an attempt to deal with everything in one swift, crushing action. He needed to move the body and look after his son's immortal soul. He would do both at once.

'Cuthbert, come here my son' he said, in soothing tones that jarred with the chaotic madness of the previous sixty seconds. 'You have done a terrible thing here today, and for that you must seek contrition. Take Father Joinson to the church and speak with Deacon Shufflebottom. He will take care of the practicalities of the body and its soul. Tell him I have ordered you on a great pilgrimage to seek forgiveness for your terrible actions. You are to travel to Avignon itself and pray within sight of His Holy Father, Pope Clement. When you have completed this great penance you shall return here to train in the work of our Lord, for only then will you prove yourself worthy of a place in his eternal home.'

'Yes, father' said Cuthbert, lengthening his vowels like a small child. The punishment for being convicted of killing a priest, no matter how innocent you were in reality, was a long and painful death that almost certainly involved parts of you expiring before you did. A lifetime of faux supplication was a reasonable alternative and Cuthbert knew instinctively he had no choice. He also knew he could simply not return if he so chose. He would take his punishment and see where it took him. He had never thought of himself as an adventurer, but he remembered a travelling wool merchant telling him that you could never fulfil your potential if you travelled on the same roads. He would find a new one, and may he be a better person for it.

CHAPTER FOUR

Before Cuthbert could set out on his pilgrimage there were certain protocols to complete. To allow the grand journey to be classed as a penance the pilgrim would have to receive a blessing from the bishop following a full confession, although Edmund was wary of turning any more attention on his family than was absolutely necessary despite the whirling scandal all around them. He had discretely side-stepped this inconvenient hoop, jumping through a different one instead. He had asked deacon Shufflebottom to hear Cuthbert's confession, selling it as a good experience for him and promising that Cuthbert would return to be mentored by the soon-to-be priest. Shufflebottom's vanity won out and he listened to Cuthbert confess to a sin he had not committed.

The long, coarse garment of a penitent pilgrim was then lowered over Cuthbert's head with more ceremony that he felt was necessary. He was also given a staff and a purse with a few small coins, strictly for emergency use only as dictated by his father. Inside the purse his father had placed two small pieces of parchment with elaborate writing painted on to them. Cuthbert could not read, but his father explained to him that the piece with a red cross on it contained petitions and was to be left in a safe place, in sight of the pope if he was able to get so close to him, while the one with a black cross was to be shown to a senior palace official in Avignon if he ever found himself in mortal danger. Only *mortal* danger. Edmund had been very clear about that. If it was only *severely* dangerous then he was to keep the parchment secret and safe and wait until his life was almost complete.

When the time came to say goodbye to his family, possibly for good, he found that he had been holding back an avalanche of emotion. What he had in Umbridge may have been of little value to him while the feelings of confinement shackled his adventurous spirit, but his they had remained and letting go was surprisingly tortuous for his heart. He kissed his sisters, making a joke about not being *too* naughty while he was away in an attempt to stem the flow of tears welling in his eyes. He hugged his mother and asked her to look after his sisters before turning to his father. They exchanged a look that said more than either of them was capable of vocalising. All that had happened, all that he had done and not done, all the misunderstandings, all the uninvited sorrow, and all the pressure he felt to appear contrite before his father and the Lord to remain blindly repentant in their Catholicism were encapsulated in the last two words Cuthbert would ever say to his father.

'I'm sorry.'

✝

ALDRIDGE-ON-THE-GRANGE, ENGLAND
December, 1347

Robert listened to Father Hambledon's sermon from the comfort of his cold stone pew. He had endured the advent services with less patience than previous years and was losing the will to pretend. He hated this time of year more than any other, reminding him of all the Christmases he had spent away from his wife and six children. What gloriously free days they were; no toddlers pulling at his trousers, no wife to build a list of jobs to do around the house during his all-too-rare periods of rest, no daily visits to the church, no toiling in Lord Norwood's fields. His days on the road were the happiest of his life and he wanted desperately to return to them, even for just a short while. So desperately, in fact, that he chose this moment to do all he could to send himself back there.

Father Hambledon was cranking up the intensity of his oration from the pulpit. *'And did the Lord not show us that it is easier for a camel to pass through the eye of a needle than for a rich man to enter the kingdom of heaven? Did he not show us that the poor woman who gave half a denarii in the collection plate gave more than the rich man who gave a hundred? He did, I tell you now, and he did all this so that we may understand the true meaning of...'*

'Bugger this for a lark!' called Robert to the congregation, just as Father Hambledon was reaching the crescendo of his sermon. 'I've never heard such nonsense. If the rich cannot enter the kingdom of heaven, why do so many of us covet the coin? Why are the priests some of the richest men in villages up and down the county? Ask yourselves *that*!'

The priest roved his eyes to find the source of the outburst, rolling them as they landed on Robert. Here we go again, he thought. 'Robert Robertson. Wait for me at the end' he said. 'When will you ever learn?'

CALAIS

January, 1348

The port of Calais was a recent acquisition of King Edward of England and the ripples of tension still waved across the town. There was a chaotic order to the docks and Cuthbert resolved to leave them behind at the earliest opportunity. He had no money to use for a roof on his first night, instead sleeping in an alley on the outskirts of the docks.

On his first morning the sunbeams found a gap between the walls, waking him from a restless sleep and sending him out into the open to begin his journey south. He saw a small church a little way down the road and stopped to say a decade of the rosary, offering it up for his safety and that of his family. When he had finished he said another one, just to be sure. It was unclear to him how penitent he should be; was the journey itself enough, or should he pray his way to Avignon, stopping at every church in his path?

As he finished his fourth decade he stood, satisfied he had been repentant enough for this morning. He genuflected and was turning to leave when he noticed a man dressed in a similar fashion to himself slumped against a wall. He was curious to hear his story and crossed to him, smelling the wine before he saw it.

'You should not be drinking in the house of our Lord' said Cuthbert, carefully leaving his tone neutral to allow the man to decide for himself whether he was being serious or playful.

'Hmmfph?' said the man.

It seemed likely to Cuthbert that this man was suffering the after-effects of drinking the night before, rather than the slumber of one still in the throes of it.

'Let me help you out to the fresh air, it will ease your suffering.'

'It will take more 'un fresshh air, I can ash... I can *asssh*... I can promise you that, young pilgrim' said the man, in what might have been an unfamiliar accent. It was hard to identify the real voice amongst the slurring and growling.

'Where will your pilgrimage take you?' said Cuthbert in an attempt to seem friendly.

The man took a swig of his wine, an action that would have emptied Cuthbert's stomach had he been in the man's position, but one that seemed to help the stranger reach something approaching a wakeful state.

'Who knows, eh? Who bloody knows? To the depths of hell as likely as not. What fun it will be though, eh? Eh?'

Cuthbert wasn't sure how to react, mostly because he wasn't sure what the man meant.

'Come on, I'll help you outside.'

He took the man under his armpits and heaved him upright before putting an arm across his back. He helped him with the tricky task of placing one foot in front of the other. Inch by inch Cuthbert coaxed the drunkard to the door and out into the blinding light of the street.

'Avignon's this way' said the man, turning his back to the port and loping away. Cuthbert followed him, beginning his long trek to the papal seat.

'So what is it you didn't do then?' said the hangover.

'Didn't do?' said Cuthbert, unsure of where to go with his answer. 'I didn't do anything.'

'That's the spirit. Robert.'

'No, Cuthbert.'

'I think I'm more likely to know that than you, with all due respect.'

'Erm…' said Cuthbert.

'So now you know mine, what's your name?' said Robert, letting Cuthbert off the hook and explaining the misunderstanding in one swoop.

'Ah, I see. Right. Sorry.'

'Funny name that, *Sorry*. Is that why you're such a natural pilgrim? You look like you were made to trudge in these itchy sacks. Enjoy it, do you?'

'Now listen here' said Cuthbert with more vigour than anticipated. 'First off, my name is Cuthbert. Secondly, who says I'm a pilgrim? And thirdly, the purpose is not for me to enjoy it, but rather to complete penance for my sins.'

'Ah! So you *are* a pilgrim then. A real one too, by the sounds of it. This is my fourth. Love them, I do. Gives me a bit of time away from the wife, know what I mean?' said Robert, nudging Cuthbert with a knowing elbow.

'I'm not sure I do, no.' said Cuthbert with genuine puzzlement.

'First one then? Don't worry, I'll look after you. I know all the best places along the road.'

'Well, that would be a great help, thank you, Robert. I was worried I may not be able to find a church each day, but if this is your fourth you must know all of them by now. Were your other pilgrimages to Avignon too?'

'A church?'

'Well of course. Where else are we to offer our prayers to the saints? We could kneel in the fields, I suppose, but there is more substance to them when you're in God's house, and anyway, we need a priest to confess to as we go.'

'Oh, so you're one of *them*, are you? You like to go a bit wild, but it's allowable if you can get to a man of the cloth before the sin soaks all the way to your soul? That could make it interesting I suppose. What's the going penance for being roasting drunk in a church these days? If we're going to do this properly it can't hurt to start with a clean slate.'

'That's not what I meant. We sin all the time, Robert, and must arrive to the Holy Father with a soul free from blemishes.'

'Is that so?'

'Of course it is. You are more experienced than I, you must know this already.' said Cuthbert, continuing to miss the obvious.

'Poor little Cuthbert' said Robert, unwisely as it happens.

'Don't ever call me that. If you say that again I'll… I'll… I'll be very unhappy about it, actually.'

'So someone back home used to call you that, someone involved in your expulsion. Interesting. Tell me, what happened to put you here, travelling along an overgrown road with a serial pilgrim?'

'Nothing, all I did was laugh at something in the gospel. The rest was chance.'

'Ah, dear old *chance*. Isn't it amazing how often a man's poor luck gets confused with his poor execution? Come on, what happened? Really now, there's no benefit in hiding behind a veil of shame. We're all here for the same reason, broadly speaking.'

'I doubt that' said Cuthbert.

'Do you, indeed? Tell me then, what did you do that is so terrible that you were sent all the way to Avignon?'

Robert was right, Cuthbert had nothing to gain by remaining secretive with other pilgrims, no matter how unholy they may appear. Part of his penance was surely to confess and accept his wrongdoings. It was all so confusing sometimes. He chose to confess. Again.

'I killed a priest' he said flatly.

'Splendid, a story to keep us entertained on the road' said Robert, utterly unfazed by the revelation. 'Please, tell me everything.'

CHAPTER FIVE

GENOA

Nicolo sat motionless as a wooden tankard flew across his eyeline. He had been staring at the dripping walls of the nameless tavern for some time, battling his inner demons. No thought bar one occupied his attention. How did Giovanni di Murta know about his past? He had not been particularly deliberate in hiding his Sicilian roots, but he was so disconnected from it now, and had conversed with so few people outside of his street-side trickery, that he was sure no-one could know of it. He had only mentioned the *south* to the doge, with no reference to Catania, nor his family. The doge himself had only mentioned the pestilence once Nicolo had introduced it into the conversation, so he put that down to the man's quick wits and not his seemingly omnipresent sources of information.

He weighed up his options. He had three, on the face of it at least; he could stay in Genoa and ignore the order of its most powerful inhabitant, he could leave the city and travel to the south, back towards his family home for the first time since his travels had begun, or he could follow his new orders and head for Avignon, residence of the Papal seat and epicentre of all power in the Holy Roman Empire. None of them particularly appealed to him. He was a man of whimsical decisions, such as he made them, and the constraints of bowing to another man's will, no matter how powerful, went against all he stood for. Admittedly, he didn't stand for very much but that wasn't the point.

He couldn't stay here, that was for certain. If he was to disobey a direct order from Giovanni di Murta then he was sure he didn't want to sit under his feet as he did so. That way only led to a short life and a long death. So, he must simply choose a direction; south to his home in Catania, or north to The Cutler in Avignon. He left the tavern and returned to his room, picked up his bag, threw in the few possessions he wasn't wearing, and took his first steps closer to home in five years.

PIOMBINO, TUSCANY

January, 1348

The port of Piombino was small, an insignificant provisions stop along the coast for most who passed through. What attracted Nicolo here was the merchant route that took traders between Sicily to the south, Genoa to the north and Marseilles and Corsica to the west. He would stay here for a few days, gathering as much information as he could about the health of the population in the south. If the doge was better informed than he then Nicolo could find his way aboard a ship bound for Marseilles and from there it was a short hop to Avignon, where he could deliver his message and be released from Giovanni's grasp. If he was wrong then it was likely the doge had no knowledge of any pestilence, his father, nor his whereabouts, and so he would go home to check on the old man, safe in the knowledge that his fictional epidemic was just that.

The sun was breaking cover on the horizon as Nicolo swung his legs over the side of the jetty. He sat between the rusted mooring posts that tethered the ships to the quay and it worried him to see them all empty. He had only been here once before, many years ago when his travels swept him through before steering him northward to Genoa, but he remembered there being a clamour, a sense of permanent urgency of which the docks now seemed bereft. He decided to wait and ask information of the cabin boy on the next ship to come in. Never ask a captain if you want the real answer, go as low as you can and you will find the truth, as likely as not. The less attention that is paid by those with iron power and loose tongues to those with neither, the quicker the valuable information passes between the two.

No ship came into port that day. As the sun turned orange he stood up from his seat at the end of the jetty and headed to a tavern. The only tavern. It was a small, grotty house with a pair of blue keys painted long ago onto the old, weather beaten door. A beggar was slumped against the wall outside, barely identifiable as human under a pile of matted blankets. He had never seen such a well insulated vagabond in all his travels.

'I wouldn't go in there if I were you, sir' said the bundle. 'There is something hanging in the air.'

'Are you being cryptic so that I may see you as a soothsayer, master beggar? For if payment is your goal you are meddling with an expert. Tell me clearly, or tell me nothing.'

'The tainted souls are counting their time, for a certain and absolute reckoning is coming.'

'Of course it is. Thank you, and good day to you, you crazy tramp.'

He did well to keep the rickety door on its hinges as he opened it, choosing to leave it ajar rather than risk the attention that removing it from its housing would bring. There was an equally withered look to the inside; a handful of small benches of crooked timber, all broken and some stained from indeterminable sources. They were placed in the only formation that would allow all of them to remain on the floor at the same time. The chaos that must regularly ensue in such a confined drinking space made Nicolo wonder how the owner survived here from one day to the next. It would have been bad enough in a small inland village, but being the only tavern in a sailors' stopover port must surely make it more trouble than it was worth. Still, the bearded and overweight man he could see through a small gap in the wall seemed like a man who could look after himself. He called over for an ale and waited.

He was well acquainted with the idiosyncrasies of tavern life. It paid well to choose your drinking companions wisely and even better to drink alone. This evening, however, he needed information and for once was disappointed to find he was the only customer. Perhaps that was information enough.

'Ale' announced the barman flatly.

'And what a fine ale it is,' said Nicolo, taking a sip as he placed a small coin into the podgy fingers of the barman. 'Tell me, why would an establishment as fine as this, with an even finer ale, be so void of life?'

'If I knew that, stranger, I would be a happier soul.'

Nicolo pressed on. 'How long has it been like this, surely your ale must have brought in more custom?'

'There has been an occasional ship from Marseilles, but nothing from the south for more than two weeks. It has been like this ever since those Genoese merchants passed through from Sicily. My mother knew they were rotten, straight off.'

'So this is not just a peculiar day? I am glad to hear that you have, at least, been busy until recent events.' Nicolo paused. '*Rotten*, you say? Do you mean rotten like scoundrels, or rotten like a ruined crop?'

'Rotten like the walking dead of purgatory. At least, that's what my mother said, God rest her soul.'

Nicolo's heart sank at the mention of ethereal conversation. He had always felt it odd that people would think they could converse with the dead. Speaking to them was fine, or more specifically speaking *at* them. That was spirituality, and that was perfectly reasonable and perfectly sensible. It implied a certain knowledge on the part of the living member of the conversation that it was a one way process, that it was something to make them feel better and to deal with whatever was the instigating catalyst of the discussion. If someone thought they were involved in a reciprocated conversation with the dead, then they were simple madmen in Nicolo's eyes.

'I see' he lied. 'Tell me, what made them seem so deathly?'

'I couldn't say, stranger. I was busy in the back pantry when they were in here. Young Angelo dealt with them, but he hasn't been here since. His father sent word that he has a sickness. I was hoping to have him back by now but it seems a moot point, there would be no work for him to do here in any case. No point in paying him to sit around all day. He'll come back when he is ready, I suppose.'

Nicolo's intuition caught a whiff of intrigue, waking up his talent and switching his mind to full focus. 'Forgive my boorish manners, signore. My name is Armando Mazzi. I have travelled the long road from Catania and have stopped here in Piombino to rest my weary body for a night before I head north again. Please excuse my discourtesy in such a welcoming house as this.'

He wasn't sure what direction the barman's response would take, but he was ready.

'It is interesting that you feel yourself rude, Signore Mazzi. You must not be a man who frequents houses of this kind, for if you were you would know that rudeness and politeness are not considerations to my customers, only ale and women. I am Signore Lievito. Come, I will cook you a hearty meal in exchange for stories of your travels. I am keen to hear of all that is happening in my homeland in the south and I have little else to do.'

Nicolo would have rolled his eyes as if to say *bloody typical*, had he the freedom to give up his secrets. It would now take more than a well placed line to get the information he wanted. He must weave an intricate tale without detail, just the kind of challenge he relished, and would be paid in kind for his troubles too. He followed the barman through a narrow doorway and into the half-hidden kitchen.

They had been swapping stories for almost two hours, Lievito's tongue loosening as Nicolo agitated his memory with vague notions of life in the south. As the conversation developed, Nicolo was able to do less and less of the talking, while Lievito regaled him with drawn out tales with no obvious conclusion. There were four empty plates and two half full tankards on the table, both men having eaten their fill of bread and fruit. Only one customer had troubled them, a simple peasant looking for work. Lievito had sent him to the harbourmaster's house with a name and no more.

'What of Angelo, your tavernhand?' said Nicolo at last. He had been a patient man, waiting for a lull in the barman's tales to allow a natural change of subject.

'He has been gone a week, as I have already told you. I can tell you no more. He is unwell, that is all I know. I am accustomed to receiving information before most but as you can see, my sources are not drinking here anymore.'

'I could visit him, to pass on your sympathies perhaps?' It was a crude approach, but the bluntest of tools can often open the narrowest of cracks.

'I wouldn't ask you to travel all the way to the Bassifondi, it is too much to ask of a stranger, though I am keen to hear of his health.'

That was enough for Nicolo, he was in.

'I fear I did not give you enough stories to justify the meal you provided, this at least will give me the opportunity to repay you, and to see another part of the town.'

'Thank you, Signore Mazzi, though it is not an area you should be so keen to visit. He lives above the tannery with his father and uncle on the very edge of the slum. I shall look forward to your safe return.'

Nicolo flinched inwardly at the implied prospect of a less than safe return from the slums. He was a man well versed in street life, but that didn't stop him from being rather attached to his limbs. He would keep his nerve and find the information he needed. Angelo was either lazy, sick, or a harbinger of something more sinister. He wouldn't find out by lingering any further in the kitchen of Signore Lievito, so left in haste and headed for Bassifondi, the slum of Piombino.

A rat scurried past his ankles as he searched the filthy streets for signs of the tannery. His nose would do all the work, a tannery being the perfect place for anyone who was challenged in the olfactory department. He passed several bakeries, all closed, and a house with a grubby street urchin sitting imploringly against its wall, surrounded by small, rough pieces of wood. The house was of brick, so he was not yet at the slums where the places were surely made of less sturdy materials, if any at all.

'Get your soul saved here, m'lord. A quarter forint for the small ones, half a forint for the large. You can't put a price on salvation, m'lord.'

'Indeed you can't, young man, indeed you can't. Trying to sell a piece of driftwood to a poor fisherman's son like me for half a forint is tantamount to gluttony and dishonesty though, wouldn't you say?'

'I don't know what you mean, m'lord. I am just a poor...'

'May I suggest you change your pricing structure?' Nicolo interrupted. 'You also need to change your product. You would do better to shape them into crosses and offer them at two for a quarter forint piece. Don't offer salvation either, offer fear. Better to have a small coin in your pocket than a piece of driftwood on the floor.' He flicked him a coin and moved on before turning once more to the boy. 'Tell me, where might I find the tannery?'

'You're almost there, m'lord. Turn the corner and your nose will show you the rest of the way. I wouldn't go there if I were you though, there is a stench you wouldn't believe. Plus it's closed.'

'Thank you' said Nicolo, familiar with the unpleasantness of a tanner's yard and considering himself quite capable of making his own decisions on the worth of his visit.

As he rounded the nameless corner in the maze of streets a wall of stench hit his nostrils. He followed it upwind to some animal skins hanging from the gutters of a house, the last in its row. There was a door there, invitingly ajar and with a wooden cross nailed to it. Nicolo pushed the door and called up the wooden stairway.

'Angelo, may I come up? It is I.'

Vagueness and assumption was his friend more often than people were. There may be several reasons why Angelo would turn a stranger away and Nicolo played the percentages as often as he could. He would let Angelo decide who had come to see him at the door, in the hope that he had more friends than enemies.

No reply came.

Nicolo climbed the stairs and turned into a stagnant room of foul odours and filthy, dull bodies. Flies buzzed unseen in the gloom. He called out a greeting but expected no reply as he crossed to a simple bed of straw, upon which was the ravaged body of a young man, presumably Angelo. His eyes were still open, with a look of pain that had outlived its creator. He was naked despite the cold of the winter, as though his body had been boiling itself alive. The pits of his arms were disfigured by large, bulbous sacs, stretching his skin and gifting the flies a great feast. His privy parts had the same, sickly boils. On the other side of the room two more bodies, older than Angelo but just as dead, showed similar signs. Nicolo was not a man to be easily spooked, but the scene he was taking in was catastrophic in its choreography. Two of the three corpses were lying prostrate, while the other was slumped into a corner. All had the same symptoms, and none appeared to have met a peaceful end. There was nothing of value in the room, just a collection of ragged blankets and a single, broken wooden bowl. He had no desire to stay a moment longer, he now knew all he had feared, and turned to leave. As he reached the bottom of the stairs he took in the cross on the door. There was a crude image of a man scratched into it. Instinctively he prised it from the door, placed it in a discreet pocket inside his tunic and stepped into the street.

Borte was an unfortunate rat. He was raised in the frozen docklands of Sevastopol and was quite comfortable there. Then one day his friend Guyuk had an idea to explore a ship that had docked in the harbour. They had reached Piombino two moons later, scurrying down the tethering ropes as soon as they were made fast to the jetty.

'I'm going to the stream again' said Borte as they crossed a gap between two buildings. 'This heat is unbearable.'

'All you've done since we've got here is moan about the weather, I wish you would give it a rest' said Guyuk.

'Well I have every right to moan, it wasn't me that got us into this mess.'

'What mess? There is more food here than we ever saw in the last place. What more does a rat want? I didn't see you complaining when we slept on that pile of turnips last week.'

'That's not the point now, is it? A rat needs some comfort in their day. I'm boiling alive here.'

'Well go to the stream then if that's what you want, but don't come scurrying to me when you get eaten by a dog. I'll be over in the churchyard, there are always nice bloated things there to keep our bellies full.'

'That's disgusting!' said Borte. 'They're dead things you know?'

'We're rats!' screamed Guyuk. 'We're supposed to eat dead things.'

'Not in this day and age. We're supposed to have a bit of refinement about us now. It was all the rage back home before your bright idea.'

'So you're vegetarian now as well as everything else?'

'Well, given the choice.'

'Right, that's it' said Guyuk firmly. 'I've had it with you. Go off to the stream and eat leaves if that's what you want, I'm going to feast on the dead like a good, old-fashioned rat.'

Guyuk sped up and headed towards the churchyard, just as a leather boot sent him flying backwards into the afterlife.

Nicolo stood in a daze, looking blankly at the tanner's shop. He now saw that the skins were dry and cracking. Crumbling houses sprawled down the street and he approached one, kicking out at another rat that scuttled past him as he crossed the empty road. The door of the house was closed and there was no window to look through. He moved on to the next, one whose door was also closed. There was, however, a small window for him to peer through. Inside were the usual trappings of a pauper's life; a stone table, some straw in two of the corners for beds, and a small fireplace with a single iron pot hanging patiently over the ashes. There was an opening in the far wall that led through to a back yard of sorts. A half opened door obstructed most of the view, but there was something on the ground there, poking out from behind the door. In the gloom it showed itself as a foot, although Nicolo was aware that it could just as easily have been a small bag of grain, his mind still whirring after the hellish vision of Angelo's room.

He moved on down the street, checking those houses with windows. All of the doors were closed and some had a red cross painted onto them. As he turned the corner he reached the peasant boy again, already working his rough wooden clumps into crosses.

'Boy' he called out. 'Why are there no people here? What has happened?'

'Been like this for days now, m'lord. People are afraid to come out on account of the dead.'

'What dead?' said Nicolo, feigning ignorance.

'They're everywhere now, that's why I'm here trying to make some coin. I tried to tell you, can you not smell it? My whole family have gone' he said, in a neutral tone. 'A boy has to eat' he added defensively.

'Show me' said Nicolo, opening an arm to indicate he wanted the boy to stand.

'No need for me to move. That's my house there' said the boy, pointing to the opposite side of the street. 'See for yourself.'

Nicolo crossed to the window, looked inside, staggered backwards and fell on to the hard earthen floor. The room inside was full of bodies, four more corpses to go with the three he had already found at Angelo's. Each had the large red boils near their armpits, and each gave an aura of a recent and painful death. He climbed back to his feet and turned to the boy.

'Take off your shirt' he demanded. 'Now.'

The boy did so without question, revealing a single, much smaller boil on his upper arm.

'What is your name, boy?'

'Salvatore, m'lord.'

Nicolo pulled a whole gold coin from his pocket and threw it at the boy. It was more than Salvatore had seen in his lifetime, and too much for him to spend in the time he had left.

'Make yourself comfortable, Salvatore, and may God have mercy on your soul.'

With that he turned and headed away from the apocalypse, wondering how he would explain what he had seen to Signore Lievito.

CHAPTER SIX

FRANCE

'Well that was quite the story, Cuthbert. Enjoyable, but surely inaccurate. Will you ever tell me the parts you missed out, I wonder?' said Robert when Cuthbert had finished his tale.

Cuthbert had, in fact, told Robert the entire truth. His reaction only served to have Cuthbert question the validity of his penance. He had always been an innocent sort, rarely questioning that which others told him. In all his life he had never done anything that could be considered antagonistic. Never, that is, until he laughed at that fateful line from the gospel. One stifled chuckle at the wrong time had led to the violent death of a priest and sent him on a journey beyond his imaginings.

Perhaps his family wanted him to leave, that would explain the swiftness with which his father removed him from the equation in Umbridge. A dead priest was a problem, and Edmund has minimised the ramifications with one swift, heartless swipe at his son. It would be several months before Cuthbert returned, if at all. He wondered which his father would prefer. If he did return then the life in the priesthood his father had thrust upon him meant there would never again be the same bond between them, that special one shared only by those living under the same roof. Maybe Robert wasn't as wild and ignorant as he first suspected. Immoral, perhaps, but what difference did that make? He had wits and an insight Cuthbert could only dream of. It would pay to keep him close, for the moment at least.

'That's all I have' said Cuthbert honestly. 'If there was more to the story I would tell you. After all, we have a long way to go and little else to keep us entertained.'

'I shouldn't worry about that' said Robert. 'I recognise this part of the land. If we are where I think we are then there is a rather fine tavern just over this hill. They have an ale that would make your hair straight and your toes curly. Come on, let's see if I'm right.'

The tavern was relatively new. Its timber walls were still pale and rough, evidence of their recent assembly. Anything that spent time in the taverns of the pilgrim road usually experienced some form of physical amendment, often the pilgrims themselves. Robert strode into the room like the landlord, made a beeline for the hatch in the wall and ordered two ales and two bowls of potage. He pulled Cuthbert over to a table in the corner of the room and bent over to him conspiratorially.

'Watch' he said, nodding towards the rest of the room.

Cuthbert watched.

'What is it I'm supposed to be watching for?'

'Just watch.'

Cuthbert watched again.

'There, did you see that?' whispered Robert.

'No, or at least I don't think so. What should I have seen?'

'That man in the grey shirt, see?'

'Which one?' asked Cuthbert, not unfairly. Everyone in the room was wearing a grey shirt.

'That one' said Robert, trying and failing to make his nod more targeted.

'I didn't catch it, sorry. What is it?' Cuthbert asked again.

'The barkeeper left a small circle of green wood on the table when he delivered the man's ale. That's our ticket to the good stuff.'

'Oh, I see' lied Cuthbert. 'Is there a special service on in the church for pilgrims?'

Robert turned to face him, staring in blank exasperation. 'If you're playing the part of a faithful pilgrim then you're doing a great job, just so you know.'

Not for the first time Cuthbert was lost. He couldn't decide whether Robert was offering him a compliment, so chose to ignore it altogether and change the subject.

'I'm afraid I don't have any money for our supper' he said.

'Oh, don't worry about that, I don't either.'

That didn't help Cuthbert's anxiety levels at all.

'Don't worry? I would have thought that would be a reason to worry more, if anything. Please don't tell me you're planning on stealing the food.'

'Why don't you pray our way out of this if you're so concerned?'

'Prayer isn't meant for that, Robert, you should know that. I'm beginning to think you're not as faithful as you make yourself out to be. Stealing is a sin, and a bad one at that.'

'Would you give it a rest for a minute? I'm trying to get us some action.'

'Action? You mean…? I don't want that kind of action, Lord no! The only action I want is one that helps to get me closer to Avignon so I can complete my penance and get back home where my family are waiting for me.'

'Are they, Cuthbert? Do you think they are leaning against a gatepost, searching the hills for your great homecoming? Let me tell you, as someone who has returned to their temporarily estranged family more than once, I can assure you they have hardly noticed you've left. Life goes on, Cuthbert; the fields will still be worked and the supper will still be dreadful, which is why we should be making the most of the time we have away from them. Action, my friend, action. Prayer can wait until after our little adventure.'

'I know this is my first one, but I'm almost certain you're missing the point of a pilgrimage, Robert.'

'Tell you what, you stay here and sort out the payment for our supper and I'll go and get us some action.'

Cuthbert weighed up his options, which didn't really help other than to make him feel vaguely pro-active.

'We should tell the barkeeper we have changed our minds' said Cuthbert. 'We could leave and find some food on the road. I'm sure there are some berry bushes around if we leave the main path a little.'

'Watch and learn, Cuthbert. Watch and learn.'

The barkeeper approached them with their potage and dropped it from a height fractionally higher than recommended, spilling some of their supper over the table. He left them without a word before returning with two ales.

'Four' he growled.

'Four, you say?' said Robert, as if rolling the word around his memories. '*Four.*'

'That's right, four' said the barkeeper. 'Come on, I haven't got all day. There's a brawl brewing, I can feel it, and I have to get the crockery in before it gets too unpredictable.'

'Four...' said Robert. '*Four...*'

'You'll have four fewer teeth if you don't hand them over, son.'

'Son?...' said Robert.

Cuthbert edged along the bench towards the door. Any head start was better than none.

'Are you a bit simple?' said the barkeeper, opening the fingers of a hand and pointing at them in turn. 'One, two, three, *four*. Come on, I'm a busy man.'

'Ah, I remember now!' said Robert, in a voice that Cuthbert didn't recognise as the one he had been using with him all this time. 'You have four children, did you know that?'

'I have two daughters, as it happens. Now you can pay for your supper, or you can take your leave. It's up to you. Be warned though, that you may be taking your leave but I will be taking your clothes. I won't stand tomfoolery in my tavern, mark my words. Let's see how you enjoy walking naked all the way to whatever shrine it is you're heading to.'

'I don't think we will be walking naked, good sir' said Robert. 'You have two daughters, but four children. How might that be, do you wonder? How could a man who has free access to the green tokens have two sons he was unaware of. I am a pious pilgrim, as you can see, but the Lord has spoken to me on the road and has gifted me with a certain... *sight* that others cannot understand. Does your wife know of your little hobby, I wonder?'

The barkeeper's confident stance sagged a little.

'Ah! I see she does not. I hope for your sake that her ignorance remains while I and my assistant here take our rest and fill our bellies.'

The barkeeper's eyes narrowed as if trying to read the mind of this stranger who may or may not know his secrets.

'I will not cause another fight in my tavern for the sake of a small serving of ale and potage, stranger' said the barkeeper. 'Eat quickly and leave, but be warned that I shall not be so malleable should you ever return.'

'Duly noted' said Robert. 'I shall remain silent on the matter, for as long as your hospitality is maintained.'

'Explain yourself' whispered Cuthbert once the barkeeper had returned to his hatch. 'How could you possibly know he had four children?'

'I didn't' said Robert, now smiling with smug satisfaction, 'but can you imagine the owner of a tavern that offers special tokens to familiar customers not having a dabble himself every now and again?'

'Of course I can, he's married!'

'You continue to amaze me, Cuthbert. What kind of a life have you had? Come on, let's get this supper down us and find a place to stay for the night. We'll have plenty more opportunities for some action along the road.'

CHAPTER SEVEN

DARMSTADT, HESSE, HOLY ROMAN EMPIRE

January, 1348

Hildegund was a bad murderer. Not an evil, sinister one, just ineffective.

Since she was a young girl growing up in the shadow of the Ratskeller tavern she had felt compelled to fight for those who couldn't do so themselves, to support the weak and heal the sick. Her father spoke repeatedly of her need to toughen up, to grasp nettles and play more roughly with her brother, but she could never bring herself to do it. At an early age she had vowed to please her domineering father, to serve final justice to those weaker than her, but her vow went unfulfilled. She would trap a spider in an upturned tankard and set it free in the bushes rather than squashing it with the base as originally intended. Injured birds would be nursed back to health rather than put out of their misery, despite her efforts to end them. She had never quite got the hang of meting out justice in the most final of ways.

Two weeks ago though she had experienced something that would set this straight. Her brother, Steffen, had been caught up in the Flagellant movement, a horde of hysterical extremists whose theories on how to be spared from the pestilence involved the violent use of barbed whips on their own backs. Not the most sensible of directions, Hildegund thought, but then the men of Darmstadt were always a little on the peculiar side.

Steffen had thrown himself from a high window above the outdoor benches of the Ratskeller to prove his worth to God. It was the last thing he ever proved but was, his peers assumed, successful. Seeing this, his brethren in the movement took their actions to greater heights, or perhaps depths, of pain and suffering. They extended their lashes to those around them, some of whom found it uniquely spiritual and joined them in their crusade of near-martyrdom. Most, however, found it bloody and painful, and in the more annoying cases, fatal.

The parish priest, Father Heusch, had hailed her brother's death as a cause for celebration, as though his guaranteed entry into heaven was joyous news for the recently bereaved. There wasn't an ounce of sorrow in his voice nor in his words. He did not comfort the family, he envied them, and made it clear that their grief was a show of weakness and of the devil steering them from the virtuous path of the Lord. No amount of faith could make Hildegund agree with him and she vowed from that day to make Father Heusch pay. She would cut the flowers in the presbytery gardens, drip wax from the church candles on to the tapestries hanging between the coloured windows, and generally cause confusion and irritation for the priest.

The longer this went on the more she discovered that irritation was neither satisfying to her, nor a deterrent to him. She would listen to his sermons each day with increased bewilderment at the vitriolic language and apocalyptic proclamations. He was a crazed, power hungry showman, she surmised at last, and resolved to raise the stakes of her vengeful game. In making her decision she had set herself upon a road from which she would never deviate. She protected herself behind an increasingly familiar emotional mask and nodded subserviently to this most vile of men as she planned her revenge. His time will come, she thought. She would avenge the death of her brother.

She deliberated at length over whether to place her revenge directly onto the neck of Father Heusch. Ultimately, though, she decided to make him suffer in this life before sending him to an eternal suffering in the next. It was futile to target the Flagellants, they would only have enjoyed her attempts in any case, as well as it handing fuel to the pulpit. The other local parish leaders were too afraid to do anything, and were unlikely to find value in her cause. She applied the same logic, and came to the same conclusion, as she imagined taking her own private crusade up the religious food chain until she thought to come at it from the other side. The most powerful man in all of the Holy Roman Empire was Pope Clement VI. What better way to avenge her brother's death, and presumably inspire her own, than by aiming for the head of the snake in the name of Father Heusch.

On a cold, frosty morning she set out from her small house on Mathildenstrasse on the very edge of Darmstadt in the general direction of the Papal heart.

SPEYER

It had taken her almost two days, but at last she felt the waters of the Rhine lapping her swollen feet. She had made the mistake of believing that walking would be a pleasurable and simple pastime, one that would be an easy way of reaching the distant city of Avignon, for all the time it may take. She would have been better to think of the difference between eating a well cooked steak and a whole cow.

There was no sure way of knowing what proportion of her journey was now complete, but judging by the familiar architecture of the few buildings she came by, there was still a dizzying distance to go. The papal seat was said to have huge sunken alcoves in the towering walls and crenulations more suited to a castle than the centre of God's power on earth. The buildings she had seen on her journey so far could have been lifted from Darmstadt for all the difference they showed, but any doubt that bubbled up through her iron resolution was extinguished with a single, fleeting memory of Steffen.

She knocked on the door of a small farmhouse on the outskirts of Speyer. She would avoid the plague-riddled population centres as best she could; there was no benefit to having more eyes seeing her and she was grateful to be away from the bustle of town life in any case. When nobody answered she circled the building. There was a chicken coop, a small pig pen and a single goat tied by a metal chain to rotting fencepost. Hildegund wondered at the effectiveness of the expensive, heavy iron when the post appeared as though it would fall down in anything stronger than a moderate gust of wind. All of the living creatures she could see either had four legs or scaly feet and so she set off into the fields to look for the farmer and his family.

She found them in a wheat field weeding their crops and called out to them in what she hoped was a friendly tone. 'Herr Farmer! Can I help?'

The farmer looked up from his work and studied the stranger; a woman, no less. He said something to his wife and children and walked over to Hildegund who was waiting politely at the entrance to the field.

'Can I help you?' he said, his long and curly blond hair seeming desperate to escape his scalp in the breeze.

'Good afternoon, herr. I am travelling southwards alone and wish to offer my services in your fields in return for a meal and a roof for the night.'

'Alone?'

A woman travelling unaccompanied was almost unheard of, but Hildegund had a rudimentary back story that she hoped would be enough to distract anyone from her true mission. This would be her first test and her most dangerous. The more homes she stayed in, and the more people with whom she practised her story, the safer she would be.

'Regrettably, yes' she began. 'My husband has a wasting sickness and I am making a pilgrimage to the holy shrine at Santiago de Compostela to plead with our Lord to save his mortal frame. He is too sick to be my companion so I must travel alone, and with all haste. He is faltering and I must do what I can to save him. If you could shelter me for just one night, and no more for I am in need of great speed, then I will pray for your eternal soul beneath the roof of the church of Santa Maria.'

She was happy enough with that. The detail needed a bit of work, and perhaps Santiago was a little too far to make it a reasonable destination, but it may do for now, all things considered. She studied the farmer's face for a welcoming sign.

'Show me your armpits' said the farmer, a request that was unique in its frequency in recent times. Hildegund understood and raised each side of her shirt, showing clean, smooth skin. There was an absence of boils that the farmer deemed to be satisfactory.

'The goat needs to be milked, and the pigsty needs cleaning. You can sleep in with them when you are done. My wife will bring you some potage before you retire.'

He turned and headed back to his family without another word.

For the next few hours Hildegund scraped matted straw from the pigsty and pulled on the underside of the goat. When she was done with her work she sat down in the shelter of the pigsty. A small, wrinkled piglet tottered over to her and snuggled its snout into her belly. She stroked it instinctively.

If she was to have any chance of successfully murdering the pope she would need to have practised beforehand. The first kill would be the hardest, she was certain. Once she had crossed her Rubicon she would surely find it easier each time, like the pulling of a bowstring. She made the mistake of looking the piglet in the eye, those innocent, brown circles imploring her to step away from the murderous brink. She steeled herself, adjusting her arms to give her a grip around the piglet's neck, and waited.

When the crucial moment came, when her power over life was to be tested against this defenceless creature, she faltered, named it Bobbins and cuddled up to it for the night.

OFFENBURG

'My apologies, Herr Rochmann' said Hildegund, bringing her mind back into the room. She had been transfixed by the flickering fire of the warm, comfortable room. It had been a week since she had been able to put something between herself and the sky and was grateful beyond measure for the kindness that Herr Rochmann had shown her since her arrival that morning. He had fed her with a rare vegetable broth and yeasty bread, given her fresh clothes while his wife washed the grubby and pungent ones she had arrived in, and had been conversing with her on a wide range of subjects; from the uses of sheep droppings to warm a house to the merits of leading a pious life in the face of adversity. They were now discussing philosophy, or at least that which constituted philosophy in this distant farmland to the east of the great Rhine river. It would be a shame to have to kill his dog.

'So if we believe that God made everything and that there is a part of God in everything around us' said Hildegund, 'does that mean that we are all God, that we are all a part of his greater being?'

'To a certain extent' said Herr Rochmann. 'He made us in his likeness and we are a part of his presence on earth.'

'What about the pigs?'

'Animals may be God's creation, but they are not made in his likeness. A pig may not enter the kingdom of heaven; that is why we control them. They are given to us by God to give us the strength to live a holy life, one that is a worthy tribute to the master of all creation.' Herr Rochmann set his drink down on the floor beside him, happy to be involved in such intelligent discourse for once.

'But when we eat them, they become part of us' said Hildegund. 'Does this mean they can enter our father's kingdom if we have them for dinner beforehand? It seems a little unfair to me.'

'If that were true, then it would be no different from our predicament. We must also die to find a place in the eternal home of our Lord.'

'Then a pig *can* enter the kingdom of heaven.'

'Well, I'm not sure about that now. A pig is a pig, with no understanding of higher levels of faith.'

'Then where does my hypothesis fall down?' pressed Hildegund. She was enjoying this, playing the role of a devout pilgrim questioning the foundation of her faith in the spirit of a curious Roman Catholic, rather than the assassin she was, on the road to destroy its captain.

'God works in mysterious ways, Hildegund, and it is too complex for our mortal minds to comprehend His plans. All that we should concern ourselves with is living a life worthy of eternal salvation.'

'What about the chickens?'

'The same goes for them as for the pigs' said Herr Rochmann. He had a feeling he was leaving safe ground now and wanted to move on. He offered

Hildegund some more milk as he considered another topic for discussion. He was enjoying spending time with this stranger, so few ever made it to his door, but he would prefer it if they could go back to discussing simpler things.

'So' continued Hildegund, 'if the chickens are God's creation, did he make the egg or the chicken itself?'

'The egg, of course. He created all things that are given life.'

'But where did the egg come from?'

'From God, as I said.'

'But eggs come from chickens, so by your reckoning God is a chicken.'

'Well, I suppose, metaphorically speaking, he is a bit of a chicken.'

'So if God is a chicken, what does that make Jesus?'

Herr Rochmann was drowning in a sea of avian logic. There was a wooden bang outside. 'I think that's Frau Rochmann back from the field. Wait here' he said, before the echo could finish. He stood up and left the room, thanking the Lord for giving him a reason to leave without causing offence.

Hildegund's gaze returned to the fire. She was grateful to Herr Rochmann for reviving her energy, despite her teasing of him. She wondered what he would make of the news of the pope's death when it reached him. Doubtless he would be like so many others, certain that the violent removal of their pope was a sign from God that His creations were not being sufficiently supplicant. She thought of her brother, of her pure motivation, and contented herself that her unholy pilgrimage, while unorthodox, was indeed a just one.

She had been at Herr Rochmann's farmhouse for only a few hours, but was already feeling rejuvenated and eager to shorten the distance between herself and her target. Despite this, she resolved to stay one night, making the most of the roof before opening herself to the elements once more.

Herr Rochmann returned with his wife and six children in tow. The youngest, Ulla, was fascinated by the wild stranger sitting on the floor of their room. She interrupted the adults' conversation several times with questions like 'do you have goats where you come from?' and 'is the sun yellow there too?' Her father soon sent her and her siblings out to play with the trees before they made his guest uncomfortable.

'Tell me, Hildegund, how long will your pilgrimage take?' said Frau Rochmann from behind a stone table. She was cleaning from corner to corner, a task that Hildegund deemed utterly pointless. 'I have never spoken to one with such a long journey ahead of them. Which direction will you take?'

'God will show me the path' she announced. 'He alone knows the importance of my journey and He alone will guide me, unless you have any advice for me, of course.'

'I have never ventured further than Colmar at the edge of the great forest, but I met many pilgrims during my stay there. Most were heading to Avignon, rather than Castille as you are, but the path is shared by both for some way. There is a shrine to Saint James in Colmar that gave them a spiritual vitality to help them on their journey.'

This was more than Hildegund could have hoped for. She could keep her story as it was, right up to the very gates of Avignon, without raising suspicion from anyone of a reasonable mind. Those without one would be a problem no matter how her story was spun. 'Thank you, Frau Rochmann. I will head for Colmar at first light, and may God bless you and your family for your kindness.'

As she gave her eyes up to sleep in a dark corner of the room, the warmth of the fire fading as her drowsiness strengthened, she felt a new confidence growing within her. She had spent hours in the company of others and passed herself off as a legitimate pilgrim with genuine and pious intent. For the first time she allowed herself to believe that this might just work.

Then she remembered the dog.

After her failure with the young swine in Speyer she was determined to kill something soon, or else she would be as well to turn on her heels and return to the anarchy of the Flagellants in Darmstadt.

She waited for the family's breathing to change to the deep, drawn breath of sleep before creeping out of the room and into the yard. She had only moved a couple of steps into the mud when the black and white dog raised and tilted its head in enquiry. She was grateful to have its name remain a mystery to her and was careful not to conjure one herself. It came up past her knees, a reasonable size for a working dog, she thought. She knelt down beside it and looked at its neck, avoiding its eyes at all costs. She was learning, little by little. For the first time she wondered at the logistics of the kill. She had no weapon, nothing with which to strike the animal. She locked her arms around the neck, causing the animal to rest its head against her thigh in the hope of receiving a little pat there. It was then that Hildegund realised the dog was far too large for her to strangle. She had no deathly instrument, not enough strength, and an ill thought out plan. The dog would survive, perhaps longer than Hildegund herself.

She patted its head, named it Tarka, and returned to the house.

CHAPTER EIGHT

FRANCE

Cuthbert could see the cross on top of the church as he crested the hill. They were still an hour or so away from it but it was all downhill from here and they could see their next few days' journey ahead of them across the pleasingly flat landscape. At the base of the hill was another nameless village and they were both keen to reach it before sunset.

'We'll find the bakery and see if the owner is a religious man' said Robert, widening his gait as the slope tilted him downwards. 'If he is, then we can spook him into giving us some of his cast offs.'

'Should we not just appeal to his charity?' said Cuthbert innocently. 'If he is a religious man then he will see we are hungry pilgrims on a pious mission.'

'Not if he's met me before he won't' said Robert, not for the first time.

They made their way down the hill and into the village, bone tired and bone hungry. As the houses thickened into a village they saw doorways selling goods and an occasional window offering services.

'Don't even think about it' said Cuthbert in what constituted a forceful voice. 'We need food and shelter, no more.'

'Lighten up a bit Cuthbert, wait until you try a real tavern with real men. Then you'll see what this is all about' said Robert before pointing to something in the distance. 'There, a bakery. Now, let me give you another lesson on how you survive on the road. You can do it this time, it's the only way you'll learn. You may not be so lucky as to meet someone like me next time.'

'Next time? I don't plan on there being a next time. I've had quite my fill of dead priests to last me this lifetime and the next, thank you very much.'

'Tell the baker you're a poor pilgrim on the holy road to Avignon with no money for food and a long way to go' said Robert, ignoring the protests. 'Tell him you'll offer up a prayer for him each day you are in the holy city. If he's true enough to his faith he'll give us something to eat.'

'I *am* a poor pilgrim' said Cuthbert, confused as to where Robert's cunning plan was hidden. 'So what you're asking me to do is tell him the truth?'

Robert hadn't thought of it like that. He was so used to being a charlatan it hadn't occurred to him that the truth could be as useful as deceit.

'In your case, yes' he conceded.

A tall man with a red glow to his thin cheeks was working at a lump of dough as they approached. Cuthbert took a step ahead of his companion, ready to plead for crusts. He watched the man for a moment, the sights and sounds of the bakery catching him in a wave of familial nostalgia.

'Is that manchet bread you're making? Looks like manchet' said Cuthbert, a little too nervously for his liking.

The baker looked up. 'Of course it isn't, where do you think you are?'

Manchet was only eaten by the upper echelons of society, a fact known to Cuthbert and one that he hoped would flatter the baker. 'It smells like manchet, but now I see it is barley bread. If it tastes as good as it smells then your customers must be grateful to you indeed.'

'It's barley bread' said the baker flatly.

'Would you have any old crusts I could try, nothing you could otherwise sell of course. My father is a baker in England and I would be grateful to sample a bread that smells as good as yours. He would dearly wish to improve his own recipe.'

The baker looked for signs of falsehood in Cuthbert's face. 'What brings you to this distant place? England is a long way from here, I know that because my grandfather once made it all the way to Calais looking for grain during the great famine' said the baker, as if this was the greatest feat of exploration ever undertaken. 'So don't think you can come here with your foreign trickery and relieve me of my hard earned crusts.'

'I am on a pilgrimage to Avignon. My father has sent me to pray at the feet of the pope himself for a good harvest to fill his granary. He must stay behind to bake the bread the village needs to survive, for he is the only one.'

'The only baker? In the whole village?' said the baker. 'I have to work all the hours God sends just to keep on top of the demand in these few streets. He must be a master baker to provide for so many. How can he produce such a quantity?'

'He has chiselled out some grooves in the side of his oven that allow him to place multiple shelves of dough in the oven at the same time. He had to make his oven taller, which cost him a day of baking, but it was worth it eventually' said Cuthbert. None of this was true, naturally, but he put it down to using his imagination rather than outright lying, so it was acceptable.

'Grooves, you say?' said the baker, turning slowly to his oven. 'I see. Yes, I can imagine how that might work. How many shelves does he have?'

'Three. He had to put some small holes in them too to allow the dough to dry enough.' He was now making it up completely.

'So he can bake three times the amount of bread in the same amount of time?'

'Precisely' said Cuthbert emphatically.

The baker stepped out from behind his worktop, walked right up to Cuthbert's face and gave him a forceful kiss on his cheek. 'You, stranger, are the answer to my prayers!'

'Well, I am on a pilgrimage' said Cuthbert, remembering at last the instructions Robert had given him. 'I shall add you to my intentions when I see the Holy Father.'

'You must take something for your travels, a man cannot walk on an empty stomach. Here' he said as he pressed two loaves into Cuthbert's hands. 'I will pray for you, kind pilgrim. Please remember me in your prayers if you deem me worthy of it.' He kissed him again before returning to his worktop, muttering as he went.

They had gone about fifty paces along the street before Robert was able to react.

'You are a natural conman, Cuthbert. Bravo!'

'I told no lies, Robert. It is better to appeal to an honest man with the truth than to deceive a liar with a falsehood.'

'That doesn't make any sense' said Robert. 'You didn't know what kind of a man he was for starters, and what if he was a dishonest sort?'

'You have such little faith in people, there are more good than bad in the world.'

'Oh Cuthbert, how innocent you are. You got lucky this time, but you'll see soon enough. Everyone is out for themselves, even you.'

'Even me? Do you think I chose to trek all this way, only to return to a life of prayer and poverty on my return?'

'Well, what would have happened if you had stayed?'

'They would have hanged me as a murderer.'

'Exactly, and you chose the more favourable of the two options to save yourself. You may not want to be here, Cuthbert, but everybody is where they *prefer* to be, given a certain choice.'

'Even if what you say is true and fair, and I'm not suggesting it is, you are saying it with a loaf of bread in your hand that was won with truth. Well, mostly the truth.'

'That, my friend, is a line worthy of winning any discussion. I defer to your self-evident skills.'

They sat under a tree and tore into their loaves, watching the occasional passer-by as they ate. As hungry as they were they could eat only a fraction of their gift, so shrunken were their stomachs after days of meagre sustenance.

Cuthbert reflected on his conversation with the baker. He wasn't sure he had ever lied before, consciously at least, and it amazed him how easily he had conjured fiction from his catalogue of facts. Perhaps Robert was right, if you could ignore the commitment of a sin that lying surely was, then it would be possible to twist a situation to your advantage.

He took a few more steps down the slippery path he had inadvertently stepped onto.

It followed, then, that the only reason to remain truthful was in order to prevent sin. This was more familiar ground for him and he relaxed a little, like a lost child finding their way out of a dark forest. As his mind tried to change the subject it fell onto something Robert had said days before. Those on a pilgrimage will have their souls absolved of any sin once the pilgrimage was complete. Something in a dark recess of his brain waved nervously to him in the gloom. The sin of lying to the baker will be removed once he completed his mission. In fact, anything he had ever done up to this point in his life would be washed away like a leaves in a flood. Lying to the baker had given him a little thrill, but even Cuthbert knew that was nothing compared with the unspoken debauchery of Robert and his recurring absolutions.

'Let's get drunk' said Cuthbert, breaking the long silence.

Generally speaking, the greater the surprise, the more animated the reaction. There is a tipping point, however, when a statement or action is so far beyond that which could be classed as merely surprising that it causes the recipient to remain motionless. Robert didn't move, no part of him even flinched. His brain still had some work to do to reconcile what it heard with who it heard it from when Cuthbert spoke again.

'Let's move on to the next village while our bellies are full, find the tavern and drink until we get thrown out.'

Robert's brain hurtled towards the monologue, desperately trying to reach it before it went any further. He needed to evolve it into a dialogue if he was to make sense of it.

'If I'm going to be absolved of my sins' said Cuthbert, 'then I'll make damned sure there are some good ones to dispose of. I didn't kill that priest, but I figure I'm in credit with as many sins as would add up to a murder. My father gave me some coins in case of an emergency, what greater emergency could there be for me than to have one chance, one opportunity at living a reckless life? Even if it is just for a few days.'

Robert reached a point where he could open and close his mouth but the right words were still catching up, panting heavily a little way back down the conversation.

'Come on, let's go' said Cuthbert, standing up and pulling Robert after him. 'The longer we stay here the less drinking time we have.'

The two pilgrims walked into the tavern of Vernot, a small and unremarkable village with more chickens than people. Cuthbert strode up to the hatch, ordered two ales confidently before swaggering over to the table where Robert was sitting, bog-eyed, at the strange spirit that now surely inhabited Cuthbert's body.

'Two ales on their way' said Cuthbert firmly. 'Let's see what all the fuss is about, shall we?'

Robert gathered himself enough to ask the question that had kept him quiet for their journey here. 'What happened to you?'

'Nothing' said Cuthbert, 'I merely saw the merit in your philosophy. If I am to be absolved of all sin, then I have a free pass up to that point. Until then, I shall taste what others have told me is enjoyable and seek redemption from the Lord. Ah, here they are.'

A boy slammed two tankards on the table.

'Two' he announced.

Cuthbert pulled two small coins from his purse and handed them to the boy.

'Now, let the fun begin' he said, before drinking half the ale in one long series of gulps.

'Don't be so hasty' said Robert, desperately trying to rein in his companion's vigour.

Cuthbert wiped his mouth on his sleeve. 'Why? All that is stopping us is coin, and when that has gone we can lie our way to more.'

'I fear you may have oversimplified things a little' said Robert. 'Lying takes practise, and you have had none.'

'Oh, how hard can it be?' said Cuthbert. 'I wasn't even trying with the baker and I got two full loaves out of it. You can't argue with that.'

'I told you before, you got lucky. You can't talk your way into riches without failing more often than not. There's a danger to it that I don't think you understand yet.'

'Pish and poffle' said Cuthbert emphatically. 'Watch.'

He drained his tankard, stood up, and headed back to the hatch. Robert watched him speak with the boy, who then disappeared. He was replaced by a burly man with dark hair and a grey beard. Cuthbert was becoming more and more animated, waving his arms around and contorting his body violently. After a few moments he stopped stock still. The barman, suddenly pale, turned to the boy and said something to him with a passion Robert had never seen in a tavern owner before. The boy scurried off, returning with two full tankards. The ale sloshed over the top as the barman thrust them into Cuthbert's hands before hurriedly slamming the hatch door closed.

'There' said Cuthbert proudly as he sat down next to his drinking companion. 'Come on, drink up.'

'What on God's good earth was that all about?' said Robert. 'You looked like the devil himself was inside you.'

'He was, in a way' said Cuthbert seriously. 'I pretended I was being exorcised without the help of a priest. Father Joinson – the one I am supposed to have killed – was conducting an exorcism in front of me when he fell to his fate. I just re-enacted it and told them it happens a lot to me when I'm near sinners. If they were bad people, as you seem to think they would be, then they would believe it to be true, as likely as not. If they were good, pious people then they would fear the wrath of the devil before them and do whatever they could to appease him. I couldn't lose!'

'And you've never deceived anyone before, you're absolutely sure about that?' said Robert, incredulity dripping from his voice.

'Not to my knowledge, no.'

'Then this is going to be a riot of a pilgrimage' said Robert, finishing his first drink and picking up the second.

CHAPTER NINE

PIOMBINO

Lievito pushed his full bowl of potage away, his appetite disappearing as Nicolo's news developed.

'Poor Angelo, may he rest in peace. Come, Signore Mazzi, let us pray for his soul.'

Nicolo was gently surprised by the ease with which he agreed as he knelt down next to the barman. They said three decades of the rosary, giving comfort to them both before standing once more. The feeling was an alien one to Nicolo. His life had been one of self-promotion for as long as he could remember, the theoretical selflessness of Catholicism remaining to him both an example of gross hypocrisy and an impractical rulebook with which to guide your life. This feeling of comfort in prayer was difficult to reconcile with all that had gone before. The rules were changing, it seemed to him. He had created a story in his mind of a pestilence rising in the south to grease the wheels of his own agenda, a plague that the doge had some knowledge of. It now seemed to be less fictional than he would have liked and the scale of its virulence was like nothing he had ever experienced. If there was to be an apocalypse on earth, and he still considered that to be a rather large *if*, then this was surely the beginnings of it. It couldn't hurt to offer up the odd prayer every now and again, just to be on the safe side.

'Poor Angelo' said Lievito for the second time.

'Poor us, more like' said Nicolo, 'They've had their suffering, ours is still to come.'

'Signore Mazzi!' said the barman, admonishingly. 'Please, some respect for the departed souls. We must do what we can to ease their passage through purgatory. Come, let us pray again.'

The novelty of prayer was already wearing off for Nicolo. The unfamiliar feeling of comfort was replaced by a feeling of numbness in his knees. He was becoming bored too, the repetition of the rosary proving to be an anaesthetic for his mind as well as his knees.

As they reached a break between prayers he turned to Signore Lievito. 'I often prefer to pray in silence, signore, I hope it will not cause offence if I do so now. I find that I can add a little more passion when silent. Please, continue aloud if you wish, I will pray with you, but will still my voice.'

'Of course. We must each pray in our own way.'

Nicolo calmed himself to allow an objective evaluation of his predicament. If the Genoese shipping lanes were dormant, while those to Marseilles were open, albeit quieter than they once were, then a reasonable assumption was that something terrible was indeed happening in Sicily. News of it would spread quickly to Genoa and Marseilles and the sailors in those places would be less inclined to travel towards the cataclysm. It was circumstantial on its own, but the vision of Angelo's slumped corpse gave it credence. When he added his conversation with Giovanni di Murta it was undeniable. Something rotten was brewing in the south. He thought of his father and for a moment considered returning to Catania to save him, but knew that any internal debate was more about justifying his decision to abandon him to the pestilence than to seriously consider a return.

South was not an option.

He could travel eastward, towards Firenze, but it was surely only a question of time until the sickness that plagued the poor of Piombino reached the throngs of that great city. The north would present him with an altogether different peril; the eyes of the doge and the punishment for his treacherous escape. To the west was Corsica, an island large enough to lose himself in, and as good a place as any to escape the wracking of his body with boils. So that was it, west to Corsica on the next ship.

Unbeknownst to Nicolo, the next ship to leave Piombino bound for Corsica would not do so for eight more months.

✝

He had been staying above Keystones tavern for three days when the first ship arrived at the small dock. Its flags showed it to be of Sicilian ownership, a fact that neither Nicolo nor the barman could decide was a blessing or a curse. They stood at the end of the jetty as the ship inched slowly towards them. Men with huge, muscular arms threw a heavy rope onto the stone floor as another jumped from a height that would maim a less maritime man. He fastened the rope around three mooring pins and waved to a shipmate. Two rats scurried down the rope and disappeared into the distance as a long wooden plank was levered onto the jetty and a stream of men clambered off.

'Welcome to Piombino one and all' called Lievito as they walked down the plank. 'My Keystones tavern is ready to quench your thirsts and fill your bellies. Please, this way.'

Sailors the world over were cut from the same cloth. Aside from women, the things they desired most when ashore was any food and drink that differed from the restricted monotony of their ship's menu. Lievito was well accustomed with their idiosyncrasies, and so was surprised when they ignored his hospitality.

'Is there a surgeon here, a barber even?' said a thick set man as he stepped onto the jetty, his voice full of haste despite their slow entry into the dock. 'Our captain is sick.'

Lievito and Nicolo exchanged a worried look.

'May I see him?' asked Nicolo. 'If it is the same sickness we have seen here then you would be better to scuttle your ship and wait for passage on the next.'

'It cannot be here too!' cried the sailor in a paroxysm of panic. 'We have travelled with the wind to escape it, nothing is faster than us on all the seas of the world. If it is here then we would be better to leave with all haste. Tell me though, before haste becomes our enemy, how does your sickness reveal itself?'

'There is a certain reluctance on our part to study the corpses of our friends' said Lievito honestly. 'Had I wished to do so I would have trained as a mortician, not a humble tavern owner, even if it does sell the finest ale in Piombino.'

'From what we have seen' said Nicolo, keen to keep the sailors on side, 'it wracks a man with a scorching and contorted pain and grows pustules on his skin, large red masses of evil that remain long after the soul has departed. It lasts only days from beginning to end.'

The sailor put out an arm to stop the train of men behind him. 'Then all is lost. Our captain has been sick for three days; his body is hot enough to warm the cold potage he cannot eat. What are we to do?'

'That I cannot tell you' said Nicolo, 'other than to say you would do well to throw your captain's body overboard to save your own. Please tell us of the news from Sicily, we are starved of information, bar the ravaging spread we have witnessed here.'

'No, he must be given the last rites and buried with all custom. We will do that here, in Piombino and will leave you to your pestilence and your fate. As for Sicily, it is an unprecedented anarchy, no more than a mountain of the dead. Those of us you see here are the last of our families. Even so, we are the lucky ones, with a means of escape and nothing left alive to bind us to the island. I can promise you this, signore; you would consider whatever you have seen here in Piombino to be a virtual paradise had you a memory of the hell on earth in Sicily, as we have. It is surely the apocalypse, God has spoken at last and none He wishes to die shall live.'

'Sounds like thirsty work' said the desperate tavern owner.

Eight days after finding Angelo in his putrid hovel, Nicolo left Piombino for the last time, giving up on his dreams of a Corsica-bound ship reaching him before the sickness did. He thanked Signore Lievito for his hospitality and begged him once more to travel with him, away from the devastation of his town. The barman refused, insisting that his place was with his townsfolk, as few of them as there now were. The Sicilian sailors had buried their captain in the grounds of the church and set sail for Genoa that same day in search of a safe haven. Nicolo had refused a passage with them, confident that a ship bound for Corsica would show itself soon. He was reluctant to travel on a plague riddled ship in any case, and Genoa was as unsafe for him as Sicily, albeit for a starkly different reason. The beggar was no longer at his place outside the tavern, undoubtedly another victim of God's rage.

Lievito had given him a leather bag, saying he could make another from the skins of the former tanner, now of no use to anyone. Lievito had filled it with as many provisions as would fit and asked only that he return one day to repay the favour. Nicolo promised to try, being careful not to explicitly commit to it for fear of being struck down from on high with the pestilence for committing a deceitful act.

He now doubted his actions. Even a man of such stoic agnosticism as Nicolo wavered in the face of this demonic plague. While he could not be said to be pro-active in his repentance, he had begun to take an active, vocal involvement in the prayers that Signore Lievito had deemed necessary for several hours a day. They spent more time in the church too, where they would occasionally meet other surviving members of the village, supporting each other with discussions on the latest catalogue of recently deceased townsfolk, as well as the mystery of both the plague and God's great plan. He could only wonder at the hysterical conclusions these genuinely faithful people were drawing.

He would travel north again in the hopes of finding a ship destined for Marseilles. If he could get that far then he would surely have evaded the clutches of the disease. From there he could choose any direction he liked, including towards Avignon if he so wished.

CHAPTER TEN

COLMAR

The shrine at Colmar was busy with the faithful. Having no experience of its popularity, Hildegund was unaware that it was busier, much busier, than usual. She wandered through the crowds as she approached the imposing walls of Saint Martin church, taking in the strange scene before her. Tall, ornate spires were connected to the church by angled stretches of smooth stone and were coupled with huge arched windows of coloured glass running along both sides. On an outside wall to one side was a high alcove housing a small statue of a man with his hands flat together in front of him and a staff against his shoulder. It was here that the rambling crowds became a solid, immobile mass. A priest was standing below the shrine, delivering an energetic sermon to the crowd. There was no way through to the front other than to wait in the throng for the priest to finish. A short, stout woman standing next to Hildegund turned to her.

'How lucky we are to be within sight of Saint James in these troubling times.'

Hildegund couldn't find a question in the woman's remarks, but answered one anyway. 'Yes, we are lucky indeed.' She was troubled beyond measure, plotting episcopicide can do that to a woman, and there were no signs here of the disease that had so ravaged the population of Darmstadt.

'I am a poor pilgrim on my way to Castille' she said, unsure of what she was going to say next but anxious to learn anything she could about the spread of the plague. 'I would be glad to learn more of this place, is that the most holy Saint James I see at the shrine, saint of pilgrims and apostle of Jesus?'

'Saint James? Goodness, no' said the woman. 'That's Father Mettler, the parish priest.'

Hildegund adjusted her expectations. 'Never mind. Tell me, what news do you have of the shadow from the east? I have heard so little since I left home.'

'Not here' said the woman. 'There are too many fragile minds. The slightest glint of knowledge can start a landslide of misinformation. Come, I must head back to the convent now anyway, I am due in the wash house shortly. I will tell you what I know in the time that we have.'

Hildegund followed the woman out of the crowd and into a field that separated the church and the convent of the Dominican Sisters of St Catherine. She considered her opening question, keen to keep the small talk brief. They could see the convent in the distance and it would be useful to know which places to avoid along the way if she was to reach Avignon before the epidemic reached her. Any other information would be a bonus.

'How long have you been a nun?' she asked.

'Oh I'm not a nun, goodness no. I'm not worthy of such an honour, I am a mere washerwoman. I keep every part of the convent clean; the floors, the walls, the clothes, the crockery. It is a pleasure to remove even such a small concern from the minds of the holy women.' There wasn't a hint of spite in her voice. It appeared to Hildegund that this woman was as pure as they came. It seemed a genuine pleasure to her to serve those she deemed more holy than herself.

'How wonderful that you have found a cause in your life worth working so hard for' said Hildegund, keen to get on the good side of this woman quickly. 'I am Hildegund, from Darmstadt, by the way.' She offered a hand to the washerwoman, who ignored it.

'Oh Hildegund, have you come from the plague? Are you well? Tell me of all that goes on in Darmstadt, I would dearly love to hear your exotic tales, no matter how banal they may seem to you. It is so long since anyone spoke to me so kindly.'

It must have been long indeed, thought Hildegund, if the conversation thus far was considered so. 'I have fled with all haste, but not from the plague, although its presence is ravaging my beloved town. My husband has a different sickness, one less swift in its execution but equally as final without the intercession I hope to warrant from my pilgrimage. The town is becoming overrun with crazed zealots who find solace and redemption for all mankind in their indiscriminate lashes. It is a place to which I would not return if it wasn't for my dear husband.'

'You are the very essence of all that is good in the world' said the washerwoman, clearly starved of perspective and company. 'I am Marguerite, and I will find hospitality for you within our walls. You must be hungry and tired. I can give you a bed to sleep on and a roof above your head. The food is meagre, as it is becoming for all of us, but you are welcome to that which we can offer. Come, I insist. We are nearly at the gates. Sister Guillemette will be eager to find me home again.'

Hildegund had not intended to enter the convent, but she had discovered little and was anxious to learn of the plague's movements before leaving Colmar. She passed through the archway that marked the boundary to the convent grounds and walked up along the side of the main building to the servants' entrance. Marguerite beckoned her through the small door and along a dark, narrow corridor. They passed several doors that Hildegund presumed led to the working areas; the kitchen, the laundry and other such places of labour. Marguerite stopped at one, heavier than the others with a large, locking bolt.

'Why do you need such a heavy lock here?' asked Hildegund.

'It is so very sad' said Marguerite solemnly. 'When I first arrived here there was hardly a need for a door, let alone a lock. Times change though, as do people's morals and vices. This is our pantry. When food is scarce it pays to protect what you have. Important work is done by the nuns here, and who else can protect us from God's wrath that spreads from town to town like the wind? The pestilence may have spared Colmar so far, Hildegund, but travellers bring with them the possibility of Armageddon. They also bring thieves and suspicion.'

'Surely no-one would steal from a place of God? They would be saving their body at the expense of their soul. They would be sending themselves straight to hell.'

'Indeed they would, under normal circumstances' said Marguerite. 'But these are not normal times, as I'm sure you are aware. Now, let us find something to fill your belly and help you on your pilgrimage.'

Marguerite slid the bolt and heaved open the heavy oak door. She stepped aside to allow Hildegund to see the food inside, of which there was none. The humble washer woman pushed Hildegund forcefully in the small of her back, sending her forwards into the tiny dark space where her head bounced painfully off the far wall. She slumped to the floor of the empty room as Marguerite slowly closed the door, locking it again before rushing down the corridor to find Mother Superior.

Hildegund took in her suddenly changed environment. It didn't take long, it was all black. She waved her arms in front of her in the darkness, hitting them off walls on all sides without needing to move her feet. She checked the locked door, despite there being no chance of it opening, and slumped to the floor. What concerned her almost as much as her predicament was that she hadn't seen it coming, not even a suspicion of it. Marguerite had seemed normal, the embodiment of what she expected from a convent washerwoman. If someone in such a lowly station could raise themselves to these treacherous heights then things were worse than Hildegund had thought. Surely it was only a matter of time before the devastation she had witnessed in Darmstadt was visited upon the souls in Colmar and beyond.

She resolved to find the washerwoman, interrogate her and kill her. Then she would leave for Avignon again, her premier murder complete and her resolve fortified. All she had to do was to get out of the cell, the one made of solid stone with a door that was locked on the wrong side.

Mother Superior looked up from her desk at the sound of knocking.

'Come' she ordered. Everything Mother Superior said could eventually be boiled down to an order. It wasn't because she enjoyed the power; it had become more of a habit than anything else after years of trying to manage an army of nuns intent on passing through this life without any pro-activity polluting their pure thoughts.

Marguerite stepped sheepishly into the room, her eyes fixated on the floor as she crossed the empty space to the desk. Mother Superior looked up and frowned. Marguerite was one of the few people in the convent who could be classified as unpredictable. Her heart was in the right place, but her head was usually in the clouds.

'Yes?'

'Mother, I come with a warning and a confession' said Marguerite.

Of course you do, she thought, tilting her head and giving a small nod to encourage Marguerite to get this over with quickly.

'I have captured an outsider' said Marguerite, pride and fear mingling nauseously in her stomach.

'An outsider you say? Where have you captured them *to*?'

'Fear not, Mother, they're in the old pantry. We're safe for now.'

'What did they do to warrant such a confinement? Were you harmed?'

'Not harmed, exactly' said Marguerite, disappointed at the notable absence of gratitude in Mother Superior's voice. 'They have travelled from Darmstadt in the east where the pestilence rages unabated. She may have brought the disease with her, or worse still its devilish contamination of the soul.'

'Let me make sure I'm following this correctly. You came upon a stranger from lands pocked with the plague and thought it best to bring them into the convent grounds and leave them in a room we hope to use again for our food. Is that about right?'

'Well, of course it sounds bad when you put it like that' said Marguerite defensively. 'I have isolated the problem and saved the town from the depravity that this curse can spawn.'

'No, Marguerite, I'm afraid all you have done is lock up an innocent woman. Does she show any signs of the disease?'

'Not as such, no. Although I haven't checked her groin.'

'I should hope not!' said the Mother, wide eyed with a vision she hadn't asked for. 'How long is it since she left Darmstadt?'

'She said three weeks, but you know how untrustworthy strangers can be, Mother.'

'Says the woman who threw her into a cell. Tell me the path she took to arrive here.'

'Well, all she said was that she kept away from the main routes to help avoid the pestilence. She is on her way to Castille to seek a miracle for her ailing husband.'

'It seems to me that all you have succeeding in doing here, Marguerite, is to scare a poor pilgrim half to death. A pilgrim, might I add, who has the wherewithal to avoid plague ridden towns along the way and had stopped at our shrine to pay homage to Saint James, saint of all pilgrims.'

'You're making it sound worse than it is.'

'No, I'm afraid not. I'm telling it precisely as it appears to me. Bring her to me at once' she ordered.

'Please' ordered Mother Superior, motioning to the seat in front of her.

Hildegund lowered herself onto the hard wooden chair gratefully and waited.

'It seems I must apologise for the actions of one of my flock. Marguerite can be a little keen at the best of times and this pestilence has only served to accentuate her vigour.'

'I hope that all of the houses of our Lord are as zealously protected as yours, Mother Superior' lied Hildegund. 'We are in unprecedented times and all preventative action should be welcomed, even to the detriment of my own freedom.'

'That is most gracious of you...'

'Hildegund.'

'...Hildegund. I fear that Marguerite had not thought her actions through carefully enough, if at all. That said, I cannot allow the ravages of this plague to reach my walls as I am sure you can appreciate. Marguerite may have executed her intentions poorly, but her principles remain sound; with outsiders comes the pestilence. We have seen it first-hand here in Colmar. I cannot permit you to stay, for only a fool would allow even the smallest chance of this disease to enter their house. In bringing you here she has set your fate.'

'I understand' said Hildegund.

'You must leave with all swiftness. I will see to it that you can use the front door, it is quicker and there are no souls there at this time of day. I am sorry to have seen you suffer at our hands, however brief that suffering may have been. Here, take this. It will give you comfort on your journey. Show it at the doors of any convent in the Holy Roman Empire and you will be given a bed for the night and food in your belly.'

The Mother placed a wooden crucifix on the small table next to Hildegund. It was fastened to a blue rosary necklace and would have been considered a great gift by most. For all her polite words she was careful not to touch the stranger.

'That is most generous of you, Mother. I do not know how to repay you' said the woman intent on killing the pope. She picked it up and slipped it over her neck.

'Do not thank me yet, Hildegund, for you have many a long road to travel before you reach Castille. Promise me only this: If you show any signs of the pestilence you will not enter a house of the Lord.'

'Of course. Should I fall to it I will find the highest hill and wait there alone for the Lord to take me to the next life.'

The nun stood and beckoned Hildegund to follow her out of the room. They made their way through the convent until the main entrance was before them.

'I wish you fair travels and may the Lord spare your soul' said Mother Superior.

'I will remember you in my prayers' said Hildegund as she crossed the threshold and walked out into the crisp air. When she was out of sight of the convent she pulled the necklace over her head and placed it in her pocket.

CHAPTER ELEVEN

MARSEILLES

February, 1348

The port of Marseilles glistened in the winter sunshine. To an eye unfamiliar with docklands it would have seemed perfectly normal, but Nicolo had been raised below seagulls and knew an impotent port when he saw one. Countless ships were docked and floating idle, while the shipping channels that would normally be a patchwork of sails were all but empty. Any vessel that moved was heading into the port, something Nicolo took as a good omen. If Marseilles had borne witness to the plague then surely there would be no incoming traffic. The devilish advocate from the pessimistic part of his mind pointed out that those arriving at the port would have no way of knowing the situation there. Indeed, there may be no departing ships because their crews were all lost to the pestilence in the slums of the city. He would have to wait until they had reached the mooring posts to learn more of the city's fate.

After leaving Piombino he had reached as far north as Livorno before finding a crew that would take him to Marseilles. It had cost him one of his lesser gold rings, but he preferred to be poorer but alive than be a slightly more valuable corpse.

As they reached the docks the first mate slammed a plank onto the jetty and Nicolo finally disembarked The Ailsaveitch. He thanked several of the sailors and wished them good health before heading straight to the markets. The ship's cabin boy had told him of a shoemaker there who was skilled at teasing information from the tightest of lips. If anyone had news of the pestilence it would be him. It was just a few streets away from the docks and Nicolo was there before he had absorbed much of his new surroundings.

On one corner of the market square was a small church with its new, smooth walls. They contrasted sharply with the ramshackle stalls that stood outside its doors, hoping to snare the departing faithful. Not since Genoa had Nicolo seen a church in such sturdy condition. Back then he would pass by them without a thought, but he had begun to step inside their walls more often now. There was a stream of people entering with him as the warm air of the nave thawed his skin, taking him back to Catania and simpler times.

His spirit sank at the scene before him. The church was almost full yet no priest could be seen at the altar. Those inside were crowded around shrines in alcoves up and down the walls, praying to whichever saint they could get close to. It was clear to Nicolo that word of the plague had reached here. He hoped that was all that had made it this far.

He knelt in the centre of the church, away from the crowds, and offered up the silent prayers that had become his routine. He said an Eternal Rest for Signore Lievito and poor Angelo, sure that the barman had now joined the mountain of dead. For his father he hedged his bets a little, saying a decade of the rosary and an Eternal Rest, just in case. For himself, he asked only that the comfort he now found in his prayers would continue for as long as the pestilence followed him.

As he left the church he had to push past the oncoming crowd, twisting and turning through the sea of hope. As the cool air brushed his face again he scanned the square for signs of the shoemaker. He passed several artists' stalls, each selling the same religious scenes drawn on a variety of media. One stall seemed to be stocked entirely with crosses carved from root vegetables while another had just a single item; a small thin slice of a tree trunk. Nicolo stopped at this one, his curiosity overcoming his preoccupation for a moment.

'You have an interesting stall, sir. What is the significance of this lump and why is it the only piece for sale?'

'This is no lump sir, oh no. This stands alone as befits a relic of such provenance.'

'Of course it does' said Nicolo flatly. 'Go on.'

'First of all, it is from the very tree that the cases of Saint Augustine's library were made. Secondly, his face appears in the grain, look.'

Nicolo didn't look, although he had not ignored the stall holder deliberately. Had he heard him he would have done so, however. He was of the opinion that imagery in natural things was either coincidental or absent. As it was, the mention of Saint Augustine had stolen his wits.

'Say that again' he ordered.

'I said his face is in the grain, look' said the salesman, sensing coin.

'Before that, and be quick about it.'

'Oh, right sir, sorry sir. I thought you would like to see the saintly face in the grain, you see. Most people who look upon it come over all funny. You know, being in the presence of such a holy relic an' all.'

'My dear man' said Nicolo, barely restrained impatience dripping from each syllable. 'If you wish to maintain your current limb count may I suggest you tell me again about the saint with all haste.'

The stall holder made three attempts to start a sentence before steadying himself with a hand on the table. He took a deep breath.

'Saint Augustine's library, sir. It had books in it, see?' said the man, with a level of nervousness that could not reasonably be described as sustainable. 'They needed shelves to store them, and shelves are made of wood, see? They got the wood from trees and this is one of those trees. It has his face on it, did I mention that?'

'Look me in the eye' said Nicolo in a tone that warned against disobedience.

The stall holder did so, or at least tried to. His sight flinched between each of Nicolo's eyes, unable to settle on one, so shot were his nerves. Nicolo placed a hand on the man's shoulder in an attempt to calm him but all he succeeded in doing was to set the man into a panic. The stallholder answered the unspoken question.

'You're right sir, please don't tell anyone sir. All of my family is dying or dead and I have no means of support bar this. Please don't turn me to the wolves.'

Nicolo wasn't sure what the man meant by this, but was happy at least to hear that he was a simple conman. He found it easier to deal with those cut from the same cloth; knowing their vulnerabilities was crucial if he was to take as much value as he could from them.

'I may yet, my good man, but I may also save your soul' said Nicolo, layering his speech with inferred auguries. 'I have an offer for you. It is the only one I will make and I strongly recommend you accept. For the moment I will not discuss the alternative.'

Nicolo didn't have an alternative, but that wasn't important yet. All he needed was for the man to believe he did, and a painful one at that.

'I will take your worthless lump of wood, and in exchange I shall give you something from which you can make some coin. Look around you, my good man. Every stall is selling religious imagery, taking advantage of the hysteria enveloping the city. What does that tell you?'

'That there are too many stalls selling religious art?' said the man, rocking nervously from heel to toe.

Nicolo rolled his eyes.

'No. People sell what people buy. There is a plague ravaging the city and those looking to make a coin have a singular product. You need art if you are to earn your meals.'

'So all you have is advice' said the stall holder, rather more brazenly than he intended.

Nicolo fidgeted inside his tunic. 'Do not be so quick to chide the very man offering you help. Here.'

He pulled out the small tapestry of the crucifixion and held it in an open palm.

'This will feed you for a month if you play it right. You should go to each of these stalls and ask the holder about their wares. They will be desperate to explain the high provenance of their goods, keen to take advantage of you. Make a note of all of them and pick something else. Make yourself different. Tell people whatever you like about it then, just be sure to include some obscure and unused shrine in its story.'

He passed the cloth to the man, picked up the wooden disc, and left. For the first time in his adult life he had traded something of financial value for something of none. He knew the wooden disc had never been near St Augustine's library, but he took comfort that it would serve as a reminder of his youth and of the days before he embroiled himself in political machinations.

He passed more stalls, each offering a particular level of protection from the plague that no other stall could offer, and certainly not for the price. He was almost at the furthest point from the church when a narrow alley drew his attention. There were more permanent shops here, using the windows and doorways of brick buildings rather than the old wooden benches of the square. There would be more chance of a shoemaker here and Nicolo headed towards it, passing a glass blower, blacksmith and a button maker before reaching a shop front that seemed to indicate an availability of skinned badgers inside.

He was close to the far end of the alley when he heard a loud bang from the last doorway. Inside was a grubby man wearing an apron that was now black but whose original colour was a matter of conjecture. The cobbler looked up at the sound of a customer and wiped his hands futilely on his clothes.

'Good morning, sir' said the shoemaker. 'How can I help you?' Instinctively, he glanced down at his customer's feet, as a milliner would study a man's head.

Nicolo, master of nuance, saw the man's clumsy attempt at subtlety and turned it to his advantage.

'I wish for you to mend my shoes. As you have noticed they are a little worn and I have a long journey ahead of me.'

'Please' said the shoemaker, gesturing to an upturned wooden box.

Nicolo sat down, took off his shoes and handed them over. 'Do you think you can fix them quickly? I am due to leave the city this afternoon and I would walk all the easier with your help.'

'I can fix them, of that you can be sure. I am a busy man though and haste comes at a price.'

Nicolo reached into his tunic and slipped a ring onto a finger. He would pay a high price for the information he hoped to gain, but a gold ring would be of no consequence on a dead finger.

'I will pay handsomely for the shoes if you provide me with certain information' said Nicolo, looking the man dead in the eye.

The shoemaker straightened his back at the glinting metal and returned Nicolo's gaze. 'My apologies, m'lord. I am not visited upon by men of your... calibre as often as I would like. I am sure I do not know any information that a man of your stature would consider useful, but I will tell you what I can, if I have anything at all.'

'Then the deal is off' said Nicolo, surprising even himself a little. 'I will not give up so fine a ring as this for information that you *can* give me. I want information you *know*, whether you would want to disclose it or not.'

'I can see you are a man of little compromise, m'lord. Tell me what concerns you and I will strike the deal, or not, as I see fit.'

With one sentence the shoemaker had revealed himself to the master of deception. If a lowly cobbler was prepared to offer an ultimatum to a man as important as Nicolo appeared to be, then he was no lowly cobbler at all.

'It is unusual for a man of your abilities to hide behind such a skilled profession, master cobbler' said Nicolo, choosing to open up the playing field for a fair fight. 'Tell me, who is your guardian?'

'I have no guardian, signore. I am but a humble shoemaker.'

'Of course you are' said Nicolo. 'Tell Giovanni di Murta I will complete my errand.'

The shoemaker, to his credit, did not crumble at the mention of the doge, but the almost imperceptible narrowing of his eyes confirmed Nicolo's suspicion.

'I have not heard of this di Murta, signore, nor your errand. I fear you have me confused with someone else.'

'Then let me explain' said Nicolo. 'You have a dirty shop, signore. Every inch of it is covered in dust and grime from your cobbling. You have covered all available spaces with depictions of our Lord and the saints, as is the current style in the face of the plague. Yet there is a lighter patch on that wall behind Saint Francis. There was a larger picture there once, one of great importance to you I am sure. The frame's edges were not the simple straight lines of a cheap frame, as would befit the trappings of a shoemaker. They were ornate, expensive.'

'I am a poor man, signore, and cannot afford such luxuries. The patch was there when I took over the shop and I have no knowledge of its history.'

'And yet the frame is still here, in this shop' countered Nicolo. 'I can see it leaning against the wall of your stockroom there. You couldn't bear to be parted from it, and I empathise with you on that front at least, for it is a fine item.'

'Ah' said the cobbler. 'That is a cheap, old frame, signore. Not all things shaped from the same mould are comparable.'

'Then you won't mind if I take a closer look. I would very much wish to learn why a man who purports to be ignorant of the doge of Genoa would keep his likeness in his shop, with or without an expensive frame.'

'But that is a depiction of the hills of my home in Piacenza. The frame is not that which graced these walls so long ago, I can promise you that, signore.'

'That may well be the case' said Nicolo, happy to concede a point that was no longer relevant. 'You should have taken more care with it, *signore*. For the corners are peeling away and have revealed your true loyalty. Even from this distance I can see the tomes of his Serenity painted into the background of what I must assume is a portrait of the great man. I have seen those books with these very eyes, and would not forget them so soon.'

The shoemaker froze.

'Now, how long will it take to fix these shoes?'

The sight of the faithful in the church would have been enough to convince Nicolo that Marseilles was not a safe haven from the plague, but the revelation in the shoemaker's shop made it irrelevant. The doge had eyes everywhere, and Nicolo's options had been reduced to just one.

He stayed one night in a cheap inn beside the docks, as much for the comforting sounds of sailors and seagulls as for the rest. At dawn he visited the church, much emptier than it had been the previous day, but still far more popular than it should have been so early in the morning. There was another long journey ahead of him, but he would travel with a tangible end to his wandering days. He would go to Avignon, despite his efforts to avoid it, and find The Cutler. He would deliver his message and leave the city, travelling as far north as it would take to reach a town still ignorant of the plague. Anywhere. That would be his home, for good or ill.

CHAPTER TWELVE

AVIGNON
February, 1348

Pope Clement VI, Bishop of Avignon, Vicar of Jesus Christ, Successor of the Prince of the Apostles, Supreme Pontiff of the Universal Church, Primate of the Holy Roman Empire, Servant of the Servants of God, blew his nose. Three men rushed to his side to ease the Holy Father's hand of the burden of the handkerchief before bowing low and walking backwards to their invisible place against the wall of the most holy administration office in all of Christendom.

'I have a common cold, not a wasting sickness!' he roared. 'Leave me now, all of you. I don't want to be disturbed for the rest of the day. And bring me my meat! Is God's representative on earth to starve to death for want of a pair of ears that will listen?'

His servants slunk silently past the carved wooden doors and out of the room.

'So, do we disturb him with his dinner or not?' said one.

'How am I to know' said another. 'There are so many twists in his riddling speech these days I don't know which way is up any more. Did you hear him this morning? He asked the old bent man in the treasury department to bring the Glory of God to his room, not an ailing Master of Coin with a lisp and a pile of parchments. The poor thing was rushing around the palace asking if anyone knew where we kept it. He ended up going back to him with that fancy red vase the Lords of Lyon gave him last year. He damn near threw the man out of the window.'

'We'll get the short one to take him his dinner, at least there's less of him to aim for' said the first.

The pope sat at his desk, looking out over the lavish gardens and its army of workers. He had sat through four meetings already today without decreeing a single thing. He needed to pass judgment on someone or something before it built up like last time. That was an uncomfortable funeral to preside over, even for a man of his standing. It was one thing to order the execution of a stable hand for the death of a nameless foal, but quite another to wax lyrically about their life in the palace when everyone in attendance knew you had all but dealt the fatal blow. He needed an outlet. He had received word last week that a visitor was expected and hoped that they would arrive today. It would be good to catch up with his old friend after all these years, perhaps it would be a salve to his growing discontent.

It occurred to him that he had ordered the servants to leave him be for the day. What would they do if his friend arrived, and come to think of it how would they deliver his meat? He decided to let them work it out for themselves. What good was it being pontiff if he couldn't test a man's priorities every now and again. He sat in his favourite seat by the door and listened.

'I'm not going in, you go in' said a voice.

'Bugger that' said another.

'Don't look at me' said a third, 'I gave him his breakfast yesterday. Look, the cut's still bleeding.'

'Fine, give it to me' said the first voice. 'What's the worst that can happen?'

The second and third voices didn't answer but the pope could hear their wooden shoes clopping into the distance on the tiled floor.

A knock at the door made him jump backwards. However powerful an eavesdropper may be, there remains an innate desire to not be caught in the act. He scuttled over to his desk and called out.

'What is it now? Did I not demand to be left alone?'

The first voice stayed quiet, waiting for an order.

'Well come in then, damn you!'

'Holy Father, forgive my intrusion but I bring you your meat and a message.'

'Leave the meat there' he ordered, pointing to a table; a nice unambiguous order that was a comfort to the first voice. 'Bring the message here.'

This was shakier ground. The message was in his head, not on parchment. Should he walk over to deliver it, or *bring it here* by saying it aloud from where he stood? The first voice was no longer second guessing himself; he was up to seventh guessing and climbing. He chose to stay where he was, reasoning that the further away he was from his master, the more likely he was to miss.

'Your visitor has arrived, your Holiness.'

'Marvellous, please send him in' said Clement VI with uncharacteristic joviality, before quickly correcting himself. 'What I mean is, why are you still here? Don't keep an emissary of the pope waiting, man. Bring him to me at once.'

The first voice backed out of the room and scurried down the corridor to the giant staircase that led down to the main lobby and the pope's visitor.

'Pope Clement, sixth of his name and Prince of the Apostles will see you now.'

'Oh, get him and his fancy titles' said the visitor. 'He didn't go for all that pomp and nonsense when we were drinking cheap wine in the cloisters of La Chaise-Dieu. How people change, eh? It seems the job may have got to him.'

The first voice remained diplomatically silent, storing the information away to regale his friends in the kitchens later. He led the guest up the stairway and along the corridor to the papal bedroom. He reached the deeply carved door, found the familiar flat spot at head height that served as the only place to knock without cutting a knuckle, and waited.

'Enter.'

'Father Bricoler, your Holiness.'

'Leave us.'

Father Bricoler swaggered into the room, rolling his head to take in the frills and fancies of the sacred office.

'Well hello there, my dear old friend. Nice place you've got here. Did you do this yourself?' said Bricoler, pointing to a tapestry on the wall. 'You've done a great job.'

'Did I do it myself? Have you forgotten I'm the pope? Popes don't do embroidery, they do decrees and judgments and other menacingly infallible stuff.'

'Well, that's where you're wrong. Is this wine free?'

'Wrong? Listen here, I can decide what is right and what is wrong, Jacques, so don't come in here with your fearless confidence telling *me* what is right and what is wrong. And yes, the wine is free.'

'Calm down. Jesus Christ you're tetchy, Pierre. Is the job getting to you? I was referring to the tapestry. Embroidery does not create a tapestry, that's weaving you're thinking of. You need a drink. Here, get this down you.' Jacques Bricoler picked up a heavy crystal jug and decanted a deep red wine into a matching goblet, drinking half before topping it up and passing it to the pontiff. 'You ought to relax.'

'Now listen here, Jacques. First of all, you do not refer to me as Pierre while you are in this place. I didn't go through the ignominy of the papal chair for you to refer to me by my old name. You're a priest in the papal palace now, not some teenager in a tavern. Have some decorum.'

'I don't remember you having much decorum with that one from La Rochelle.'

'That was a long time ago now. I am the most holy man on earth and must behave as such. Back then we were all just lost travellers on the road to salvation. I have found the true path and am all the more enlightened and contented for it.'

'We both know that's boll...'

'May I remind you that you are in the presence of the Lord's representative on earth' interrupted Pope Clement before the curse could escape Jacques' mouth. 'That kind of language would see a lesser man hanged. Do not test my principles any further, old friend.'

'What difference does it make if I use nice words or blasphemous ones? There is only you that can hear me and you can fabricate anything you like without a soul questioning your honesty. I may as well get a few out of my mouth while I can, it is so suffocating being a priest; people expect you to be so polite all the time.'

'Why did you choose the life of a priest then, Jacques? There were options for you back then.'

'Well' said Father Bricoler, 'It's an easy job, isn't it? Say a few words on a stage and people think you're their ticket to redemption. I got a lovely fruit cake from Madame Perruque last week too, so I can't complain. Plus the tax breaks help, what with us having a *noble profession* and all.'

'I'm not sure you've grasped the purpose of the priesthood, Jacques' said the pope. 'You are a servant of Christ, a healer of the sick and a comfort to the poor.'

'Are you going to be like this all weekend? Because if you are I'll bugger off back to Marseilles.'

'I have changed, Jacques. We were insignificant young men the last time we met, now I'm an important figure in the jigsaw of the world. If you do not wish to spend time in the presence of such a shadow, then you can indeed, as you say, *bugger off.*'

Jacques looked at his old friend, mischief glinting in his eyes.

'I have an idea.'

'I'm still not sure this is such a good idea, Jacques. What if someone recognises me?'

'Don't be such a wet blanket, Clem, they won't notice a thing, and even if they did what could they say? You seem happy enough to hold the power here, so wield it. What is the point of being the most feared man in the land if you don't use it to your advantage? Get out there and see what your flock is doing. If you see something you don't like you can decree it to be ungodly tomorrow and they will think you really are the eyes of their omnipresent God.'

'*Our* God, Father Bricoler, *ours*' said the pope pointedly.

'Of course, of course' said Jacques, waving an arm dismissively. 'Listen, how can a man lead his people when he doesn't understand their lives? You need to get out there and see how the real people of your city live. You will discover the reality, a tale untainted by layers of prejudice added by those who would protect you from the truth.'

'Well, when you put it like that' said the pope, 'I suppose it would be fun to spy around the city for a while. Do you think I could go to the church of Saint Pierre? I would dearly love to see their Stations of the Cross, I've heard they are a sight to behold. All who venerate there are said to feel the comfort of our Lord as they reach the sixth Station, you know, the one with Veronica in it?'

'Can you hear yourself?' said Jacques, exasperation pouring from his tongue. 'You have the freedom of the city, the freedom to do whatever you choose for the first time in five years and you want to go to a church, like a lumberjack heading to a forest for his Christmas break.'

'Yes but it's different for me…'

'Yes it is' said Jacques before the pope could finish his rebuttal. 'You are drowning in a pious gaol here, take a break and live a little.'

'I can do all I wish in the eternal life that is to come' said the pope, trying desperately to reclaim some of his authority from the grappling hands of his friend.

'I'll send you there now if you don't lighten up a little.'

'Careful now, Jacques. If there's any killing to be done here it will be me that orders it. I am the pope, after all.'

'Then you won't want to send this friend of yours to hell by ending his life before he can repent his many sins, would you? Come now, put this on and let's begin your adventure.'

Pope Clement VI, Bishop of Avignon, called out to his servants on the other side of the bedroom door. 'Listen, all who have ears to do so. My friend is sick, he has lost his voice and is visiting a physician in the city. Do not ask him to converse with you as you guide him out, nor on his return. Any who attempt to do so will feel the vengeful wrath of the Lord for mocking a man with such an unfortunate ailment. Also, I am taking a break from my papal duties for the rest of the afternoon, I have a bit of a headache from this cold and a good sleep is all that is required. Do not send anyone to me and do not bring me food or drink. Any who disturbs my rest will be sleeping for considerably longer than they would like before the day is out. I mean forever by the way, in case my subtly was lost on you.'

'Smoothly done, your Holiness' said Jacques. 'Very... you know?'

'Yes, yes. Do I have to wear this veil over my face, I can hardly see where I'm going?'

'How else would you suggest we disguise your face?'

'Fine, but I'm not wearing that hat.'

CHAPTER THIRTEEN

AVIGNON

February, 1348

The most significant centipede in the known world crawled ignorantly amongst the undergrowth. Hildegund held her stone high above it and waited. She was close to Avignon now and could not arrive there without at least one murder under her belt. The animals at the farms were, with hindsight, too great a task for her inexperience, but starting with the pope was surely a foolish strategy. Once she had disposed of the centipede, she would find a vole or a mouse and serve judgment upon it. From there it would be easier to build up to episcopicide.

The centipede slid up and onto a sturdy piece of fallen branch. Hildegund closed her eyes and smashed her stone down onto it, or at least where the centipede had been a moment earlier. She prised her eyes open cautiously as the insect scrabbled off the branch and away from her. A feeling of diluted rage flushed her and she ran after it, reaching it in four paces and stamping on it with a forceful thrust of her leg.

She lifted her foot to inspect the underside of her shoe, finding a much flatter centipede peeling slowly off it. Her anger was replaced by the exhilaration of accomplishment and she marvelled at how this tiny show of power could elicit such emotions in her. Killing the pope is going to be a hoot, she thought.

The walls of the great city showed themselves between the forest of trees. Hildegund had been on the move for longer than she cared to consider and was ready for some rest now that she had reached her final destination. She would use her time well, scouting the city from the taverns to the palace for signs of a way to the pope. There was also the small matter of settling on the method she would use to murder him. Her murderous ramble – it wasn't quite a rampage just yet – had progressed in the days leading up to her arrival; from insects, through small rodents, up to a stray cat that she had mercifully slain with a sharp stick and closed eyes. She was sure she would soon be able to keep her eyes open at the crucial moment, though not just yet.

During her days on the road she had modified the crucifix the Mother Superior had gifted her. She had sharpened the longest part of the cross to a point and crafted a cap to replace the removed wood, sticking the two pieces together with sticky sap from a tree. This allowed her to carry it in plain sight without arousing suspicion. She had not used it yet, preferring to save it for her final act, and could only hope it was long enough to cause a fatal wound when the time came.

She walked through a huge archway in the city wall and was met with a stench for which she was utterly unprepared. She had always imagined Avignon to be a clean city, full of culture and glistening awe. The reality was a brisk shock, in this part of the city at least. On either side of her were lines of stalls, all manned by dirty salesmen with anxiety on their faces and death on their minds. They were punctuated by ominous gaps in the long line, the compacted and worn mud on the ground evidence of past vendors and present mortality. Arms stretched out from all sides, imploring her to give up a coin for their goods. There was no shortage of beggars here. The lowest of the low sat under tables and against walls like flies on a sausage, filling every available space with their catatonic desperation.

About halfway down this pathway of fear was a bald man, standing confidently behind a table of glass ornaments. He was dressed poorly, but not so much as to imagine he was without a choice when he dressed each morning. Hildegund was drawn to the distinction. She stepped over a recently expired dog that lay half eaten on the path and picked up a small blue and white lump of glass from the seller's table.

'This is a nice looking... thing you have here' she said.

'It is ornamental' said the man.

'What does it do?'

'Its purpose is to brighten your home and your soul. Please, allow me to demonstrate.'

The salesman took the item from Hildegund's hand and lifted it high up to the sky, catching the sunlight and flooding his table with a blue hue.

'Have you ever seen a thing of such beauty in such a swamp?' said the man.

Hildegund wasn't sure she had, it was a very pleasing effect. 'I'm not sure I have' she said. 'It is a very pleasing effect. Does it do anything else? Can you use it to clean your trousers? You know, to scrub them.'

'Well, no' said the man. 'Its purpose is one of emotion rather than practicality.'

'So let me get this straight' said Hildegund. 'This thing is supposed to just sit on my windowsill until such time as the sun crosses it. Then I will get a few minutes of this blue light before it disappears for another day?'

'One cannot put a price on the happiness of the soul in such unprecedented times' said the man, losing patience but keen to make the most of this rare customer. 'One should protect one's mind as well as one's body.'

'Should one, indeed?' said Hildegund.

'What else is there to do' said the man, showing his concern for a moment.

'I have travelled far to worship in the sight of the Holy Father. That is what I shall do to protect my mind and my body' said Hildegund, delicately steering the conversation. 'Prayer is a powerful protector, my friend, and our Holy Father will protect us all when the time comes.'

'Then you must not have seen the havoc this pestilence can bestow on its victims. Our lives of debauchery and sin have awakened God's vengeance, laid bare before the eyes of all people. Much prayer will be needed to stem this wave of judgment; I hope your knees are ready.'

'I have seen more than most' said Hildegund truthfully, 'although I confess to my ignorance of its activity here.'

'Where have you come from?'

'I have journeyed from my home in the mountains of the east to pray within sight of our beloved pope. My husband has the wasting sickness – not the ubiquitous pestilence that haunts us all I should say – and I must do all I can to seek intersession from our Lord.'

'There are many who ask for a similar miracle, but I believe yours may have a chance at success. If this plague is indeed God's vengeance then offering up prayer against it would be like asking a marauding butcher to spare your only lamb. You, at least, may be heard.'

'Then I am grateful that my husband is dying of an unfashionable illness' said Hildegund with false bitterness. The more she repeated her story the more naturally her reactions came.

'My apologies, I did not mean to cause offence' said the glass seller. 'I merely wished to convey my optimism for your pilgrimage.'

'When does the pope say mass?' asked Hildegund, spotting an opportunity to get something from the man.

'You would be doing well to find the pope at the altar' said the bald man. 'His cardinals do most of the services now, and they are on a permanent loop these days. The demand for salvation and protection is unabating.'

'Does he say it in the morning or the afternoon?' she insisted.

'If the pope's diary is of such concern to you then I am reluctant to give you information that may prove to be misleading.'

'It is my only concern. I am here for the pope and no other.'

'Then my advice to you is to visit the cathedral and discover his routine for yourself.'

'I will do that, but may I ask one more thing of you before I go to the cathedral to begin my work? Where should I look for shelter in this great city? A woman travelling alone must be careful in these troubling times.'

'Not here in the Merchant's Quarter, of that I can be sure. I would advise you to go to the opposite side of the city if you can afford to. There is no hiding from the pestilence any more, but there you should be safe from the unsavoury elements of the populace.'

'I will take your advice, and promise to return for this before I leave' said Hildegund, pointing at the lump of blue glass.

'Then I wish you the very best of health to you and your husband. Perhaps the radiance of this beautiful piece will ease his troubled soul' he said, hefting the blue glass in his hands once more.

Hildegund left the man and headed for the far side of the city. As she entered the more residential parts she sensed a change in the ambience. With hindsight the Merchant Quarter was full of nervous energy; the unacknowledged gaps in the line of stalls being the only indication that the city was creaking under the strain of a plague. Here, though, it was unavoidable. Several doors displayed crude red crosses, painted there to warn off the healthy. The scenes were the antithesis of how death had ever been handled.

There was a commotion ahead of her. A group of men were carrying a cumbersome weight out of a doorway, while others looked on from a distance. As she neared the scene she could make out three figures huddled together in the window of the house, one much taller than the others and visibly shuddering. The men outside swung the weight towards the house and then back to the street, heaving it up and onto a cart. Hildegund stopped dead at the scene she knew so well. She was taken back to Darmstadt, to the piles of dead and the wails of those left behind. She thought of her brother and all that this damnable pestilence had done to him.

She felt in her pocket for the crucifix, imagining the hidden point at the base, and clasped it hard. She would kill the pope for what his church did to Steffen, and may her punishment be what it may.

Hildegund had been in Avignon for several days before stepping into the cathedral. She had used her time well, studying the mood of the city and the movements around the Palais des Papes. She only saw the pope twice, on the second and ninth days, and took this to be his routine. He would say mass himself once a week and let his cardinals do the rest. If she was right, then she had just five more days to prepare the details of her plan. There was also a significant chance that she too had the same five left to live.

It wouldn't have changed her actions either way.

She sat at her table in the Boar's Arrow tavern and ordered a small bowl of potage and a mug of ale, as she had done each day since her arrival. She absent-mindedly studied the dark wooden timbers that crossed the ceiling and went through her plan in her mind again, struggling to add any sort of detail to it, as though complicating matters would reduce her chances of success. So far she had surmised that she must commit her final act, for that is what it would surely be, on the altar of the cathedral. There was nowhere else she could get close enough to reach the pope's heart and she knew it would end with her certain death, whether at the hands of officialdom or an enraged mob. She also knew the pope said mass once a week, so would wait for the day and sit at the front of the congregation, anxiously willing their Holy Father to come just that one step closer. It felt a little thin on planning, but then sometimes the simplest of actions produce the greatest of ripples and she was in no doubt that these ripples would reverberate for as long as her name was spoken.

An old woman approached her, sitting next to her before an invitation was offered. She screwed up her milky eyes and ran her fingers over Hildegund's face.

'What do you think you're doing?' said Hildegund. 'If you insist on fumbling over a woman's face you should at least seek permission first.'

'Do you say that to everyone who looks at you? For all I am doing is looking. That my eyes are of little use is unfortunate, but not motivation for you to interrogate me before I have introduced myself.'

'Then do so' said Hildegund flatly.

'I am Edith, a humble pilgrim from Lyon.'

'Only a pilgrim with something to hide would introduce themselves as humble' said Hildegund, a woman who knew a false persona when she saw one. 'If you were truly humble you would not announce it.'

'I see you are a woman of a similar disposition, for a person who is true to themselves would not be so hasty in their judgment' said the old woman.

Hildegund couldn't help but be drawn to the woman. There was an unexpected charisma there and an instant connection born of similar temperaments. She called to the barman to bring another mug of ale.

'I am Hildegund. What brings you to Avignon?'

'I am lost' said the old woman.

'We are all a little lost these days, are we not?' said Hildegund honestly. 'The pestilence has changed a good many things, not least of which are the routines that guided us during less turbulent times. There is an unpredictability in the air, one that sets whole cities on edge. It is a shame to see so much history and tradition crumble around us.'

The old woman gave Hildegund a peculiar look. 'Well you're a bit intense, aren't you? I merely meant that I'm *physically* lost' said Edith, 'and not because my sight fails me before you go jumping to conclusions. I have spent the summer in Montpellier visiting my sons before I am no longer able to make the journey. I am on my way to Lyon but seem to have arrived here in this great city unplanned. I prefer the lesser villages and hamlets along the way, you see. There are fewer walls to bump into for a start.'

'Then I shall enjoy your company while you are here and leave you to your journey when the time comes.'

'That's more like it' said Edith. 'Lighten up a bit and you may find that more people will want to share your company. I have been here for two days and have heard you in here on your own four times already. Perhaps your aura betrays your desire?'

'Now who's being intense?' joked Hildegund. 'And anyway, for you to hear me four times you would have to have been here too, so you may cast your aspersions elsewhere.'

'That does not mean I have been here on my own, which was the point I was highlighting to you.'

'Then who were you here with?'

'Nobody, I was on my own, but that isn't important.'

'So we are both loners, for the moment at least.'

'What brings you here?' asked Edith, changing the subject before the gravity of the conversation sank towards seriousness again.

'I am here for the pope' said Hildegund, telling the truth without the detail.

'To what end?'

'Does not everyone come to this place to lay their eyes on the Holy Father?' said Hildegund. 'Or ears' she added diplomatically.

'That is not what I asked' said Edith.

'Then you may make your own assumptions.'

'I would advise against that' said the old woman. 'I am of an age and disposition that does not lend itself to the acceptance of traditional opinions.'

'So you are a self-professed cantankerous old woman then?'

'That would be a fair and honest assessment' said Edith with a smile that reorganised the wrinkles in her face like earth beneath a farmer's plough. 'It is pleasing to hear you do not hide behind a veil of politeness. Too many are constrained by manners in this modern world.'

The barman slumped a mug of ale onto the table and trudged back to his place on the far side of the hatch. Edith took a long drink before slamming it down with a satisfied sigh.

'Now' she continued, 'tell me why you are drinking in an Avignon tavern with an accent from the east and coy responses to straightforward questions. There is more to you than meets the eye, especially to eyes so clouded as to heighten the owner's wits.'

Hildegund couldn't fail to be impressed by this woman, despite her unappealing appearance.

'I have already answered you. I am here for the pope.'

The old woman seemed to look past Hildegund to some far off place. She nodded gently a few times, as if conversing with herself, before finally bringing herself back into the moment.

'It seems unlikely that you would be here to cause problems for the pope' she began, 'but that is the conclusion I have drawn. I can tell from your reaction that I have seen through your riddle at the first attempt. How intriguing.'

The old woman reached out a hand and closed Hildegund's sagging jaw.

'How did you...?'

'I guessed you would be surprised at my evaluation, an emotion that often elicits a dropped jaw. It is simple reasoning.'

'What? No, I mean how did you know of my intent?'

'I didn't until now. Thank you for the enlightenment.'

Hildegund cursed herself. She wasn't sure she had done anything wrong necessarily and she had certainly not let her mask slip deliberately. The aura of this woman was like nothing she had experienced before. Her outward appearance held no clues to the sharpness of the mind within. She rolled the dice for the first time since she left Darmstadt.

'Let me be clear, and I am not suggesting your conjecture is accurate, but I have been starved of intellectual debate for many weeks and would be grateful for some, no matter how wild the idea may be. Tell me, would you be inclined towards a similar intent? Hypothetically speaking of course.'

'Hypothetically? Why don't we place our cards on the table my dear Hildegund. If you intend to do harm to one of such power then you would do well to plan your move with considerably more care than you feel is required. There are many cogs in the workings of the papal machine. I may be one, for all that you believe me to be nothing but a withering bat.'

'Are you?'

'No, but then I would say that in either scenario, would I not?'

Hildegund wasn't sure where this was going, nor the direction she hoped it would take. She was also reluctant to give up all she had worked for, but the entirety of her plan thus far could be summarised in a single sentence: Get close to the pope during mass and pass the sharpened crucifix as far through him as she could manage. There wasn't a lot of depth to it, and she wasn't sure what this stranger could offer, but a conversation would do no harm if she kept her words neutral.

'What would your plan be?' said Hildegund, treading the delicate line between vagary and frankness.

'I couldn't say' said Edith. 'I haven't given it much thought. What I can tell you is what I would not do, and that is to target the individual with violent intent. It is rare that someone so well protected can be destroyed by a tactic so devoid of subtlety.'

'And what level of interest would you have in such a subversive scheme?' said Hildegund.

'I'm not long for this world, by plague or old age, and frankly I'm rather bored. I would rather go out with a bang than a whimper. Hypothetically speaking, of course.'

'Then I should reassess my plans' said Hildegund, slamming all of her cards and most of her soul on the table in one tremendous statement.

'Oh marvellous' said Edith. 'I do enjoy a good plot. We need more to drink, there is no better lubricant to the workings of murderous mischief than a few tankards of Avignon ale.'

'Who said anything about murder?' said Hildegund, grasping at the last shreds of the pretence as it careered away from her.

'If we are to arrive at a conspiracy that holds the slightest chance of succeeding then we must at least agree on our preferred outcome. Are we trying to hurt his feelings or are we trying to send shockwaves across an empire? There is quite a difference, as I'm sure you can appreciate.'

'My brother will not die in vain,' said Hildegund defiantly. 'Let us send shockwaves to all corners of the Holy Roman Empire.'

CHAPTER FOURTEEN

PALAIS DES PAPES, AVIGNON

God's representative on earth stepped out from the lobby and into the cool air outside his palace. He didn't notice the two guards at the doorway, so still were they remaining and so ubiquitous had they become to his existence. He walked the long path out to the boundary of the palace grounds and stepped unaccompanied into the wider landscape for the first time in five years. He had no idea in which direction the city lay and a blend of exhilaration and trepidation swirled around his stomach as he tried to choose a course in which to travel. It was precisely this kind of knowledge that was the peril of the ruling class; deemed too trivial a detail for men of power, yet vital if the entourage was to make it to that party with the free cake before sunset.

He set out in an arbitrary direction to an undetermined destination, taking in the scenery that passed at the speed he deemed most enjoyable. He stopped at a small bridge and leaned over the edge to see the running water below, taking an unexpected pleasure from the simple scene. A wave of nostalgia sloshed over him; of days gone by when the weight of the world did not rest on his shoulders, of endless weeks when he could do as he pleased, within reason, and walk the streets unrecognised. He stopped again a few paces along the road, this time to look at two squirrels that seemed to be having some kind of fight. He marvelled at their ferocity, when to anyone passing by it would seem a futile effort to be staking a claim to such a small patch of woodland at the side of a road. When he realised they weren't fighting at all, and were in fact doing quite the opposite, he turned away quickly and carried on along the hard-mud road towards the city.

It had taken him about half an hour, but he was now within smelling distance of the Merchant Quarter. He wandered up and down the streets and marvelled at how much things had moved on since his pseudo-captivity. He marvelled all the more at how they had, against all historical evidence, moved backwards rather than forwards. There seemed to be fewer merchants than he remembered, not more, and the range of goods on sale was much narrower than before, almost linear. Those houses selling food seemed to be exclusively offering bread and grain. Those selling goods seemed to be almost entirely stocked with religious artifacts, a sight that should have filled him with pride and stroked his ego, but they were too saturated in their frequency to be a result of his leadership alone. Something else was happening here and he wasn't sure he was going to like what it was when he found out.

He stepped up to a crooked doorway with myriad religious items on display, coughing to get the attention of the dozing shopkeeper.

'Whuh?'

'Quite so. Now, tell me young man, what would you like to sell to me today?' said Pope Clement VI, Master of Avignon and would-be winner of the inaugural Naïve Shopper of the Decade award.

The shopkeeper was a little taken aback. It sounded like a trick question, so he answered honestly. It was the only way he could respond with such an educated accent jangling a metaphorical purse in front of him.

'All of it.'

'All of it?'

Yes, all of it. That's what I'd like to sell to you today.'

'Well, yes' said the pope, unsure of where to take the conversation from here. 'So, erm, how much would that be then?'

'How much? Bloody hell' said the shopkeeper, staggering a little. 'I mean. Right. Yes. Erm. Well, these crosses here are…' He paused in his calculations as he began to run out of fingers. 'Hang on, give me a minute. Joan! JOAN! I need your fingers. NOW!'

A plump women of indeterminable age sine curved her way to the front of the house with her fingers outstretched. 'Here, and hurry up, Leonard. I have a pot on.'

The shopkeeper took Joan's hands and tapped each of the fingers, glancing periodically at the crosses on the floor. Mathematics was never his strong point and so soon gave up, chose a number he thought was tantamount to robbery and added a bit on top. Then a little more.

'A hundred forints, and I'll throw in these rosary beads for nothing. Can't say fairer than that now, can you?'

Clement VI was ignorant of both the fairness of the offer and the value of a forint, and so agreed. He turned to his right to nod at his guard to pay the man.

'Ah' said the pope.

'Too much?' said the shopkeeper, happy to haggle at these lofty levels. 'I tell you what, you can have two rosary beads, this pocket sized statue of Saint Francis, complete with smiling dog, and my most prized item.' He picked up a small piece of decomposing wood, no bigger than an egg, and lifted it up towards the sky in a show of unabashed salesmanship.

'Is that part of the true cross?' said Clement, a man who knew a rotting relic when he saw one.

'It's even better than that, my wise man. This is part of the very cross that the good thief suffered on next to our Lord. Now tell me, how many times have you been offered part of that, eh? Houses up and down this street can offer you a piece of the true cross and unless our Lord was hoisted onto a cross the size of the papal palace it can be safely assumed they are not all... *legitimate*. How many times have you been offered a piece of the cross next to Jesus though, eh? This is a genuine relic, one that has been seen by our Lord himself, and I'm giving it to you for nothing. *Nothing!*'

'Well that is very tempting' said the pope, with genuine intrigue. 'Unfortunately I have come out without my guard... I mean, purse. Purse. I have come out without my purse. Can we agree on this sale and I shall return to you another time to complete the exchange?'

The shopkeeper had given his best performance for some time and all he received in return was an answer he had heard dozens of times before. He could feel a barbed response rising from his chest, battling with his inner salesman for control over the end of the conversation.

'You're as bad as the pope, feigning interest in people just to toy with them like a marionettist. I look forward to never seeing you again, good sir' said the shopkeeper, despite himself, 'but may the venom of his Holiness pass over your head to your enemy nonetheless' he added, just in case.

Clement was pulled in every emotional direction. He had never experienced such a personal attack since his ascension to the papal seat, yet a response in his usual all-powerful manner was out of the question if he was to remain anonymous. It would be unproductive. He could not allow such a perception of himself to go unchecked, however.

'Dear lowly shopkeeper' he began, stepping on his words carefully like a child walking on a wet floor. 'I do not feign anything, including threats to those who slight my sincerity. Let me be as clear as I can to avoid any unintentional… *misunderstandings.*'

Clement had thundered back into a familiar demeanour. He raised himself to his full height, towering above the shopkeeper and casting his ample shadow over the now cowering man. He was an expert at looming ominously over people, and enjoyed it almost as much as the casting of judgment itself. The pope wasn't the only man who could intimidate people in this city, he reasoned. He could be enjoyably menacing without necessarily being the pope. That was sufficient to convince himself it was safe enough to open the floodgates.

'I will have these trinkets, with or without payment. For your part you will be glad of this day, for in time it will become your means of life. People of weak substance will come to you for guidance and comfort as the man who met me on this day. Let it be enough for me to say that, as it stands, it may also be your means of death. I would choose your next words carefully my kind, lowly shopkeeper.'

'I'll give you one cross to bugger off, you lunatic' said the shopkeeper. 'Here.'

'I'll take it, thank you' said Pope Clement, enjoying this shopping experience much more than he was a few minutes earlier, 'and a good day to you too, kindly shopkeeper.'

He continued along the street with a feeling of freedom so exhilarating that he couldn't help but grin like a maniacal frog. As well as the religious salesmen and the bakers there were beggars, slumped here and there against the walls of the houses. He considered whether he should show them charity with the toss of a coin or two, but on remembering again that he had none, decided that he definitely would have done, had he some to give. The thought was as good as the deed, he concluded, and passed happily by those most in need of his help. Amongst all this activity he noticed a bejeweled hag in a pile of filthy blankets. He stopped and looked down on her.

'You are finely dressed for a common beggar' he commented.

The old hag looked up from the rumples of cloth, revealing small milky eyes buried deep in a manger of wrinkles. 'Speak not of me in such a way as this' said the voice with more pomp than Clement thought was necessary. 'I can see that which mortal souls dare not. Come, I will tell you what you most fear, the answer to the question that wracks your spirit.' She grabbed at his clothes, feeling the material with her bent fingers.

'Oh come off it' said the pope, stepping back from her clutches as he did so. 'You're just a blind old bat with more time on her hands than her mind knows what to do with. Go and get a wash, there is a stench from you that would perish all the apples in the orchard.'

'The senses of men have betrayed you' she said with practised gravity. 'I can see beyond the light and hear that which remains unspoken.'

'Now you're just talking nonsense. Good day to you, withered woman' said Clement, opening his legs to move away from the strange creature at his feet.

'You speak in tones unworthy of your standing' said the woman.

Clement's departing foot stopped as it landed on the floor. He spun back to the woman and glared intensely into her white eyes. 'What would you know of my standing, peasant?'

'You have no purse, yet you walk in fine clothes through these grubby streets. That makes you out to be a noble, a man of the cloth, or both. You speak with a voice of unbridled authority, so you are no mere priest. What is more, even nobles find fruit a luxury in this new wasteland. There is but one place in all of Avignon so out of touch with the common people, and the constrictions of our burgeoning populace, that it may still give up space in its lands for an orchard and not find it peculiar. God moves in mysterious ways indeed if he had sent his representative to the street of merchants to mock the afflicted. I shall let you pass, your Holiness, and may God send you to nicer places than this next time.'

Clement was impressed. This old woman was as astute as any of his highly paid advisors in the palace. She seemed to use her deductive skills for entertainment rather than money too, for she had not asked for payment of any sort thus far. It would only be right to show such an altruistic soul the true meaning of charity, and what a useful piece of charity she could become.

'Follow me' he said. 'I have seen your future.'

'You get five minutes of freedom and you buy a cart load of cheap souvenirs and bring a vagrant back to the palace!?' said Jacques.

'I haven't bought them yet, I have made an *agreement*. I did get this rather fetching cross for nothing though. Not bad for a first attempt, wouldn't you say?' said the pope defensively, and with obvious pride at having secured a transaction on the streets without assistance.

'Nevertheless, there is now a stinking pile of enigmatical blankets spreading wild pronouncements and proclamations throughout the palace' said Jacques. 'That's your job!'

'Calm down, I am merely safeguarding the church from those who would seek to undermine its authority. And anyway, she's locked in the dungeons. What harm can she do?'

'Undermine its…' said Jacques, unable to finish the sentence before another barged past it. 'Do you mean to tell me you intend to round up every gutter rat in all of Avignon and give them board and lodgings in the palace? Come on, Clem. That's insane, even for a pope.'

'Not all, Jacques, no' said Clement. 'Just those who have seen me on the street dressed as a common priest.'

Jacques closed his eyes and dropped his head to his chin. 'Bugger.'

'Quite so, Father Bricoler, quite so.'

CHAPTER FIFTEEN

FRANCE

February, 1348

R obert and Cuthbert stopped running and bent down to put their hands on their knees, panting.

'That was a close one' said Cuthbert. 'Check my back, will you? I think that scythe may have caught my shirt.'

Robert inspected his friend's simple garment. 'It's fine. You worry too much.'

'You did your fair share of worrying when the farmer picked up that pitchfork.'

'That was just for show. If he thought we were going to run off in panic he might have stayed where he was.'

'He didn't though, did he?' said Cuthbert. 'Next time we should plan our escape *before* we try to steal a chicken.'

'Next time? Marvellous!' said Robert enthusiastically. 'Welcome to the party.'

They had been travelling now for almost a month and were close enough to the holy city of Avignon to begin considering their arrival plan. Their journey had taken them through a wide spectrum of iniquitous dens, with Cuthbert taking a firmer hold on their decisions as they progressed. He had embraced his new philosophy with a passion Robert had never seen in him before. There were now several villages they would have to avoid on their way home, should they wish to make it back with the same number of teeth.

Having started out as an unpromising companion, Cuthbert had become a more intensely hedonistic pilgrim than Robert himself. No tavern was safe from his exorcism routine, and no tavern declined him free sustenance bar the one in Saint Rambert. That was a tricky exit to navigate and not one Robert hoped he would ever have to make again. It had taken days for the smell to come out of their clothes and his opinion of female tavern hands would never be quite the same again.

The next day would see them arrive at the great city, one whose foibles were familiar to Robert. Cuthbert's understanding of it, on the other hand, remained shrouded in the mysticism and hyperbole that befits a place often discussed but rarely seen.

'Are there taverns there or are they forbidden in such a holy place?' asked Cuthbert as they lay beneath a hilltop oak overlooking the Rhône. 'I bet the ale there is better than anything we've tried so far. Are the women as free as we have seen or are they chained in a concentration of morality?'

'That depends on your definition of free, my friend. Compared to your recent rampages they are as tamed as the statues in the cathedral. I think, however, that they will suffice.'

'Then I shall look forward to them, and to the hospitality of the city. May it be a fitting climax to our pilgrimage.'

'No churches then? I seem to remember you wanting to visit as many as you could on your journey down. Have the last vestiges of piety left your soul so quickly?'

'Yes, yes they have Robert. What good is a decision if it is executed with half the passion and half the determination? Do, or do not do.'

'Well you certainly did do, of that there can be no doubt. Indeed, you will be a long time in the confessional box if you still intend to wipe your slate clean of your shenanigans this past month. Come on, let's find one last tavern before we enter the maelstrom. I think we should pay for this drink though, for luck.'

The two travellers stood up and made their way down the hill towards the village. As they reached the maze of streets they sensed a mood in the air unlike anything they had experienced on their journey thus far. There was an eerie quietness to the place. Not quite a silence. Not yet.

A priest walked past them, squinting at doorways as he went. He reached one a little further ahead that made him come to a sagging stop at the threshold. He took a deep breath as if steadying himself before pushing the door open and plunging into the house. Cuthbert and Robert looked at each other in bemused ignorance.

They studied the village a little more closely until they too stopped still.

'Robert?' asked Cuthbert nervously.

'Yes?'

'…'

'I thought the same' said Robert. He spun around to face the way they had come before quickly doing the same in reverse, as if the answer to the riddle was hiding in his shadow.

'I don't like the feel of the air here' said Cuthbert, voicing a shared concern. 'Where are the villagers?'

'There's one' said Robert. 'Let's ask him.'

A tall, thin man was approaching them and Robert raised his arm in acknowledgement. The man looked up drearily from his daydream. He narrowed his eyes slowly as if evaluating the two strangers, opened them again wildly, turned on his heels and ran at full tilt into the distance. He turned sharply at the first corner, almost tipping over on the road as he did so, and disappeared.

'I don't know this village' said Cuthbert, 'but I'm fairly sure that isn't normal behaviour.'

'Come on' said Robert, breaking into a run. 'He's part of the riddle, and so part of the solution.'

They ran to the corner and turned into a long, narrow street just as the man turned right down another entry. Robert was making better ground and made it to the turn before Cuthbert, leaving his friend to take a different course in the maze of alleys and passageways. The man was nowhere to be seen but Robert could see a crossroads a little further up the street. He sprinted to it and flashed his head right then left, seeing the man's foot as it disappeared down another lane.

Cuthbert had carried straight on the road but knew he had to take a right turn if he was to catch up with their prey. He hurtled along the hard road, taking corners at random until he was truly lost. He stopped for a moment to catch his breath, leaning on his knees and panting hard. A moment later he was thrown to the floor by a careering stranger, both landing in a heap on the floor. Robert appeared, shortening his gait before stopping as he reached Cuthbert and the man.

'Don't touch me!' shrieked the stranger, flailing an arm as Robert grabbed his shirt. 'Get away from me!'

Robert lifted the man, hauling him to the side of the alley and slumping him against the wall.

'What's going on here? Why did you run from us? Where is everyone?'

'You're strangers!' said the man, as if that was all the explanation required.

'So what if we are? Are strangers a portent of doom here in… wherever we are?' said Robert.

'Yes' came the unexpected reply. 'The pestilence has reached us.'

Robert stepped back sharply from the man. 'What pestilence? We have travelled from the north and have heard no news of it.'

'It is a scourge unlike any other. It approaches from the south and sends a man to his maker before a week is through.'

'What about the women?' said Cuthbert innocently. 'Are they sent to their maker too, or is it just the men?'

'It is God's vengeance on His sinful world and nothing can stand in its way.' said the man, avoiding the question.

'So we could just dress as women and pass through safely?' said Cuthbert.

'What? Half our population has perished. Now is not the time for semantics' said the man.

'It is if the surviving half is all women' said Cuthbert relentlessly.

The man's face showed the confusion that came from having a concept presented for appraisal for the first time. He had never really considered women to be important enough to count among the piles of the dead.

'Both men and women have perished' he said at last.

'Right, so that's that plan out' said Cuthbert. 'Perhaps we should just leave.'

'And keep our souls tainted for all eternity?' said Robert. 'No thank you, Cuthbert. Not after the journey we've just had. Without absolution at the end of our pilgrimage your depravity has sent us on a trip to hell. We must complete our journey before escaping this blight.'

'Ah, so it's a pilgrimage now, is it?' said Cuthbert. 'I thought you were just playing the system but all this time you've been as much of a believer as I was. *Am.*'

'It's whatever it needs to be to help us get back home cleansed of sin and free from this disease.'

'Now that's the Robert I know. Come on, let's head into the village.'

He moved to help the man up but he was already gone, sprinting down the muddy alleyway and out of sight.

'I'm sure he was exaggerating, nothing can kill half a village. Let's find the tavern for one last meal and this time tomorrow we'll be in Avignon. It is surely the safest place to be if God's judgment is to be cast.'

'Or the most dangerous' said Robert.

CHAPTER SIXTEEN

PALAIS DES PAPES

Pope Clement VI took off his vestments and picked up a crystal goblet. He half filled it with the best wine in Christendom and drank two gulps before pouring the rest out of a window, giving a departing churchgoer the most expensive shower of their life.

News of the pestilence had not only reached Avignon, it had manifested itself in some of its inhabitants. Panic was brewing in his city. As the days passed and the plague spread his people were discovering the ceaseless horror of the disease. The stories they had assumed to be crass exaggerations were, if anything, downplaying the sheer dread that now filled their core. Families were being decimated, literally in one case, such was its size. They had turned to him for answers and he had none. In these times of desperation he turned to a philosophy he had always held dear to his heart. If you can't satisfy those who look to you for guidance, fake it. If he was going to bluff his way through this, though, he would need help, and there was one person even better at deception than he was.

'Bring Father Bricoler to me' he called out to the door.

The familiar sound of wooden shoes on the tiled floor clopped into life and grew faint. A few moments later it returned, followed by a knock.

'Come.'

'Father Bricoler, your Holiness' said the first voice.

'Leave us.'

The door closed with a resonating thud as Jacques crossed the room to Pope Clement, arms open as if welcoming him back from a long journey.

'Sit, Jacques. There is much for us to discuss.'

'Oh Clem, you're not going to get all serious again, are you? We were just starting to get you relaxed.'

'Now is the time for me to lead, Jacques, not play children's games.'

'You're going to get all high and mighty after the fun you had in the town?'

'I am high and mighty, I'm the damned pope! If I can't get all mighty every now and again, what's the point in being pontiff?'

'What's the point!? What isn't the point, more like. You don't have to hang around here watching this sickness close in on the palace. You don't have to tell people God's wrath is descending on account of them playing around with their neighbour's wife. Or at least, you don't have to *keep* telling them. Once should do it, if you're as mighty as you think you are.'

'What are you suggesting, Jacques? That I abandon my people in their time of need?'

'That's exactly what I'm suggesting.'

The pope looked past Father Bricoler to a tapestry he hadn't woven, staring through it in deep contemplation.

'It is a bit of a nuisance having to say half a dozen masses a day' he said at last. 'You'd think they'd have had enough of me by now.'

Jacques pounced on the opening. 'If they were truly penitent they would have, only those with more to repent than meets the eye would spend so much time in God's house. The cleanest of souls need the least purification. It stands to reason that those who spend the most time listening to your ruminations are the very ones who deserve it least. Abandoning them would be to show them the true error of their ways. You would be helping to save them.'

'Some would say they are the very ones I should work harder to save' said the pope.

'Some also say the world is round, Clem. There are many opinions on many things, but not all are worthy of consideration. If a man can only seek repentance when he can see his fate, should he be granted the same blessing as those who lead a good life for its own sake?'

'You have a sharp mind, Jacques. Perhaps you could stay here in my stead while I abandon my city to the wolves' said the pope sardonically.

'Perhaps I could' said Jacques seriously, surprising his old friend with the tone as much as the content.

'Where would I go?' said Clement, sidestepping the unexpected and possibly hollow offer for the moment.

'You could go to your residence in the hills, away from the maddening vociferation of the people. You should take your physician, Guy, with you. If the pestilence somehow makes it to you he will do all he can to keep you well.'

Pope Clement poured himself another drink, nodding to the decanter as he did so. Jacques went through his now familiar ritual; filling his goblet, drinking half and filling it again. The two friends retired to the corner of the room where two chairs sat at angles at one corner of an ornate, pale wooden table. They sat in silence for a moment, each musing over the possibility of a papal relocation.

'I can't leave my people in their hour of need' said Clement, breaking the stillness.

'You don't have to. Or at least, the pope needn't.'

'I can see an idea filling your throat. Spit it out before it chokes you to an early grave.'

'I don't think you'll like it' said Jacques, determined to manage his friend's expectations before revealing his plan.

'I never expect to like anything you say. Now less than ever.'

'Well, I was thinking… What if you moved to a safer location but the pope stayed here?'

'Why don't I go to Rome too? Then I would truly be the earthly embodiment of our three person God.'

'I'm serious, Clem. You are merely a human representation of the papal seat. It is not you the people need but your position.'

'*Merely*!? I am the damned pope, not some insignificant priest' snapped Clement. 'Watch your words Jacques, I may be your friend but I still outrank all around me.'

'Oh relax, Clem. You're so uptight these days. Go to the hills, take a break and come back when this little drama is over. I'll look after things here.'

'I was joking about that' said Clement. 'And anyway, people would notice. They expect me to be omnipresent at the altar.'

Jacques cleared his throat as one does before delivering the winning blow of a debate. 'No, they expect the pope to be there. I can play your part as well as anyone, all I need is a veil and a deeper voice.'

'Let me make this absolutely clear, Jacques. You're not going to be pope' said the current pope. 'At least, not while I live. No offence.'

'I don't want to be pope' said Jacques, 'but if I can save the pope, I will. I will put myself in the vulnerable position at the centre of the storm while you are protected at a distance. If I am to die, what better way to ensure my passage to the heavens?'

'Aha!' said Clement, pointing to his friend as if winning a game of hide and seek. 'So that is why you are so keen. Now that death is climbing the stairs to your room you are playing catch up with your soul.'

'Of course I am' admitted Jacques happily. 'Also, it is an undeniably altruistic move, wouldn't you say?'

'Is it?'

'Then it's settled. I will conduct your business here in Avignon as the pestilence rages around me' said Jacques. 'There are two important matters we should attend to before we begin our plans, however.'

'Is there indeed?' said Clement dubiously.

'Yes. We need more wine, and I need to practice your voice.'

Jacques took a few steps towards the door before turning back to Clement.

'What do you call them? Your servants, that is.'

'I don't really call them anything, I just tell them what I want them to do.'

'Right, thanks.'

He turned back to the door, calling out in a deep voice to the servants on the other side. 'I need a veil to protect me from the imbalance of humours that surround the city. It must depict the cross of our Lord in fine material. If you can't find one then order the... the Master Weaver to make one with all haste. And bring me more wine immediately and double the amount.'

He crossed back to the table and chairs and sat down beside the pope.

'Master Weaver? *Master Weaver?* Where do you think you are, an artisan's loft?' said the pope. 'You need to do better than that if you want to see me ride off to the hills.'

'Oh that was just the beginning, Clem. I'll find my touch, don't worry. Now, we have work to do.'

Pope Clement VI left the papal administration office with the pope. They passed by the servants without comment, although they would have been equally silent had they suspected the ruse. Jacques wore the traditional red stole of the papacy and the crucifixion veil he had ordered. Clement was dressed in the simple black of a priest, a white veil masking his features.

They made their silent way to the stables and waited for the opulent papal carriage to be drawn up to the finest of horses. Clement would travel with his physician, Guy, and two of his most trusted aides, sworn to secrecy on pain of excommunication. The journey would last no longer than a day but, crucially, it would take them to a land so sparsely populated and so removed from the main thoroughfares that it would take an extraordinary stroke of misfortune were they to be visited upon.

'Wait!' called Jacques, turning to a servant and cursing himself for not deepening his voice. He cleared his throat and dropped his chin a little. 'Send the carriage back to its storehouse. Put these horses back in the stables and bring our four worst steeds to me.'

The pope looked at Jacques with furrowed eyebrows and narrowed eyes. He then opened them a little wider to convey to Jacques his desire for an explanation.

Jacques leant in to his friend and lowered a corner of his mouth to allow a surreptitious whisper. 'A golden carriage is not the most inconspicuous of choices for a scuttling man.'

'What about my things?' said Clement, as distressed as a child over a lost doll.

'You can take a burdened mule with you. Think of it as a re-enactment of Christ's Passion. In fact, if anyone recognises you, that's what you can tell them. It's perfect. God does move in mysterious ways, doesn't He?'

'Not as mysteriously as the seat of my pants by the time I get there' said Clement, not unfairly.

'Now, don't worry about things here' said Jacques, moving things along. 'I've checked on the wine cellar and everything seems to be at full stock. I'll keep my promise to have mass said at least once a day and I'll try not to frequent too many taverns.'

'You will not try' said Clement sternly. 'There will be no tavern excursions while I am away, do you hear me?'

'Relax, I was joking. Jesus, Clem you need a holiday. I'll send word when there are some of note to deliver, and may God bless you on your journey.'

'Don't get all pious now, just because you're a charlatan pope.'

'I need all the practise I can get. Now, be gone; your carriageless carriage awaits, Holy Father.'

'I'm telling you, he's like clockwork' said the first voice. 'He'll have drunk the wine by now and pretty soon his stomach will ask him for more of that bread he likes so much.'

'He's never been like this before' said the second voice. 'Maybe that cold he had has gone to his head. His voice is certainly different, perhaps his humours are imbalanced after all.'

'They must be' said the first voice. 'I can't think of any other explanation. He must be trying to even out his fire element. Ah, I hear him moving, are you ready? Three... two... one...'

'MANCHET!'

'There you go' said the first voice. 'Right on cue.'

Jacques rubbed the sleep from his eyes. He had been awake for about an hour, but had only just finished his wine and was still a little groggy. He hoped the bread would revive him. Clement had been gone for almost a week now and the battle between papal responsibility and the papal wine allowance had been a brief one. The greatest perk of any higher order role is the ability to delegate, and Jacques had delegated the living ghost out of this one. His days were now spent eating rich food and drinking expensive wine. He would occasionally leave the papal bedroom for some fresh air in the gardens, but that was usually to clear his head of the previous evening's revelry.

He had promised Clement to have mass said each day, not that he would do it himself, so he was on safe ground there when the final reckoning was upon him. He had passed the responsibility on to eager young cardinals who had to be reined in from their requests to perform multiple masses every day. Jacques had warned them, through letters delivered by the voices outside his room, that panic could not be seen to be permeating the palace.

Clement didn't know how lucky he was, thought Jacques. There was only as much responsibility as you put on yourself, and the workload was effectively optional, such was the clamour to be the pope's representative across the city. Cardinals and archbishops from all corners of the empire would have walked across the sighing corpses of their colleagues just to have a chance to clean a papal goblet. No wonder so many of Clement's predecessors died violently.

There was a knock at the door, doubtless the miraculous manchet, he thought.

'Come!' he boomed in as deep a voice as he could manage.

The huge doors opened and the second voice walked in.

'You have a visitor, Holy Father'

'Does he have bread?'

'I didn't ask. My apologies I shall return to him immediately' said the second voice, cursing inwardly at the random nature of the pope's questioning.

'Don't bother. If he is without bread then you are to bring some to me before our guest has had time to take of his coat. Does he have a name?'

'He said his name was not important.'

'Did he, indeed? How very brave of him. Bring him to me at once.'

CHAPTER SEVENTEEN

AVIGNON

Nicolo had finally arrived at Avignon. He lay on his straw mattress and stared at the ceiling. What little hope he retained had fuelled him on his journey from Marseilles, the thought of scraping the demon of di Murta from his back proving to be an effective motivator. He had joined a band of merchants heading for Paris, relieving them of a small amount of coins along the way. He could have taken more, but he needed their friendly company as they plotted his course to Avignon. He found a surprising comfort in playing Simple Stones again, despite his saturated boredom of it only a few short weeks ago. Sometimes that which is mundane and tiresome is transformed into a healing spring for mental vitality when adventure is driven by fear.

He had used these coins to place a roof over his head for a few nights. Now that he was here, all that was left was to find The Cutler, deliver the message, and leave to the north with all haste. If he completed his mission before his rent expired, then he would be happy to forego a few coins for the chance to escape both the pestilence and the doge. He wasn't certain which of the two he was looking forward to fleeing from more.

Either way, he needed to find The Cutler, and the sooner the better.

Now that he must find him, Nicolo pondered the etymology of the man's name for the first time. It could have been literal of course, although someone as devious as Giovanni di Murta would surely veil his connections with more sophistication. He eliminated this from the list of possibilities for the moment. When he realised it resulted in his list being empty he reinstated it at the bottom.

It could be a reference to his means of dispatching his victims, or his acerbic tongue. Indeed, it could be a nod to any number of sharp characteristics. Perhaps he had a particularly pointy nose. Nicolo had failed to narrow down the possibilities so instead thought like a spy. Regardless of his name he would be a servant to the rules of espionage. He would be unlikely to have an advertised past, or at least not one based in reality. He would have few friends and, as likely as not, no family in the city. Nicolo wasn't sure how this deduction would help him but he stored it away anyway for later reference.

As he tried to determine a starting place for his search, his thoughts kept returning to the taverns. Would a spy avoid them at all costs; the perils of drink to a clandestine mind being too great a risk, or would they gravitate towards them for the same reason? His search had to start somewhere and the less arbitrary that start was, the less time it would take to track The Cutler down, in theory at least. In the absence of any other ideas, he pulled on his tunic and headed to the nearest tavern to get drunk.

✝

'Ale, please' said Nicolo to the bearded barman in the Greave Dunning tavern.

'Less of the *please*, if you don't mind' said the barman, confusing Nicolo with impressive efficiency. 'I get all nervous when customers use nice words. It ain't proper in a place like this. No offence.'

'Right, I see. Sorry.'

'And no apologies neither.'

'Ah, right.'

The barman thrust a tankard of ale towards Nicolo.

'May I thank you?'

'I'd rather you didn't, if it's all the same to you.'

Nicolo was unsure how to close off the conversation so left it open, taking his ale to a table and scanning the room for a suitable drinking partner. He would avoid the more drunken customers; he required the utmost integrity in any information he gleaned, and for it to be uncommon enough to be useful. Those with ale in their bellies would offer up neither.

A young man was sitting sheepishly in a corner, stooped over a full tankard. Nicolo crossed the room and sat down opposite him, causing the man's head to rise in slow surprise.

'Good morning. Mind if I sit?' said Nicolo with as pleasant a tone as he could muster.

The head lowered itself again.

'Is the ale good in this town? This one will be my first and I'm hoping for something with more taste than ship's water.'

The head looked up, opening a single eye with more effort than Nicolo had thought possible for such a simple task.

'Hoowuh yoof. Leughfmuh low' it said.

'I'm sorry, I didn't quite catch that.'

The head let out a large sigh and wobbled its cheeks vigorously with both hands before slapping itself. The eyes shot open, then took a few seconds to focus on the newcomer.

'I said, who are you?'

'I am Nicolo Anatra from Sicily' he said, using his name for the first time in months. He had no need to stay in the shadows anymore and it may help to bring The Cutler to him, if he was aware of his name.

'I also said leave me alone' said the head. 'So if you could bugger off over there I'd be most grateful.'

'I can see you've had a rough night' said Nicolo, desperate to make progress despite the state of the man. He had at least caught him at the right end of the drinking process.

'Have I?' said the head. 'So it's morning then, is it?'

'Not for much longer. What on earth were you up to last night?'

'Now if I knew that I wouldn't have enjoyed it as much, would I?' said the head.

Nicolo knew better than to pick a battle with the man's logic, choosing to engage him in an alternative conversation instead.

'Are you familiar with the city? I am searching for an old acquaintance and would appreciate any help you can offer.'

'I'm a visitor like you' said the head. 'I would be familiar only with its taverns, had I the memory of them to recall. We've been a little... frivolous since our arrival.'

'We?'

'Oh' said the head. 'Are we not both here?'

'You are alone, my good man' said Nicolo, wondering if this man was as sane as he would have liked. 'Should there be someone else with you?'

'Ah yes, that's right' said the man, as if finding a small piece of the previous night's jigsaw. 'I arrived with a fellow pilgrim. I'm fairly sure he was with me last night, but the evening is a little foggy.'

'Then it seems we have similar problems. I will help you find your friend, if you then help to find mine.'

'Buy me another ale and you've got yourself a deal' said Robert.

✝

Nicolo and Robert passed the large, four-spouted fountain that acted as a grand centre piece to the busy market square, scanning left and right through the crowd for any sign of Cuthbert. He had been missing for almost half a day now and Robert had begun to worry about his wellbeing. His friend's debauchery had spiralled beyond anything Robert had seen in a pilgrim before. On their last night together Cuthbert had chosen to debate rather too vociferously with a huge man with eyebrows the size of a horse's mane. His ill judged motion concerned the benefits, or lack thereof, of executing the largest men in each city to help ease the extreme food shortage. He reasoned that those who ate more than the average should be removed from the equation altogether, thereby reducing both the volume of consumed food and the demand for it.

Logic has no place in the mind of the drink-addled, however, and the unfortunately eyebrowed man had won the argument emphatically with a surly swipe of his arm across Cuthbert's inadequate chest. The two friends drank more heavily then, led by Cuthbert to better numb the pain throbbing in his torso. At some point Robert's memories sank below the surface and all that he could now recall was that Cuthbert wasn't in their room when he woke that morning and was now lost somewhere in this debauched city.

'It's no good' he said to Nicolo. 'There's no chance we'll find him among so many.'

'Well not with that attitude we won't' said Nicolo. 'I say we stop looking in the obvious, open places. If he was as drunk as you think then he isn't likely to be going for a nice stroll in the open. It's more likely he's lying in a gutter somewhere sleeping his hangover away. Let's split up. I'll take the alleys around the market stalls, you go and check up by the big houses. Perhaps he thought to take some coin from the rich folk while his bravery was exaggerated. Check every nook, he could have sidled into any space that would keep him steady.'

The two men parted ways, agreeing to meet at sunset in the Greave Dunning. Nicolo headed downhill towards the city gates, searching in the shadows as he went. The journey took no more than ten minutes, but he passed three separate victims of the pestilence being passed on to carts all the same. The disease was tightening its grip and commandeering all waking thoughts of the people. Nicolo had had less chance to think about it than most, other than to remind himself of the importance of finding The Cutler and escaping its ravages. He would look back on this time as the strangest in his life; surrounded by a relentless killer that failed, against all sagacity, to be his most pressing concern. Instead he must find a stranger and deliver a message whose contents remained a mystery to him.

First he had to find Cuthbert.

The stalls at this end of the city were more scant than those in the main square. There were gaps where the pestilence had snatched sellers away from their wares and fathers from their families. Judging by the matted clothes of some of those still alive, it had also snatched several wives and children. Nicolo passed around the back of the stalls, checking in the narrow passageways that lined the buildings for signs of a hungover English pilgrim.

He stepped into one and waited for his eyes to adjust to the gloom. There was a shadow about twenty paces away that may have been a man. Stepping deliberately along the filthy floor he saw that it was indeed a stricken figure, covered in an old, worn blanket.

'Cuthbert?' he called into the relative darkness. 'Is that you?'

The blanket didn't answer. They rarely do.

'Cuthbert? My name is Nicolo, I am helping your friend Robert, he is desperately searching for you.' Although not as desperately as I, he thought.

Nothing.

Nicolo tapped the blanket lightly with his foot, then more firmly when no reaction came. There was the slightest of movements from within the rags but no voice followed. He reached down and pulled the matted blanket away from its owner, throwing it away from him in the same movement as he saw what lay beneath.

A pitiful figure had crumpled herself against the wall, boils showing on her stretched, bare skin as the pestilence roasted her body. Whether she had been abandoned here or had sought to distance herself from her family Nicolo couldn't say. What he could say was *urgh*, and he did so rather loudly with a blend of shock and disgust.

'Have you been given the rites from a priest, woman?' said Nicolo, but there was no reply. 'I will find one and bring him to you. Wait here' he added pointlessly.

Albert glared at Norman with patient infuriation. He had never wanted to look after his brother but his father was an imposing flea and it was the less fatal of his two options at the time. His brother's ailment of choice today was an upset stomach. Never before had this been a problem for a flea, but Norman was a ground breaking master of medical complaints.

'Don't look at me like that' said Norman, 'it's not my fault I had a dodgy lunch.'

'It was the same lunch we've had every day for the last week' said Albert.

'Yes but this one was off.'

'I'm not so sure it's possible for a rat to be off while it's still alive. Unpalatable maybe, but *off*?'

'You're not the one with a sickly feeling in their stomach.'

'You're a flea for dog's sake! You have rat's blood for breakfast, lunch and evening meal. It's all in your head.'

'There was a funny taste to it, I remember thinking that at the time.'

'Well you kept it to yourself well enough. Anyway, I had the same thing and I'm fine.'

'Thank you for your comfort and support' said Norman, hoping that sarcasm would win his brother over.

'You're welcome' said Albert, turning his body away from Norman in a show of stubborn haughtiness.

'I think I'm going to be sick' said Norman.

'Well don't do it here' said Albert, taking a few steps away from him. 'There's a human over there against that wall, maybe you can drink their blood when you've finished and we can carry on with our day?'

'Fine. I will' snapped Norman. 'Don't go anywhere now, do you hear? I'll be back before you can blink.'

'But I can't... oh forget it' said Albert, choosing to keep that line of conversation closed for the moment.

Norman hopped off the rat without another word and headed to the human.

Nicolo left the alleyway and headed to a small church a few streets away. Once there, he entered a place of fervent and pious panic. From one side of the nave to the other was a deep wall of the faithful, anxious to redeem their soul. The altar was empty, but that was no longer a surprise to him; churches up and down the city were devoid of their leaders, instead taken over by those in desperation. He made his way to the very front of the church, squeezing passed rocking bodies as he did so. The thick wooden door to the sacristy was closed and would have remained so in less exceptional times. Nicolo opened it without knocking, assuming that any priest within would be reluctant to acknowledge its sound in any case.

He had never seen the inside of a sacristy before and was surprised at the relative opulence of the place. There was an antechamber leading to a main room, the two spaces separated by a narrow opening in front of him. To his left was a wardrobe that took up the full length of the first room, filled with vestments of various colours, each for a particular period of the religious calendar. To his right was a flat worktop with a green felt surface. A scattering of chalices and candles took up most of the available space and there was a small wooden bowl piled high with communion hosts. He moved through the opening and into the back room where a middle aged man was slouched motionless on a wooden bench with his head in his hands.

'Father?' asked Nicolo, unsure whether the priest's posture was more unusual than his acceptance of a layman in his sacristy.

The priest raised his head as though it was made of iron and twice the size.

'You cannot be here' he muttered without conviction.

'I have found a woman near the market stalls, she is sick with the plague and must be give the rites before she passes. Come, I will show you where she lies' said Nicolo.

'I cannot do it. What is the use? The ground is darkening with bodies and I cannot reach all of the souls that need my blessing. God has punished us all for our sins and no man can stand in His way. I will no doubt join her before long and may God alone judge my actions when the time comes.'

Nicolo had never heard a priest speak in such a way before, even allowing for his once tempered view of them. A priest's role was to give hope to those with none and if they were now afflicted with the helplessness that maimed the people then the very foundation of society was under threat.

'If not you, then who?' said Nicolo. 'Get up from your melancholy and save the souls of your parish.'

He heaved at the priest's arm to raise him up. The priest pulled hard in resistance, a stark contrast to his soporific behaviour thus far, freeing himself from Nicolo's grip and slamming his elbow into the grey stone wall behind him.

'Bugger!' he shouted, rubbing energetically at his arm and standing up to loom over Nicolo. 'Now look what you've done. Get out of here, you peasant! If you feel so sorry for this creature, give them their rites yourself.' He snatched a small, stoppered jug of oil from a windowsill and thrust it into Nicolo's chest. 'There are too many dying and too few priests. The pope has decreed that delegation can be applied in extreme cases, and quite frankly I'd be happier to see someone else rub their fingers over the heads of the cursed. Now get out!'

Nicolo was aware that his opinion of religion was much changed since his visit to Piombino, but this was the moment he would always look back on as the most significant of his religious life. He placed the jug into the pocket of his tunic and left the priest to his demons.

'I have been blessed so I may give you your last rites on this earth' said Nicolo to the possibly dead woman. 'May the Lord take you in his arms and forgive you of your sins.' He wasn't sure what he was supposed to say, having never witnessed the sacrament before, but that sounded like it was more or less the gist of it.

There was no movement and he was reluctant to touch her for fear of catching the disease himself, despite his altruism thus far. Amongst the debris around him was a broken table from a market stall, one that was likely to have outlived its owner. Picking up a wooden plank from the broken pile, Nicolo reached out from a distance and gently prodded the woman. She opened her eyes slowly and tilted her head ever so slightly, acknowledging Nicolo's efforts and saying goodbye in one small, subtle and heartbreaking gesture. He watched the woman become a corpse and turned away, unable to look at her any longer.

CHAPTER EIGHTEEN

PALAIS DES PAPES

'It's not him, I'm telling you' said the second voice. 'It doesn't sound like him and he's drinking more than he ever has.'

'Wouldn't you be if you were expected to lead a city consumed by death?' said the first voice.

'And it's free, don't forget that' said the third voice.

'Yes, and it's free' agreed the first voice.

'It's always been free' countered the second voice.

'Well yes, but...' argued the third voice. He was usually the first to give in when a conversation got too technical.

'Maybe he consecrates the wine first?' said the first voice. 'That way he would be drinking the blood of Christ. Perhaps he's readying himself for a great defensive effort against the plague. If anything, his drunkenness could be seen as a holy crusade.'

'Yes, a holy crusade' agreed the third voice, trying admirably to contribute.

'I'm not sure that's the most likely reason' said the second voice. 'And anyway, what about the voice?'

'Have you ever heard a man after a night of revelry?' said the first voice. 'With the amount he's been drinking he should have a voice deeper than the wrinkles on the hag's face.'

'Wine doesn't change a man's accent' said the second voice defiantly. 'Whoever this guy is has spent a significant amount of his life near Marseilles I would bet. Pope Clement is from Limousin in the north.'

'So you're saying that there is an imposter from Marseilles in the papal office, is that about right?' said the first voice.

'Well, that's a very categorical way of looking at it, but yes, on the balance of probability I would say that the weather may be clement, but the pope is not' said the second voice with just enough ambiguity to help support his denial later.

'In that case' said the first voice, pulling a short iron bar from his stocking and swishing it in the air, 'I'm awfully sorry about this.'

'Your visitor, your Holiness' said the first voice.

'Marvellous, you may go' said Father Bricoler.

The second voice bowed to the guest and backed out of the room, the wooden clip-clop of his shoes fading away as he headed to the bakery.

'Please, sit' said Jacques, gesturing to the opposite side of his enormous desk.

'I will stand, if it's all the same, *your Holiness*' said the brave man.

Jacques knew a power play when he saw one. He had, after all, just completed one of the greatest in all of history.

'It is not. Please, sit.'

The visitor recovered. 'Of course, Holy Father.'

'Now, tell me why the pope should hold a private audience with a man who refuses to announce himself' said Jacques with the confidence of a man who had recently talked his way into the papal vestments.

'With respect, I couldn't say' said the guest.

'With respect' countered Jacques, 'there is only you or I who could and I will not play games with a man of little etiquette.'

'I fear you may have asked the wrong question' said the man, 'for you asked why the pope should hold such an audience, and I have not come to see the pope.'

'Then why are you here, you fool? The kitchens are in the basement, perhaps you meant to go there?'

'If I wished to see the pope then I would not have come here. I would have visited him in his country estate.'

Jacques wobbled.

'And yet here you are, in the Palais des Papes and in front of the pope, the most powerful man in the world. Is it your intent to offer riddles for my entertainment, or is there another matter you wish to discuss?'

'How interesting that you do not dichotomise the two' said the guest. 'You may be the most powerful man in the world today, Father Jacques Bricoler, but the pope you are not.'

The floor of the papal office broke away, sending Jacques Bricoler's stomach through several storeys before hurtling back up again, almost emptying itself in the process. His guest was incomparably well-informed, and delivered his message with a patience and skill reserved for spies and heads of state. In the instant of his revelation, Jacques knew there was little difference between the two. A spy is simply the physical representation of a leader's will. If this man was a spy then he was, to all intents and purposes, a leader of men.

'That is an interesting thing to say' said Jacques. Regardless of the accuracy of the man's statement, it was not one he could ignore. 'What would make you say something so strange to someone as powerful as I?'

There was a hidden threat in there that the guest read like one of his books.

'It is strange indeed, Jacques, though not as strange as your move on the papal throne. I am curious as to why a man of such diluted faith would covet that which requires the strongest concentration.'

Jacques was in a corner, but it was his corner and his papacy. This stranger would need to play his hand well if he wished to leave the palace with a beating heart.

'I have faith in my tools, stranger, and their ability to reveal to me a man's most deeply held secrets. I can show you if you like, I suspect you would appreciate them. Professionally speaking, of course.'

'There is no need to lower yourself to threats, Jacques. I am here to help.'

'Telling me your name would help stay my hand' said Jacques.

'I am sure it would, but first I would like some assurance from you that I will not be flayed alive for my actions thus far. I am familiar with papal... whimsies, and I would rather be safe from them than not. I can promise you that you will be glad to hear of my identity when the time comes.'

'If you can prove your identity as well as claim it, then I will not punish you for your time here. Anything before or since will be a matter of fresh judgement. Now, I recommend you remove all shrouds from your talk. Who are you to have found an anonymous route to the papal office?'

'I am Giovanni di Murta, doge of all Genoa, and I bring grave news.'

'If you come with news of the pestilence then you will have seen that you arrive behind your leverage, Giovanni di Murta' said Jacques. 'I am ahead of you, protecting the pope and comforting the faithful. What news could you bring that would turn my attention from this Godly act of vengeance?'

'For all your positioning, Father Bricoler, you are not a master of the art. You should be reticent to give up your strengths, to do so is to hand the keys of power to your enemy' said Giovanni. 'I should tell you that I am not your enemy, nor you mine. I come with news you are yet to hear, for if you had I would not have gained access to you so effortlessly.'

'The plague is a risk I am prepared to face if it helps to keep the Holy Father safe' said Jacques, remaining faithful to some of his ruse at least.

'I do not refer to the plague. I am also in possession of certain information that would undermine your claim of pious altruism, information gleaned from merchants familiar with the shared shipping lanes of Marseilles and Genoa.'

Jacques knew that could have been guess work, though even a basic knowledge of his roots in Marseilles would be a significant concern.

'Then step from behind your curtain of diplomacy and deliver the message with which you have travelled so far.'

'Among the chaos of this sickness rides an assassin, one who targets the visible pope, false or otherwise.'

'There are many issues that concern the Holy Father' said Jacques. 'The pestilence rages in his city and the people are teetering on a knife edge. They may turn to the church as their salvation, or make it the target for a ruinous revolution. How the pope acts may determine the fate of all. An assassin would be joining at the back of a rather long queue with no refreshment stall, so you may take your petty threats and return to Genoa where I am sure your people are looking to you for guidance.'

He was rather happy with that, all things considered. As manipulative as Jacques had proven himself to be, he was always happier enjoying the spoils of his deviousness than the act itself.

'I would advise against drawing any rash conclusions, Father Bricoler' said the doge. 'This assassin is different in almost every way and they will most certainly succeed should you remain ignorant of their secret. I'm sure I needn't remind you that you are, despite the incongruous nature of the facts, Pope Clement VI and you will surely fall without my help.'

'I do not bow to those with cloaks and daggers, your Serenity. Reveal your secret, if such a thing exists, and allow me to judge for myself. As you say, I am to all intents and purposes Pope Clement VI and as such I can wield the same power as he. I am no monster, so I will offer you a choice; give up your secret and allow me to judge its merit for myself, or have judgment cast upon you without revelation. If your information is worthy of this political chicanery then you have nothing to fear. A charlatan I may be, your Serenity, but a man of my word I remain.'

'Then it seems I am left with no choice but to give you the information that may save your life, Father Bricoler, with one condition.'

'You are in no position to bargain, di Murta. Accept my offer or accept your fate.'

Giovanni raised his hands in a peaceful gesture. 'All I ask is that you say a mass for my intentions on the feast day of Saint Giovanni, the twenty fourth day of June.'

'If you had investigated me as deeply as you would have me believe then you would know of my aversion to such things.'

'You may be averse to saying mass, but you are not so foolish as to gamble your life to avoid one.'

'Then it seems we have a deal. Now, deliver your message.'

'The one who schemes to kill you is no man.'

'Oh come on!' cried Jacques. 'I hope we haven't danced around for the last ten minutes only for you to tell me that God is my judge and my executioner. I've had enough of that from Cle... the Holy Father.'

'I would not travel so far to deliver something so asinine, Father Bricoler. It is a woman that wields the weapon that tracks you, *our Holy Father*.'

'Is that it? Am I to wander in mortal fear on account of a woman, *your Serenity*? I would do as well to fear a beggar on the street. What harm can a woman do?'

'Fear the motivation, not the appearance. If one is so determined to complete their task there is little that can stand in their way. I am here to offer protection, for I know the appearance, if not the weapon.'

'Well you should have started with that then, shouldn't you? If someone comes in here and tells me they know what my would-be murderer looked like then I'd take them a little more seriously right from the off. You need to work on your overture, Giovanni.'

'I must respectfully disagree. My overture, as you put it, is precisely how I intended it to be and my protection of you while I am here will be the last line of protection for you and this most important of institutions.'

'And how is a man from Genoa, for a man you remain, Giovanni, better informed than the pope, whatever *appearance* he may take.'

'If you understood the world of high politics, Father Bricoler, then you would know the answer to your question. As it is, I shall humour you a short while longer. The world of leaders is governed by money and fear. I rule with money, while the pope rules with fear. There is only so far the papal purse can stretch, and the fear you sow in your people keeps you safe from those who would seek to destroy you far better than any amount of gold. Intelligence is less valuable to you, under normal circumstances. I, on the other hand, rule for money and information is the key that unlocks the treasures of men. I have invested far and wide in those who can bring me news, information that may seem insignificant to peasants and princes alike. While you may not appreciate the skills, nor the motivation, it is something that has saved your life, for the time being at least.'

'What of her appearance, then' said Jacques, keen to move the conversation along before he became inescapably entangled in diplomatic semantics. 'Am I to run from every woman who seeks a blessing from their Holy Father?'

'She is from Darmstadt in the east and has not changed her clothes in two weeks.'

'I'm not sure that's entirely relevant, Signore di Murta.'

'Oh Jacques, how naïve you are. It is most relevant. It is likely she will remain in her clothes until her attempted assassination of the pope. Murderers are such superstitious folk.'

'Well I should damn well hope so!' exclaimed Jacques. 'A woman without clothes would be spotted by all, assassination target or not.'

The doge of Genoa took a deep and patient breath, as if discussing the intricacies of iron smelting with a dog. 'The *same* clothes, Jacques. It is likely she will remain in the *same* clothes.'

'Ah, yes. Well, I suppose it makes more sense when you put it like that. Is that all, I'm to look out for a stinking woman from Darmstadt?'

'You are behaving like a spoilt child, Father Bricoler. Embrace my information and allow me to finish, if you would.'

'Then tell me all you know and cease with this percolation' replied Jacques, desperately trying to cling on to some high ground as he tumbled down a power play hill. 'If you could make it a nice, snappy list that would help us both out, I'm sure.'

'As you wish' replied di Murta with the gravity of one who has comfortably enough cards up his sleeve to release a few into play. 'She is taller than average, with blond hair that is tied in a bun on top of her head, but sits just below her shoulder when she wears it down. She wears a long tunic of plain grey cloth with pockets on either hip. She is fond of the famous Avignon soup in the Boar's Arrow tavern at the bottom of the hill and has eaten it every day since she arrived. This differs from her journey here, when she ate anything that could be given to her from the various farms and houses that acted as her shelter during those first difficult few weeks. She wears soft shoes, more in keeping with a man richer than her, but essential for one with such a long journey behind them. She sees no value in items that serve no practical use and is continually monitoring the movements of clergymen throughout the city. She has no faith to speak of, yet spends more time on her knees in the Cathedral than the most pious resident of the city and she intends to assassinate you in five days' time, with a weapon that is yet to be revealed to us.'

'Does she have a name?'

'I give you all that and still you doubt me?' said di Murta with incredulity.

'Oh, I believe you, signore. I just want to know what to call her while I have her on the rack.'

'She goes by Hildegund and has enough motivation to defeat you if you do not take my instruction.'

'And what, dare one ask, would your instruction be?'

'To answer that question with the fullness and respect it deserves would take longer than an uninvited guest should spend in a man's home.'

A timely knock came from the door.

'Then join me for dinner, guest, and tell me all.'

'Your meals' announced the third voice.

'You may leave us' said Jacques, lifting his veil as the door closed behind the servant.

The two men sat at the large light wood table, overflowing with dried meats and soft fruit.

'I will give you until this meal is ended to persuade me, Giovanni. I would counsel you to choose your words wisely; do not fill your speech with flattery and spin. Get to the point at this table, or you may find yourself at the end of one before the day is out.'

'Come now, Jacques. Are we not friends? Have I not shown my intentions to be honourable and true?'

'You have shown your admirable skill with words and diplomacy and no more. I will need more than a few well placed lines from you to be convinced. For now, however, that is all you have so make them count.' Jacques speared a morsel of mutton and pointed it casually towards the doge before putting it in his mouth, as if to say *well, what do you have for me?*

'I have trusted men across the city' began Giovanni, 'each harvesting information and delivering it to me through conduits that I will keep to myself for good or ill, no matter how persuasive your tools may be. They watch all corners of all places for me and each has circled in on this Germanic woman. She is an amateur, of that there is no doubt. Had she been more than that it would have taken longer to track her down, but as it is we have her. The routines of the cathedral have become her routines. She is predictable in her movements and overt in her preparation.'

'Then we have nothing to fear. If she is as predictable as you say then we can capture her whenever we choose' said Jacques.

'Not so, for she spends most of her time within the walls of the cathedral, and when she is not there she is in a busy tavern or sleeping in a room with a dozen other women. I do not believe she does this to hinder our approach, rather that they are the cheapest places to spend her time. Her inexperience is what sets her apart from her more accomplished peers.'

'So I should hope for a ruthless assassin rather than an uninitiated one? I'm not sure I agree with you, with all respect your Serenity.'

'With all respect to *you*, Father Bricoler, of the two of us sitting here at this table I am the more familiar with the nuances of political machinations. I am the one who has come to you with this information.' He stood up, looming over the priest with a volcanic anger at the point of eruption. 'I am the one who can save the papacy! Not you! I could snap my fingers and you would be pinned down by two men before the echoes had diminished to silence. Do not test me any further.

Do as I say or you will not be alive long enough to learn I was right.'

Jacques sat dumbfounded. This man had been the epitome of diplomatic politeness, despite the rage that bubbled under the surface. He was either a crazed fool, or there was truth in what he said. Either way, Jacques was in another corner, this time one that required a manoeuvre worthy of a seasoned escapologist.

'Then click your summoning fingers and prove your intent.'

The doge stared forcefully down at Jacques, then lowered his head in disappointment. His fingers clicked. The doors opened. The first and third voices charged in and threw Jacques to the floor, pinning him down and tying his hands behind his back with rough leather bands.

'Oh ye of little faith' said Giovanni di Murta, doge of all Genoa and owner of the power of the papal seat.

Pope Clement VI, the real one, stared out of a window in his vast country home. His gaze ignored the intricate ornamental garden and its rudimentary reconstruction in poppies of the Palais des Papes and the cathedral that leaned against it. It was painstakingly maintained by a virtuous gardener all year round on the off chance that his holiness might cast a brief glance in its direction once in a while. Clement also ignored the fishing pond that had taken twelve men four months to install following a throwaway comment he had made about the presumably relaxing qualities of angling in one's own garden. He had never used it, and never would.

Instead, his gaze was locked onto a nest of three starling chicks. He had spent hours watching their parents come and go with worms, grubs and other such juicy meals for them. He was almost sure they were due an attempt to leave their nest soon, although what he based this assumption on was not clear to him. Never before had he shown the slightest interest in ornithology, if you didn't count a brief obsession with birds during his time at the abbey in La Chaise-Dieu. He wasn't sure that was quite the same thing, though.

He considered the chicks' confinement, helpless creatures with no means to support themselves and no escape from their predicament bar hurling themselves from a great height in the hope that the noises coming from their parents was their way of saying *jump would you, for God's sake!*

He was not so dissimilar to those poor starling chicks, trapped as he was in his glorified prison. Safe from the plague he may have been, but he was most certainly not safe from the mental ravages of isolation, nor the sure and certain knowledge that he was failing those who looked to him for leadership. Was his whole purpose as pope not to give comfort to the infirm and to offer guidance to those souls in need of direction?

A movement in the nest brought him back from his daydreaming. One of the chicks was peering over the edge. It backed away to the safety of its siblings before slowly creeping forward again, leaning further this time. It turned to its siblings and tweeted before throwing itself from the nest and into the concealed shadows of the trees.

Perhaps that was what he must do. Playing the percentages didn't get him to the lofty branch of the papacy. He had taken risks once, gambles that had paid off with an almost alarming effectiveness. He often reflected that the timing of his move on the throne was incredibly fortunate, but without taking the chances he had it wouldn't have been relevant at all. He was flirting with no amount of jeopardy while he remained in this prison and for all he knew the pestilence may still reach him, even here. Sitting in this opulent nest would not be a fitting end to his reign, but jumping off and learning to fly may be.

'Guy!' he called to the walls. 'Bring me my quill.'

CHAPTER NINETEEN

Nicolo worked up and down the line of stalls, enquiring of the sellers for clues to Cuthbert's whereabouts. None were helpful and all were on edge.

Salesmen are, by definition, masters of spin; able to find the positive in almost anything. The benefits of whatever goods they happened to be selling today were tailored to the needs of the customer and sometimes vice versa. The problem these days was that everyone had the same need; to escape the clutches of the relentlessly encroaching pestilence. An ornate washboard could not be considered a reasonable defence, no matter how effective the salesman might be. The line of stalls was being continuously thinned by this demonic plague, whether by taking stallholders from this earth or by scaring them from their jobs. Those who remained were struggling to earn a coin for their families and for most of them hunger was the only thing biting. Their desperation was mirrored in Nicolo's actions. He had to find Cuthbert if he wanted to triple his resources in his search for The Cutler and he had made no progress. He resolved to try one more stall before heading back to the tavern in the hope that Robert had been more fortunate than he.

He approached one half covered in colourful glass ornaments, picking one up and studying it as he wished a good morning to the owner. When no reply came he looked up, only to see the back of the bald man as he disappeared down a nearby alleyway. If the salesmen are spooked by strangers in this vast city, thought Nicolo, then these are undoubtedly unique times. He placed the glass down on to the table and headed back to the tavern. He needed a drink if nothing else.

Nicolo opened the tavern door and glanced straight to the empty table in the corner where he and Robert had met a few hours earlier. He took the same seat and ordered an ale. The barman was not the man who had served them before and Nicolo wondered if it was simply a shift change, or something more sinister. This plague was soaking into every conscious thought.

The barman returned with the drink and left Nicolo to his thoughts. Perhaps he would be as well to abandon Robert and search for The Cutler alone. At least then he wouldn't have to give away any of his secrets, no matter how irrelevant they may be here. By way of a final attempt to help find Cuthbert he considered what his actions would be had he been suffering the after effects of being blind drunk in a strange city. All he knew about Cuthbert from Robert was that he was a pious man who had embraced a temporarily debauched lifestyle over the last few weeks. There was no evidence to suggest this trajectory had been altered, and the only logical conclusion Nicolo could draw was that he would continue with his drinking once his body allowed him to do so. It was as likely as not that he would find his way to this same tavern, as Robert had done, and concluded that the best thing he could do was to sit where he was and continue drinking. Once he had established that Cuthbert was not already in the tavern he would simply call out to those coming in until one of them answered to the name.

He looked about the room. It was sparsely populated, with most choosing to recoup earlier sins through prayer in the cathedral and churches across the city rather than doubling down by drinking their way through this test of faith. Of the six men he could see, three of them were grey haired and withering, much too old to be Cuthbert. Two others were talking spritely to each other about the condition of their fields after last summer's heat. One man sat on his own and was young enough to fit Cuthbert's description. On closer inspection Nicolo could just about make out what may have been a pilgrim's cloak, if you ignored the rough tears and ground in dirt. He picked up his mug and headed over.

'Lovely morning!' said Nicolo to the filthy man, taking a seat opposite him.

The man looked up, anger glaring in his blue eyes. 'What would you know of such things? If you can see into a man's heart then you would do well to use your skill in better places than this. People need hope. If you are a charlatan, then be gone with you and leave me to my drink.'

The instantaneous vitriol took Nicolo by surprise, even allowing for the location. 'Who says I'm a charlatan?' he said, a little too defensively.

'I do. The weather may be pleasant but that is no reflection on my current demeanour. I would warn you against aggravating me any further.'

'Well you're quite the joy, aren't you? Enjoy last night a little too much, did you?'

'I didn't enjoy it at all, thank you very much' said the man. 'Or at least, I don't remember enjoying it. I have a sore back and a sore head for my troubles and would appreciate a little space to level myself up again, if it's all the same to you.'

Nicolo knew that hundreds of men would be feeling a little worse for wear every morning in a city the size of Avignon, and these days many more than usual, but his question would be harmless.

'Cuthbert, I assume?' he said.

The man looked up from his tankard without moving his head.

'How interesting you would ask a stranger such a specific question? You must have a great need to find this *Cuthbert*, no doubt. Fill my mug and I will answer your question.'

Nicolo clapped his hands together slowly, but not sardonically. He knew this wasn't Cuthbert, but appreciated the man's ability to turn things to his favour. He would happily reward him with a drink; a respectful nod to this conman from one who was moving further away from the trade with each passing day.

As the barman placed a fresh ale in front of the filthy man the tavern door swung open and Robert walked in looking forlorn.

'Robert!' called Nicolo. 'Any news?'

'Robert!' called the filthy man.

Nicolo looked between the two in surprise.

'Cuthbert!' called Robert.

'Cuthbert? Ah, yes! Cuthbert! I found him, Robert. Look' said Nicolo, keen not to lose any credit he may have inadvertently earned.

'Cuthbert, what on earth happened to you?' said Robert, sitting down beside his friend and clasping his arm across his shoulder. 'We were worried sick!'

'You know this man?' asked Cuthbert.

'Of course! This is Nicolo, he has been helping me find you.'

'Well it seems he has luck on his side then.'

'What happened to you?'

'You're asking the wrong person' said Cuthbert honestly. 'I remember you getting involved with a heavily eyebrowed giant. I'm fairly sure I saved you from him.'

'I may not remember much' said Robert, 'but it was most certainly you who got us entangled with the eyebrow, not I. Anyway, it's not important, as long as you're safe and well.'

'*Well* may be stretching it a bit, but it's nothing a few mugs of ale can't cure. Come on, I've already managed to get one free drink this morning, even if it was from this new friend of yours.'

'It's the afternoon' said Nicolo, 'and you have to earn your next drink.'

'He's right' said Robert. 'I promised we would help him to find his friend if he helped me to find you.'

'I don't have to earn anything' said Cuthbert to Nicolo. 'I wasn't consulted in any deal you may have made with Robert here, so you can leave me out of it.'

Nicolo knew a man of self-interest when he saw one, he had seen his own reflection often enough. He also knew which buttons to press.

'You're correct, of course' he began. 'Robert here made the deal and he will, I am sure, stand to his word and help me in my time of need. For your part, I would rather see you help me for your friend's sake, but I am willing to offer you a reward, such is the urgency with which I make my search. If you find my quarry before sunset tomorrow I will give you this.' He pulled the second finest piece of jewellery he owned from his pocket and placed it on the table. 'You can exchange this for as much drink as your stomach can handle for the rest of your holy pilgrimage.'

Nicolo slipped the ring back into a pocket and watched the cogs in Cuthbert's mind work overtime. The pilgrim picked up his full tankard of ale, drank it all in just a few large gulps, slammed the mug onto the table and wiped his mouth with the arm of his sleeve.

'Prove your virtue by filling this mug and I would be honoured to help you, dear friend' said Cuthbert.

'Barman!' called Nicolo, clicking his fingers to show he was not to be kept waiting. 'Six ales here, we have a long stretch ahead of us.'

Six tankards dropped onto the table in the gloomy tavern, spilling more than Cuthbert would have liked.

'So who is this friend of yours?' said Robert.

'He is less of a friend and more of a...' Nicolo hesitated, unsure how to describe the man when all he knew of him was his name. Not even his real name, at that. 'He is a friend of a friend.'

'Ah, so this is a business operation?' said Cuthbert. 'You would not be so deliberate in your description if it were a leisurely pursuit you were on.'

Nicolo looked at Robert. 'Is he always this cynical?'

'Only recently, you should have heard him when I first met him. He would have won awards for naïvety if it wasn't for a baker in Chambry.'

Part of Nicolo wanted to ask the obvious question, but there were more important things for his mind to focus on.

'It is both business and personal' said Nicolo. 'I like to make it my business to protect my personal heartbeat. Finding The Cutler will enhance that protection greatly.'

'So you're in trouble then, and this Cutler can get you out of a sticky situation? Is that about the size of it?' said Cuthbert.

'That would be oversimplifying it rather a lot, but I believe you've grasped the crux of the matter. If we find him, then I will be free to go about my business. I intend to flee north and escape this ruthless pestilence.'

'If we are to be of any help to you' said Robert, 'then you must tell us your tale, and all you know of The Cutler.'

Nicolo let his mask slip properly for the first time since the crypt of Saint Augustine the Meek all those years ago. He told them of his trade, his travels and his unfulfilled grand plan to extort the doge of Genoa of a significant portion of his wealth. When his story reached Robert and the tavern he took a drink and waited for their response.

'So let me get this straight' said Cuthbert. 'You're an honest conman who wants our help to find a mysterious stranger, a stranger intimately connected to the most powerful man in all of Genoa. In return your life will be spared, and those of your family. Is that about right?'

'That's a reasonable summary, yes' said Nicolo.

'Then I very much doubt that your life is worth a single ring, let alone those of your family. You will need to double the stakes if you are to triple your resources.'

Robert looked at Cuthbert and, not for the first time in recent days, wondered at the change in him since Calais. Nicolo looked at him with an altogether different mindset. Cuthbert reminded him of a younger version of himself, one he no longer reflected on with any significant pride. Still, the man was good, there was no question about it.

'Then I will increase the stakes' said Nicolo. 'If I find The Cutler I will pay you the gold ring, as promised. If either of you find him for me then I will pay you with three.'

He pulled three rings at random from his tunic. In truth, he would have given everything he owned to find the man and relieve himself of the burden. He knew how to make something from nothing and would be happy to start again, even if it meant returning briefly to *Simple Stones* until he had enough money to keep himself honestly.

'Then we have a deal' said Cuthbert with finality. He picked up his last tankard and drained it in one. 'Well come on gentlemen, what are we waiting for? I grew up in the poorest part of town so I'll search the slums. Robert, you're a seasoned pilgrim with enough wit about you to open the tightest fist, so you can work the market areas. That leaves the rich parts for you, Nicolo. You have experience getting past guards in important places and you'll need it here.'

Neither of the other men could fault his logic, again.

'Then we will finish these drinks and go our separate ways for now' said Nicolo. 'It is late, and I for one would be grateful for a full night's sleep before beginning another hunt. Let's meet at the fountain at midday tomorrow and share what we've learned.'

CHAPTER TWENTY

Cuthbert wasn't ready for sleep and had headed straight to the slums of Avignon, breathing through his mouth as he walked. The pestilence was rife in this part of the town and was the catalyst for a nightmarish scene of which the rest of the city seemed largely ignorant. Back in Umbridge he would find any reason to blame the rich of the village for the ailments of the poor, and for the most part his aim was true, but everything was different here. For once he couldn't blame those with money for ignoring the cataclysm happening on their doorstep; who would want to even acknowledge this hell on earth, let alone come to see it with their own eyes?

Cuthbert walked in the centre of the pathways that criss-crossed the sprawling slum, such was the level of activity at the hovel openings. With alarming frequency he witnessed bodies being heaved onto heavy wooden planks and carried away. The old Cuthbert would have knelt on the spot and prayed for the souls of the departed, but the new one simply covered his mouth instinctively and walked a little quicker. Quite where he would find a clue to the identity of The Cutler was as great a mystery to him as the man himself.

It is said that a man can eradicate the pain of an arrow piercing their leg if only they are given a greater pain on which to focus their attentions; an unexpected amputation of their arm, for example. It was a reflection of this philosophy that led Cuthbert to his decision. There was no obvious benefit in staying here in the disease ridden cesspit of the poor. No man of real power, no matter how much that power must be kept in the shadows, would remain here for longer than was necessary to complete their mission. There was no value here. No reason for being. No life. If a man wielded power then he would surely wield it somewhere else.

The slums were a dead end, literally and figuratively. Under less mortifying circumstances it would have been an ideal place for a man of secrecy to hole up, but the growing piles of corpses that polluted the air were surely a deterrent to even the most hardened of spies. He left the slums to wander aimlessly along the dark streets of Avignon. His search had taken a passive turn, as if The Cutler would tap him on the shoulder and offer him food, board and an invitation to a sing-along.

It was past midnight and the crowds at the market were either asleep in their homes or praying in the churches. There were one or two desperate stall holders still lingering behind their tables and Cuthbert approached one, as much to break his boredom than to advance his search.

'Good evening' he said to the trader. 'You are here late today.'

'I have nothing to return home to, pilgrim. My house has been emptied of my wife and children and I am as well spending time here as in a place now void of anything but painful memories.'

This wasn't quite the light conversation Cuthbert had had in mind.

'I am sorry to hear of your loss, sir. The boil sickness?'

'No' said the salesman, surprising Cuthbert and giving him a renewed interest in the conversation. 'Sometimes I wish it was, at least then I would have kindred souls to support me through my mourning. People continue to die of other causes you know? It may be a powerful and relentless force, but it has not yet taken control over all death. Only God wields such a thing.'

'Of course, my apologies. May I enquire as to what took your family from you?'

'Sheep.'

'Sheep?'

'Sheep.'

Cuthbert had no choice. 'How did the sheep... do it? Was it a particularly large sheep?'

'Sheep, sir, not sheep. Sheep plural.'

'Ah, I see' said Cuthbert. 'So how did the *sheep plural* do it?'

'They herded my family to the edge of a steep rock face and pushed them over it.'

'They can do that?'

'Do you think I made it up?' said the widower sternly.

'Well, no. I mean, of course not' said Cuthbert, struggling to regain his composure. 'I didn't mean to cause offence, it's just that I have never heard of anything like that happening before.'

'There is good reason for that.'

'I'm sure there is. Please, my apologies.'

'It's because it never happened' said the salesman, a wonky grin appearing on his face.

'Pardon?'

'I said it's because it never happened. A flock of sheep herding a family over a cliff indeed? Honestly, some people shouldn't be allowed out on their own at this time of night. I can't believe you fell for that one! Fell for it... hah! See what I did there?'

'No wonder you're still here at this time of night trying to scratch a living' said Cuthbert. 'I know death is at the front of all of our minds these days but making light of it will not warm customers to you.'

'I was only joking.'

'I know, and that's rather the point.'

'I mean I was only joking about the sheep. My family have been taken from me by the infernal pestilence and all I have left is this stall and a small square of wood to sleep on in the slums. Some days I have to work such long hours that I turn around as soon as I get home and come straight back here to start the next day's work.'

'That's better' said Cuthbert, but go easy on the sleep deprivation part, people won't believe that.

'Right you are sir, and thank you. Here, you don't fancy one of these do you? They're from the one true cross.'

'No thanks, I've had enough passion recently to last me a lifetime. See what I did there?'

The black floor in front of Cuthbert was yet to begin its daily conversion to grey as he woke. He had fought off fatigue for as long as he could, talking to anyone who would listen in the hope of finding a clue to the identity of The Cutler. He had finally succumbed and given in to sleep, as ignorant of his identity as he had been when he started. He made his way to the fountain and sat down on the floor beside it, stretching his legs out and resting his head against the cold stone. His eyes drooped and sleep took him again.

When he woke the sun was past its zenith above the buildings of the market square and people were milling around him. He cursed himself but knew Robert and Nicolo would have woken him had they arrived. Something had surely happened to them, and it was unlikely to be good news. One of them may have found The Cutler, he supposed, but that would not explain their combined absence. The most probable scenario was that Robert had gone drinking and lost track of time, as one does when drinking through the events of the night before. Nicolo may have found trouble, their prey, or both. If Robert was indeed drinking to cure a hangover then he would most likely be in the Greave Dunning or possibly sleeping in their rooms above the fletcher's workshop. Cuthbert headed to the tavern, grateful to have a tangible lead to follow.

Robert scanned the lines of stalls in the thin morning sunshine for a starting point to his investigation. He had little to go on bar his wits but knew Cuthbert was right to suggest he work the market. As he made his way down the hill he considered his approach. He knew The Cutler was linked to the Genoese political landscape in some form, though not the level. He would pass himself off as a new resident, keen for information on the city and loose with his tongue.

There were fewer stalls than he remembered and the range of goods was narrower. Reasoning that those stallholders with more acumen would have changed their offerings to those in demand, he approached one of several now selling religious goods and picked up a stone with a cross painted crudely on one face.

'Nice stone' he said to the greying salesman.

'It is sir, quite the nice stone as you say.'

'What else have you got here' said Robert, feigning interest in the other items on the table. 'Oh, I like this.' He turned a metal crucifix over in his hands as if studying it.

'I can see you have a good eye, sir' said the salesman dutifully. 'That's real iron that is, not the cheap stuff you'd get from the others.'

'Yes, it's clear you have an altogether better quality of wares here' said Robert. 'I have heard of such quality from my brother but I have never seen it myself. He is living in Genoa, in the old quarter if you know it.'

Robert peeked up at the salesman for a sign of interest. He wasn't sure what the sign might have been, but he felt as though there should be one if this man knew anything.

'I'm afraid I am an expert in Avignon matters only, sir. The lands beyond these walls have remained a mystery to me. I'm the first in my family to have their own stall, can you believe that? Someone offering goods as fine as these and I'm the first. Almost beggars belief, wouldn't you say?'

Robert sensed the man was both ignorant of the information he required and on the verge of a rather long and tortuous ramble. He placed the iron cross back on the table.

'Thank you for your time, kind man, and I wish you and your family well in these troubling times' said Robert, using the parting remark that was becoming ubiquitous among the living.

He continued along the stalls, stopping in turn at a baker, a jug seller and a stall that seemed dedicated solely to the repair of socks. He came next upon the only glass items he had seen so far and stopped with a genuine curiosity, despite his desire to glean information of any kind for their dawn meeting at the fountain.

'This is a fine collection' he said to the bald man behind the table. 'The finest I have seen since my arrival here.'

The man stood a little straighter as he subtly looked the man up and down. 'That is most generous of you, stranger. You are new to the city?'

'I arrived two days ago on a pilgrimage from the north' said Robert. 'I knew a little of the sights here, for my brother passed through on his way to Genoa some years ago, but his tales did not prepare me for the reality of this great city. Even as the pestilence grows there is beauty to see. It is heartening.'

The bald man knew a fictional back story when he heard one. After all, he was acting out his own as he stood in the filthy streets of this godforsaken place.

'I am glad to hear that my city warms your heart, stranger. Tell me, what does your brother say of Genoa? I have not experienced it's majesty for myself, although friends have seen it and speak well of the markets.'

This was the first meaningful reaction to his mention of Genoa since his search had begun and Robert was quick to latch on to it.

'He is enamoured with the atmosphere there. He was a fisherman at our family home so spends his time at the docklands catching food to sell to those who can afford it. Alas, I fear he will never return. The Genoese fish agree with him, financially speaking, and the work is easier. For one, there is a cutler there who produces the finest gutting instruments. Our father always told us that the most worthwhile investment a fisherman can make, no matter how poor they may be, is to find the right cutler. There is a message in there for all of us, wouldn't you agree?'

If Robert had the freedom to show his true feelings he would now have been leaning back and squinting, as if bracing for an impact.

'Is that so?' said the bald man. 'Then I believe there is something you would be most interested to see. Come with me, stranger, for I will take you to the greatest cutler in all of the Holy Roman Empire.'

CHAPTER TWENTY ONE

Nicolo strained his neck to take in the glorious masterpiece of Avignon cathedral. It leant against the Palais des Papes and was an enormous structure, taller even than the Palazzo Pubblico in Genoa. It bore more resemblance to a castle than a cathedral, the crenulated walls speaking of defence more than reverence. His mind wandered back to Catania and his escapade in the crypt. He had considered the church of Saint Augustine the Meek to be the greatest building he would ever see, in proportions at least, but each new city presented him with a new benchmark. Avignon was the pinnacle, and he couldn't help but remain fixated by it, awestruck at the sheer scale of the construction.

A beggar girl pulled at his tunic, snapping him from his reverie and instinctively sending his hand to cover his pocket. He swatted her away and moved on towards the main entrance, a simple, small doorway in distinct contrast to the grand scale of every other part of the great place. Inside a mass was in full swing, the cardinal at the altar raising the communion host as Nicolo took a seat at the back of the congregation.

Time plays by different rules when you are listening to a monotonic voice delivering an oration in Latin. Every word seemed stretched, every syllable like a sentence. Nicolo's eyes drooped, the events of recent weeks combining with the relative warmth of the cathedral to send him lower in his seat and closer to an unintended nap, despite the previous night's rest. He entered that drowsy phase shared by waking moments and minute sleeps. Each time he woke he struggled to gauge how much time had passed. Had he been asleep for a few seconds or an hour? It was difficult to tell, such was the continuous nature of services in the cathedral on this morning. The cathedral, in contrast to its surrounding churches, seemed to be doing its best to supply what the people craved, but when that demand is insatiable the supply can never be enough. The cardinal was raising the host again. It was a different cardinal now, one with boil-laden arms and the face of his father. He looked around the congregation and saw several Roberts in various states of supplication. There were Cuthberts and Lievitos, Angelos and Salvatores, all venerating themselves energetically in front of his cardinal father.

A loud bang woke him.

To his left a drunkard had knocked over a pew and was trying valiantly to stand himself upright again. Nicolo massaged his face and took the opportunity to leave. He needed a drink before he could start questioning people. Perhaps the cathedral wasn't the best place for him to have started, all things considered.

Nicolo sat at his table in the Greave Dunning, fingering the rough sides of his wooden tankard. He had always used past experiences to shape present decisions and this time would be no different. His grand plan in Genoa was ultimately flawed and unsuccessful, but he had learned a great deal from it nonetheless. There was no advantage to be gained by slowly climbing the ladder of power. He should aim at the top and work down from there if needs be. His main concern was that the top in the case was the pope himself. It is one thing to aim at the leader of a city state but quite another to enter a pit of snakes that houses the leader of a religion.

This time he had no choice. This time he would test his fate against the leader of the Holy Roman Empire. All that was left to do was to choose whether to arrive at his door as friend or foe.

He peered through the branches at the entrance to the Palais des Papes. In the previous three hours he had seen large numbers of servants come and go, and several important looking men with entourages longer than a summer evening. No beggars had troubled the doors in all this time, an unexpected development for him and one that raised doubts about his chances of success. If a beggar man sees no value in prostrating himself in front of the epicentre of Christian charity then perhaps there is no charity there at all. Perhaps the guards have stone hearts. It was enough evidence to convince Nicolo he should use means other than sympathy and empathy.

He had considered many different strategies that may grant him an entrance to the palace. He could buy some trinkets from the market and announce himself as a delivery man for some anonymous figure in the relics department. He could put himself forward as a dignitary from some far off land with a pre-arranged appointment with the pontiff that must not have been put in the papal diary. Neither of these seemed likely to allow him access though and he eventually settled on a singularly direct approach that would incontrovertibly answer the question that was scorched onto his mind.

It was almost midday when he landed with a thump on the undergrowth, dusted himself down and walked out of the far side of the trees. He took a circuitous path back to the road, ensuring the guards could not see his route, and strode confidently into the palace grounds and towards the guards at the entrance.

'Make way!' he commanded gruffly in the general direction of the guards while still some way off.

'We do not make way, we are the way' retorted the first guard haughtily as Nicolo reached them.

'I thought that was Jesus' said Nicolo.

'He is the way to heaven, we are the way to the palace, now speak your business or we will have Satan cast you out' said the second guard.

'You have a direct communication with Satan? Here, at the palace?' said Nicolo. 'I would think this was the one place in all of Christendom he wouldn't be seen dead at.'

'Satan's the dog' said the first guard. 'Big one too.'

'Ah'

'Shall I get him?' said the second guard. 'I don't mind, he's just over there.'

'I don't believe there is a need for that. I will announce myself and then you will understand that the pope will insist on an audience immediately.'

'Will he indeed?'

'He will.'

'Who are you then, Satan's nephew?' said the second guard, nudging the first and giving him a smug look.

The first guard didn't appreciate the humour and stared at the second guard for a few disapproving moments before turning back to where Nicolo had been.

The stranger who was not Satan's nephew almost tripped on a discreet step as he hurtled into the palace, his arms flailing as though he was falling from a cliff. He sprinted through the lobby, stopping briefly to establish the best direction in which to charge, and flung himself up a staircase. Halfway up he grabbed a banister and swung himself around to the right, covering the last few stairs with giant leaps. At the top was a central doorway leading to a corridor that ran perpendicular to the stairs. He headed right to keep his momentum going and ran at full speed towards a left turn at the end. He didn't notice the priceless artwork softening the walls, nor the ancient pottery on small tables below each window. Unfortunately for Nicolo, there were also two men he didn't notice as he turned the corner, slamming into them and sending bread and wine in all directions. The men jumped on his prone figure and pinned him to the ground.

Nicolo slumped in defeat. He licked a dark red liquid from his lips, taking the most expensive drink in his life as he did so. 'Bugger.'

'Who are you?' said one of the former wine carriers.

'I am The Cutler' said Nicolo, 'and the pope must see me at once.'

'Oh, *he* should see *you*? Is that so?'

'Maybe you did not hear me, for I have announced myself as The Cutler. Tell that to the pope and he will be here licking the wine from my face before you can say *sour grapes*.'

'I am of no doubt that the one in the papal office would be most interested to hear of your announcement, Nicolo Anatra.'

'Ah.'

A knock interrupted them.

'What?' called Giovanni di Murta to the knock.

The first voice walked in. 'You have a visitor, master, and I think they will be of great interest to you. They found a way past the guards but we were able to apprehend him as he made his way here.'

'Does he have a name?'

'He says he is The Cutler.'

'Oh that is marvellous. Clean up the charlatan pope here then bring him to us.'

'I still don't understand' said the third voice. 'Should I call him his serenity, his holiness or simply master? Come to think of it, I'm not even sure which human to address, let alone which title they're currently holding. It's like a game of foxes and chickens in there.'

'You just keep an eye on our petty conman there, I'll deal with the important people' said the first voice.

The third voice retreated to a chair next to the bound limbs of Nicolo. His torso was a little further away, such was the contorted way they had tied him. This was more to do with their inability to tie a decent knot than for any arbitrarily spiteful reason.

'Any chance you could loosen these a little?' said Nicolo, lifting his wrists an inch towards his captor. 'I think my fingers are turning blue.'

'I never could get the hang of knots' said the third voice, ignoring the petition. 'I can spear a mouse on horseback but can't tie a simple knot. Funny really. My dear father, God rest his soul, used to tell me it was more important to master the difficult things in life than the easy ones. That way I wouldn't turn out like his brother, God rest his soul. He could tie a knot as well as any man in the Holy Roman Empire, and a good many other things of that nature too, but ask him to train a boy to spy on his masters and he'd be as useless as a flea on a rat.'

'I've never seen a mouse on horseback before' said Nicolo. 'How do they hold on?'

'I can spear a mouse while *I* am on the horse, not the mouse. Dear God, no wonder you got caught.'

'Ah, but I wasn't caught by those who were chasing me, and that is what really counts if we are evaluating my abilities.'

'Not while you're lying on your back like a turtle it isn't' said the third voice. 'Now shut up before I show you some of my more advanced skills.'

✝

'The Cutler' announced the first voice to the room in general.

Giovanni di Murta sat at the pale wooden table with his legs crossed and the elbow of his right arm resting on the pine. His left hand fidgeted with something in an inside pocket of his dark green and black doublet. His eyes watched the doorway expectantly.

A part of Nicolo was excited to be meeting the pope. Admittedly it was much smaller part than that which was deliberating on how the wine carriers had known his name. He hobbled along the last few paces across the corridor, the third voice helping him to stay upright, and reached an ornate wooden door with one small flat spot on which to knock safely.

The doors opened from the inside and Nicolo was pushed into a room of such riches that it would have caused him to faint at the prospect of stealing it all, had the sight of Giovanni di Murta not got there first.

A shower of cold water brought him back to consciousness. He wished they hadn't bothered. Above him, and consuming the entirety of his field of vision, was the doge of Genoa; commander of that great city and master of Nicolo's immediate future.

'Signore Sigliano, how nice of you to drop by' said Giovanni.

Nicolo waited for a question.

'Do you not have anything you wish to say to me?' asked the doge.

'I could use a mug or five of wine' said Nicolo.

Giovanni clicked his fingers and a voice appeared with two crystal goblets filled to the brim with the most expensive wine in the world. The doge took them and slowly poured the contents over Nicolo's face.

'May it never be said that I treat people unfairly' he said, 'and I intend to treat you with precisely as much fairness as you deserve, Signore Sigliano. Some may say it is of such a level of fairness as to be called *justice*.'

'Ah yes, your message' said Nicolo. 'It is right here in my pocket and I am here in Avignon to deliver it, as you can plainly see. If delay is your concern, then may I suggest you give your messengers a little more to go on next time. It would have been much more effective had you given me an address. If I knew to deliver it to "The Cutler, Second Room On The Left, Just Above The Shop With The Funny Looking Flowers, Avignon" we would all be home drinking ale from a deer's antler by now.'

'Ah, but then how would you have explained away the time you spent in Piombino, Signore Mazzi?'

'Bloody hell, have you got a little man living in my damned pockets!?' cried Nicolo. 'I appreciate you're a well connected man, your Serenity, but how on God's good earth do you know about Piombino?'

'I told you I have eyes everywhere, Nicolo. That you didn't believe me is your problem, not mine. Needless to say my network shall remain a secret to those without it, although there is one I may reveal to you before our paths are untangled once more.'

'If it isn't The Cutler then I have no interest in learning the identity of one of your common spies' said Nicolo defiantly.

'Oh I shouldn't worry about that, Nicolo. There is one you will be most interested to discover, of that I have no doubt.'

A shadow coughed politely from a gloomy corner of the room.

'Ah yes' said Giovanni, summoning the third voice from the corridor with a click of his fingers.

The third voice strode up to Nicolo with a dagger the length of his hand and cut the string that bound his wrists and ankles. He handed a rag to Nicolo and bowed to the doge, then again to the gloomy corner before backing out of the room and resuming his position on the chair.

'Thank you. May I?' said Nicolo, gesturing to the pocket of his tunic as he wiped his face with the rag.

'By all means' said the doge.

Nicolo fumbled in his pocket for the small cylinder of parchment that held the doge's message. He twisted it round in his fingers to be sure the unbroken seal would face Giovanni as he passed it to him, and cleared his throat.

'I have a message here that I am under orders to pass into your hands only, with an unbroken seal, on pain of death to me and my family in Catania.'

The doge's mouth opened wide as he bellowed an enormous laugh, rocking back and forth with uncontrolled hilarity until his forehead banged on the table, stunting his passionate display and reinstating his sober demeanour. He wiped a tear from his eye before catching his breath and steadying his voice.

'My dear Nicolo, how naïve you are. You think that I am The Cutler, that I have played games with you across vast distances. No, you are not so important to me. You may become so, but for now you are a speck of dust on my shoe.' The doge took the message from Nicolo's outstretched hand and foraged in his doublet once more, producing another small scroll with the same dark green seal. 'When you learn the identity of The Cutler, give this to him and instruct him to open it immediately.'

'Are you going to tell me what was in the first scroll?' said Nicolo, defiant in his curiosity despite the gravity of the situation. 'I will not be your constant messenger until our Lord takes me from this earth. Tell me, or find another lackey.'

'You truly are a feisty one' said the doge. 'I will show you the message, but let me be as clear as I can; it is not because you delivered an ill-advised ultimatum. I will show you because then you may understand the cunning of those who control you. Maybe then you will have a more appropriate perspective of your place in matters that exceed your competence.'

Nicolo swallowed his response, prioritising an effective retaliation over a hasty one. Giovanni pulled the original scroll from his pocket again, breaking the seal and unfurling the small piece of parchment. He turned it to face Nicolo and watched his expression change from defiance to subservience.

The simple note read:

"If he has announced himself as Nicolo, kill him"

'Perhaps now you understand me a little better, Signore Anatra?'

'What is on the second note?' asked Nicolo.

'Do not take me for a fool! Deliver your new message and I may free you from my service. Should you choose not to follow my instruction I will free you from this life.'

'You *may* free me?'

'Indeed. I can see many things, Nicolo Anatra, but that which has not yet happened remains a mystery to all. When the time comes I may require your services again. If I do not, then our acquaintance will be complete and you will be free to go about your own business once more. There is no negotiation here, fisherman. Find The Cutler and deliver my message, or seal your fate.'

There was a commotion in the corridor outside. The sound of men clamouring and arguing reached the room before the doors burst open. Two men collapsed on top of each other in the doorway, one pinned face down on the floor while the other looked up at Nicolo and the doge.

'Nicolo?' said Robert, keeping his weight on the other man's back for the moment.

'Robert?'

'How interesting' said the doge.

Robert shoved his adversary's back closer to the floor as he stood, releasing a groan from the man's throat.

'What are you doing here?' said Nicolo.

'What am *I* doing here? I'm finding the damned cutler is what I'm doing here. What are you doing here?'

The prone man lifted himself onto his knees, only the back of his bald head visible to the others. He raised himself to his full height and turned to face them. Nicolo's eyes widened with incomparable shock.

'Father?'

CHAPTER TWENTY TWO

uthbert opened the door to their room and sagged. Everything was as they had left it and there was no sign that Robert had entered the room since they were last here. His friend had not been in the tavern either, nor any of those nearby. He slumped onto the faded straw matting and stared at the dank wall.

Nicolo was his own man and could clearly look after himself. Cuthbert also owed the stranger nothing, excepting their agreement. Robert was a different matter. Cuthbert was grateful for his friendship and for all that he had done to help his recent social development. He would help him now and repay some of the debt.

Robert had been canvassing the market area from the square down to the city gates, although he would surely have moved on from those areas by now. Still, it would be prudent to search there in case he was simply sleeping in an alleyway. If that proved to be a fruitless search he would head to the more grandiose areas of the city. Robert may have found information worth sharing immediately and gone there to find Nicolo before dawn.

He pictured the worst case scenario in his mind. If he couldn't find them then he would be alone in a strange city with only his wits to help him survive hunger, the pestilence and an impossibly long journey home. If they had been captured by this Cutler then they may give up his name and description. What then? He had been an innocent young man when he left his home, and even the debauchery that had followed was on a small scale with minor players. This was an altogether different scale of mischief, possibly including the Avignon elite and certainly the leader of the Genoese empire. Dealing out deathly sentences to anonymous peasants would be of no consequence to men with such power. He lay back on the straw and stared at the ceiling, a sudden feeling of helplessness overwhelming him.

Then he remembered the parchments his father had given him.

Cuthbert spent a few short minutes searching the passageways close to the market areas. He was doing it as much to be able to say he had tried than because of any conviction that he would find Robert. When he drew a blank he headed back up the hill to the cathedral. Nicolo would either be there or not, it made little difference, but that was where he would find the senior officials for certain.

He crossed the narrow threshold of the enormous building, enjoying the familiar change in temperature as he did so. It took him briefly back to Umbridge and simpler times. Dull times to be sure, but straightforward and predictable. What he would have given for some predictability now.

There were people praying throughout the great nave; some standing reverently near the altar, others kneeling at alcoves up and down the walls. An old man carried a basket of candles, replacing those whose wicks had reached the iron floor of their holders. Chandlers were profiting mightily during the height of this plague, as though the lighting of a candle could stave off the fury of God long enough to offer up sufficient repentance.

It surprised Cuthbert that no mass was being said. The lesser churches across the city were devoid of liturgical activity but the word on the street was that those in charge of the cathedral seemed to end each mass for the sole purpose of starting another one. Now, though, the altar was bare. The old man in charge of the candles seemed to be the most senior person in the building. He had heard that the cardinals themselves were saying mass but there wasn't so much as a deacon muttering a prayer to himself. Something was amiss. At a time when the faithful were looking to the clergy for theological calibration and comfort, all they had was an empty altar and too few candles.

He waited there for an hour, watching the faithful plead their cases to God. Some were silent while others were apoplectic in their volume, but all were doing so without a man of the cloth there to witness it. He had seen enough. If Avignon cathedral was no longer a place for officialdom while a pestilence destroyed its flock then there were only two assumptions he could make. The first was that the whole city was in mortal danger, not just himself, and he could legitimately justify passing his father's parchment on to an official, should he find one. Secondly, if he could not find anyone suitable to pass it on to here then there was only one place he could go.

He left the cathedral and headed to the Palais des Papes.

'You can't come in here' said the first guard as Cuthbert approached them. 'There has been a papal decree. No man is to enter the palace without an order from the pope.'

'Then I shall go home and bring my wife here' said Cuthbert.

The two guards furrowed their eyebrows.

'I don't see how that would help your cause' said the second guard.

'You said no man can enter, so I will bring a woman.'

'I think the Holy Father means anyone at all' said the first voice.

'Well he should have said so, shouldn't he? If you're going to issue decrees willy-nilly without properly considering the wording then you shouldn't be allowed to *decree* at all.'

'Don't play with our words, young man' said the first guard, placing his spear between them in a show of power. 'No-one else is getting past us today.'

'No-one *else*?' said Cuthbert. 'So you are acting all professional because you let someone get past you earlier, is that about right?'

'No semantics, do you hear me?'

'Then I will not force your hand. I am merely here to pass a message on to a senior official here at the palace. I do not mind whether that is done inside the palace or here on these steps. All that is important is that I place it into their hands directly.'

'Who is the message from?' said the second guard.

Cuthbert had only one name he could use, and knew no detail of the man in the event of an interrogation. He had no other choice.

'I come with a message from Giovanni di Murta, doge of the Genoese empire.'

The two guards looked at each other then lunged at Cuthbert, locking his arms behind his back and frogmarching him into the palace.

The first guard pushed Cuthbert forcefully down a corridor, shoving him into a room and throwing him to the floor.

'What is this message, and no funny business' he snapped.

Cuthbert pulled out his purse and opened it, revealing the two small parchments. The guard snatched the one with the red cross and ripped open the seal. He read a few of the words and slapped Cuthbert hard across his cheek.

'Who is Mrs Tumble? Do you take us for fools?'

'That is a list of petitions' said Cuthbert, desperately trying to regain control of his wits.

The guard slapped him again.

'Explain yourself!'

'That is not the message. It is a list of prayerful intentions my father gave to me to leave within sight of the pope at the end of my pilgrimage. The other parchment is the one I must hand to a senior official.'

The guard leant over Cuthbert and pressed his face against him.

'If this is a shopping list then I swear to the almighty creator you will pay for your mischief.'

He took the scroll with the black cross and ripped it open. He read the few words scrawled onto it and froze, letting it drop to the floor. The second guard bent down and picked it up, reading the message as he straightened his back.

He nudged the first guard. 'Have you seen this?' he said, breaking his colleague's catatonia.

The first guard turned to lock his gaze onto the second guard. 'Have I seen it!? Of course I've seen it. He must be informed at once. We will bring Cuthbert with us.'

Cuthbert stared at the man. 'How do you know my name?' he asked as the guard lifted him from the floor.

'Your father is a well connected man. He may just have saved your life, if not your soul.'

'You must have me mistaken for some other Cuthbert. My father is a poor baker's hand in England. The only connection he has is with yeast and a loaf tin.'

'Then you do not know him as well as you think' said the first guard. 'Come, you will have an audience with the most powerful man in the city.'

As they made their way up the palace stairs a servant approached the second guard and handed him another two scrolls. The guard opened them in turn, raised his eyebrows, and rolled them back up.

'I'll go in first' he said. 'There is urgent news.'

The second guard rapped on the flat spot of the door.

'Can it wait?' said an irritated voice from the room.

'No' said the second guard bravely.

'Then wait.'

There was a scuffling noise from inside the rooms, followed by loud gasps and exclamations. The second guard tried not to listen. He never liked to hold information he should never be privy too, only trouble came from it.

'Come' said Jacques.

The second voice opened the door and stepped into the room. Two young men were tied up in a corner and a stranger sat at the pope's table. He took in the scene, made a judgment call, and addressed the charlatan pope.

'I come with two messages, your holiness. No, three. Three messages.'

Jacques turned to Giovanni. 'Watch them. If they move, kill them. That goes for his son too.' He stepped out into the corridor and looked further down the hall to where the first guard was waiting with Cuthbert. 'Well?' he said to the second guard. 'What is so important that you felt the need to disturb me?'

'I have three messages to deliver, Holy Father.'

'Yes, yes. You said that already. Get to the point, man.'

'Right, well, the first is that Cardinal Whimsy has fallen to the pestilence. There are now no more than six remaining and they are refusing to enter the cathedral to say mass for the people.'

'Pah. That is no concern of mine. Quickly now, come on.'

'I have received word from your country residence' said the second guard, handing Jacques the parchment.

The pseudo-pope gave a curious look before unravelling the paper. He read the few words that took up most of the available space and looked back at the guard. 'You have read this?' he said.

'I have, your serenity.'

'Has he?' he said, pointing to the first guard.

'Yes.'

'Then you are relieved of guard duties indefinitely. You will join my private entourage and never speak of this to anyone. 'Forget you ever read it.'

The second guard nodded and cleared his throat.

'The last message concerns that man there' he said, pointing to Cuthbert. 'He arrived at the palace to deliver a message to a senior official. Says it's from Giovanni di Murta.'

'And why, pray tell, is he now within spitting distance of my room?'

'Because of this' said the guard, handing him the scroll with the black cross.

Jacques read the message without reaction. 'Bring this Cuthbert to me.'

The second guard beckoned them over.

'Let him stand freely' said Jacques.

The guard unhandled Cuthbert and took a step back before following them into the room. Several sets of eyes danced around each other. Nicolo looked at Jacques, then Cuthbert. Robert was still staring at the bald man from the market stall when Nicolo nudged him. The sight of Cuthbert added too many layers to the calculation for the part of his brain in charge of facial expressions. He stared blankly at him instead. Cuthbert looked at Nicolo and Robert in turn, then the doge and finally the bald man. The guards looked at Nicolo, then Robert. Jacques tried to recognise the faces he had only glanced at on his way from the gloomy corner to the door.

Only Giovanni was smiling.

'Gentlemen' he said, raising his arms slightly in a show of calm. 'Let us sit. We have much to discuss and little time in which to do so. Jacques, the parchments if you please? Servants? Wine!'

The voices scuttled off to the cellar, returning with two large jugs and extra goblets. They set them down on the table before pulling out each of the guests' chairs in turn. The richer the owner of a chair, the less able they are to use it without assistance; a rule known to servants the world over. When the group were seated and their goblets filled the subservient voices left the room as silently as ever, closing the large doors behind them as they went. The table was full, Giovanni and Jacques at either end with Nicolo, Robert and Cuthbert on one side and Nicolo's father on the other with the two guards.

CHAPTER TWENTY THREE

THE DUNGEON, PALAIS DES PAPES

Edith grimaced as she straightened her back for the first time in an age. She threw the filthy, matted blankets into a corner of the small, stinking cell and stretched her limbs one by one. Blood found its way through veins it had long considered abandoned. The smirk that crossed her face as she felt the prickling sensation in her limbs was an uncomfortable juxtaposition for her. She had been in character as The Bejewelled Hag for longer than intended, but was thankful that it had reaped far more than she could ever have dreamed. Their plan was centred around snaring passers-by to elicit information from them. What that information could have been was unclear to her, but it had seemed like the sort of thing that an assassin's aide would do during the planning phase of an operation. That the pope himself should pause to speak with her was incalculably improbable. So much so that she would have been sure there was an omnipotent puppeteer in the heavens playing marionettes with her fate, had she any faith left with which to believe.

She organised her things, a task that involved the folding of her blanket and no more, and sat by the door. It was locked and a guard was posted outside, presumably for fear that this blind, helpless old woman would rampage throughout the palace like a demonic goat. All that she could do now was wait and listen. Once she had enough information she would escape and find Hildegund to deliver what she had learned. It was to be her last grand statement, one final show of contrariness for its own sake. She wasn't against the church as Hildegund was, she was more of a natural irritant, content to ruffle the feathers of whatever notion passed into her consciousness. The Bejewelled Hag would be her great finale.

She pushed the small wooden plank that acted as her plate through the gap underneath the cell door. She took up her now familiar place against the wall and tilted her head back onto the cold stone. Another guard always came along after lunch to take away the plank, one of the few times each day when she had a chance to eavesdrop on a conversation rather than trying to start one with the lump of meat on the other side. A faint clip-clop came from the end of the corridor, followed by the gentle thud of a closing door.

'Morning, Alf' said the lump of meat to the clip-clopper.

'Brains' stated Alf, nodding his head in greeting. 'Anything to report?'

'Yes there is, as it happens' said Brains with the excitement of one who has only ever answered the question in the negative. 'A rat came scurrying past earlier and nibbled on my toe. Huge one, the size of a small chicken, as God is my witness. I named him Orteil. I think he's going to be my friend.'

'That's what constitutes news down here, is it? A rat in a dungeon?'

'You should try spending half your day in here, Alf, it's enough to send a man to drink.'

'You've been drunk since you were old enough to keep a mug steady' said Alf.

'Which is why I always need one when I leave.'

'You finish at dawn, Brains. You should judge the merit of your actions by how many others are doing it at the same time. I bet there aren't many who share your breakfast drinks in the Goose's Head.'

'So that means the merit of God's action is the same as my drinking, does it? He's the only one doing all that vengeance stuff these days.'

'Well there's three of him, and he's bigger.'

'I would think the merits of his actions were more than three times mine though, wouldn't you say?'

'I haven't got time for this nonsense Brains' said Alf, leaning down to pick up the empty plank. 'Cardinal Malveillant wants me to clean his quills. You know how spiteful he gets when he's kept waiting.'

Brains watched Alf walk back to the door at the end of the corridor before repositioning himself on his chair for the long wait ahead. Edith lay down in her cell and pressed her mouth to the narrow opening at the foot of the door.

'Brains!' she called. 'I have an answer to your riddle.'

'Quiet, wench!' boomed Brains. He liked booming, it gave him a sense of importance that was disproportionate to his place in the world. He was good at it too, and loud. People often commented on the loudness of his booming specifically.

'You have a loud boom for one so bedevilled by chance' said Edith enigmatically.

'It is a sin to waste a talent, so my old mother used to tell me' said Brains. 'That's why Deacon Bleu first gave me the honour of guarding the important prisoners in the deepest dungeon. He said I should use it to make them uncomfortable. *A booming nuisance* he called it.'

I can imagine, thought Edith.

'Do you think a withering old hag with but the smallest wick on her candle of life is a threat to his holiness himself?'

'It's not my place to say' boomed Brains.

'You shouldn't boom all the time' said Edith, slipping out of character for a moment. 'It makes it less effective.'

'Is it a nuisance?' boomed Brains relentlessly. ''Cos if it is then I'll boom all the more.'

'If you boom constantly then it ceases to be a nuisance at all, that is my point' said Edith. 'You could boom every third sentence until you get the hang of it. You'll soon work out which to boom and which to... not boom.'

'Well if it isn't a nuisance then I guess you're right' conceded Brains. 'No point in booming if it isn't a nuisance.'

'Oh no, it isn't a nuisance at all if you're always doing it. I should know, I was married to an ogre for long enough.'

'You were married to an ogre?' said Brains in a volume just below that of an erupting volcano. 'Must have been a strange household and no mistake, what with you being a witch and all.'

Edith was about to correct her use of the word ogre to something more literal but stopped herself. 'Oh yes, He was the height of two men and had a body like a pulpit.'

'He was made of stone?' said Brains.

'Why not' said Edith. 'We had bats too, lots of bats.'

'Do you have a cauldron?' asked Brains. 'All good witches have cauldrons.'

Edith was trying to be a hag, not a witch, but had no intention of correcting him on that front. 'I had two' she said.

'Oooooo' said Brains, impressed.

'I lost one when my dragon tried to help me with a potion, melted it to nothing in the blink of an eye' said Edith, hamming up the charade with surprising ease. 'I had cats too, dozens of them. All black.'

'I should hope so' said Brains, taking comfort from the news that she was a proper, traditional witch. 'No good going round all witchy with one of those funny orange cats now, is it?'

'I wouldn't be seen dead with an orange one' said Edith truthfully; she hated cats of any colour.

'Have you got a broomstick?' asked Brains.

'How dare you!' snapped Edith. 'It is most improper to ask a witch about her broomstick, have some manners.'

'Begging your pardon, I didn't know' said Brains.

'Just be more respectful in future' said Edith, slowly climbing to the high ground of the conversation. 'If you're so interested in them I could *possibly* show you one when I get out of here, if you're good. It's a real beauty. I can even show you how to fly a little on it. Not too high though, they're tricky little buggers if you get above the tree line.'

Brains was swept along. He hadn't known a witch's broomstick was such a delicate matter, but now that he did he was desperate to see one. 'Really? You'd show me your own broomstick? I would be honoured.'

'I can do better than that' said Edith, her mouth pressed against the gap in the door. 'If you come with me now I'll give you your own. Do you know what you could do with your own broomstick?'

Brains was contorted with conflict. He had a job to do but hadn't realised until now that he had needed a broomstick. She was also blind and he was a guard of the Palais des Papes. What harm could she possibly do to him? She may be a witch, but she doesn't have the tools of her trade with her and everyone knows a witch needs at least an eye of a newt and a small pot to do even the slightest bit of witchcraft.

'If you promise not to do any funny stuff I might let you out for an hour. I'll have to march you there myself mind you, and if you try anything it'll be the rack for you, mark my words.'

'An old blind witch can't cause any trouble with a strapping lad like yourself watching over her now, can she?'

'Exactly, and you've promised not to do anything too, so that's that.'

'Have I? I mean... *Have* I! Of course I have' said Edith, changing the emphasis a little too late.

'Wait, you haven't' said Brains, catching up with his own thoughts.

'Oh, well I certainly meant to' said Edith. 'Would you like me to promise again? I can if it would make you feel better about walking with a poor old blind woman.'

'That won't be necessary' said Brains. 'Once is enough.'

Edith wrinkled her forehead a little as she tried to make sense of the last few moments.

'Right then' she said. 'Let's get you a nice broomstick.'

She stood up and grabbed her blankets as the key rattled in the lock, quickly stooping again and lifting her head from her crouched shoulders. She would have to look like a witch now as well as sound like one. The door opened slowly and Brains reached in, grabbing Edith's wrist and pulling it around behind her back.

'Sorry about this' he said as pulled on her other wrist and moved behind her to frogmarch her out of the door.

There would be no point in trying to win Brains over by sheer force, nor in the open where others would see. She took the most promising avenue open to her and kicked her leg back, successfully aiming her heel square between the legs of the soon-to-be writhing guard. Even a kick from an old woman can be excruciating if targeted accurately enough and the guard fell to the floor holding the most sensitive part of his body in his cupped hands. Edith kicked the prone figure again to buy a little more time, took the keys from his fingers and stepped out of the room, locking the door behind her as she went.

She half walked, half ran down the corridor of cells as only a woman of a certain age can. A loud plea came from the penultimate room slowing Edith to a trot.

'Help me!'

She approached the cell door, conscious that anyone down here was likely to be at the dangerous end of the predictability scale.

'Why are you down here?' she asked the door.

'Don't you want to know who I am first?' said the prisoner.

'What difference would that make?'

'Well you may be more inclined to help me out of here if you knew who I was.'

'I have heard enough. You are a shallow man without ears to hear the folly of your doom.'

She wasn't trying to play the role of The Bejewelled Hag for this anonymous captive but some of the idiosyncrasies had seeped into her own persona. Also, the evidence suggested the man's status had taken a rather sharp fall towards the gutter in recent times and she would be damned if she was going to help one of *those* men up from the floor.

'I heard that commotion just then' said the man. 'A woman could get into a lot of trouble if word was to get out of her assaulting a guard of the papal palace.'

'Do you know who I am?' said Edith.

'No' said the man.

'Then you can bugger off.'

She left him to his regrets, taking the last few steps to the end of the corridor and the heavy wooden door that sealed Brains in for most of the daylight hours. She pressed her ear against the door but could hear nothing. Her visual affliction had heightened her hearing considerably and she was confident there was nothing but a couple of scampering rats on the other side. She could hear a feather landing on a bowl of water given the right conditions.

She pressed gently on the door, opening it slightly and sending countless specks of dust to dance in a pale sunbeam that penetrated the space in front of her. For a moment she felt like a bird flying high above the city, watching the energetic panic of the people as news of the pope's death spread. Then she remembered how much she hated all that natural spirituality nonsense and admonished herself quietly.

There was a flight of stairs to her right and she climbed them, being sure to remain bent over in case of a chance encounter with an official. She had no idea how she might talk her way out of any such meeting but that was for a future version of herself to sort out, if it materialised at all. At the top of the stairs was a small archway leading to an impossibly long corridor with enough doors leading off it to make it seem plausible that they represented all the rooms in heaven. She made her way along it, searching for a clue to the whereabouts of the pope as she moved. She would find him and give a performance of The Bejewelled Hag that would make his eyes curl. Her escape plan from that point on was still to be determined, the unspecified mechanics of such an exit being a rather large flaw in her increasingly improvised scheme.

She wound her way through the palace, checking a door or two occasionally as she explored the labyrinthine corridors. She was yet to come across another soul and wondered at the absence of such an expected obstacle. As she reached another stairwell a noise from somewhere above stopped her in her tracks. She tilted her head a little more, straining her hearing. She could make out several voices in the distance and headed towards them, listening intently as she moved.

CHAPTER TWENTY FOUR

'It seems we have arrived at an interesting convergence of fates' began Giovanni. 'I am sure there are many questions you each feel should be answered before any other. For now I will satisfy two, for fear that our little meeting will be ineffective while they hang in the air.'

The two guards fidgeted nervously in their seats, unfamiliar as they were with the protocols involved. Cuthbert looked obediently at Giovanni, waiting for the story to unfurl itself. Robert watched the bald man, wondering about his recently revealed identity. Nicolo's gaze was also locked on to his father. There was no set of circumstances he could think of that would legitimately place him in the room. Only the fact that he himself was holding an audience with both the pope and the doge made him believe it to be happening at all.

Giovanni clapped his hands together loudly, winning the attention of the table. 'The question of the guards' recruitment can wait. Your curiosity in that regard will have to remain unsatisfied.'

He looked at each of the men while pointing at the bald one. 'You may know that I cast a wide net to ensure I remain well informed. This man here is Nicolo's father, Franco, and has been in my service since he was a young man. The pestilence forced him northwards from his home, towards Genoa and the whims of his master. I sent him to this place and instructed him to report back to me on the news of Avignon. In particular, I was interested in the talents of a confidence trickster who had found a way into my private office without any knowledge of the inner workings of high society. What better way to ensure my man remained in the shadows than to assign him to his own son?'

'How did you know my identity in your rooms in Genoa?' said Nicolo, fumbling for something his mind could hold on to in the swirling maelstrom of revelations. 'I gave you no clues.'

'Ah, but you did' said the doge benevolently. 'You speak with a Sicilian accent, no matter how hard you try to extinguish it. There are not many that travel so far without a sailor's badge.'

'I do not believe that you could identify me from my accent alone' said Nicolo. 'There may not be many who travel so far, but I am the only one with this man as his father.'

Franco looked at him neutrally. 'Your face gave you away.'

'You saw me?' said Nicolo in astonishment. 'Why didn't you come to me?'

'For the same reason you stopped coming to see me in Catania, son. Our relationship has not gone the way either of us would have wanted, but that does not alter the reality of the dynamic.'

'So all this time you were a spy for the very man who sent me on this damned crusade. You could have advised against it, you had his ear!'

'Nobody has my ear, Nicolo Anatra!' boomed the doge. 'I am a man of unilateral decisions. That your father was in the palace for your arrival was a happy coincidence, a characteristic that litters the great political moves in history, as I am sure you are not aware. Being as you are, a simple fisherman's son.'

'I am a man who found his way past the security of a paranoid dictator with nothing more than a pauper's ring' said Nicolo defiantly.

'*Paranoid dictator*?' mocked the doge. 'How much you have to learn little boy. Show me a leader without paranoia and I will show you a grave.'

'Then you will live a long life, Giovanni.'

'Address me by my title, or address me from a rack. The choice is yours to make. You are getting ahead of your station, my little pawn, so we shall move on from this touching family reunion and discuss matters of more import.'

Giovanni turned to Cuthbert. 'I am sure you are keen to learn of the message from your father.'

'I am' said Cuthbert with difficulty, like an adolescent boy struggling with a breaking voice.

'I will relay to you the exact content and will leave you to extrapolate its meaning for yourself. As I have already mentioned, I am a man with a wide net, wider even than some of you here may believe possible. He sent a message that was meant for a lesser cog in my machinations. You are lucky it was received into my own hands so efficiently.' Giovanni unrolled the parchment theatrically. 'It reads:

"Cuthbert, Of My Parental Endowment, Now Stands As Testament – Edmund Downey."'

'I don't understand' said Cuthbert honestly.

'Oh I wouldn't expect you to' said the doge, taking pleasure from wielding even this insignificant amount of power. 'It is a message from the one living man to whom I am in debt, in a simple code naturally. It asks that I protect you from whatever peril you have thrust yourself into. It is another most pleasurable coincidence that your little adventure brought you to my door. Read the message again, your father has now been *compensated* and the debt paid in full. Once you don't fall foul of my enemies, of course. I shall protect you while you are here in Avignon and repay your father. Anything from then on is your own doing.'

'But I can't read' said Cuthbert pitifully, retreating back to the boy who left Umbridge.

'Then the code shall remain a mystery to you. Take comfort in what it has done for you and leave the nuances of the letters to those with greater wits.'

'I still don't get it' said Cuthbert, desperate to have an understanding of what was happening around him. 'How could my father possibly have a connection to you? He is a simple baker's hand! We have almost starved most winters since I was a boy.'

'*Almost* starved, Cuthbert, almost. I am not in the business of narrowing my network for the want of a husk of bread.'

'So you held the power to send an army of cows to us and you let us tiptoe across the line between life and death?'

'An army of cows?' said the doge with a thespian laugh that failed emphatically to break the tension. 'I'm not sure they are quite so... *organised*, my poor little Cuthbert.'

Cuthbert's expression solidified. 'What did you call me?'

'My, my. You are quite the brave one, *poor little Cuthbert.*'

Cuthbert's chair flew backwards as he stood and leapt towards the doge in one motion. His face was instantaneously red and was heading for a full blooded purple. He wrapped his fingers around the throat of the doge and squeezed with all the pent up frustrations of his childhood. People shouted at him to stop, pulling his arms and legs to drag him off the most powerful man in two empires, but like a man who finds his prize goat under a cartwheel he found untapped reserves of strength, squeezing harder and harder until the doge's eyes showed fear at last.

'Call me that again and I will send you to your maker, doge or not' said Cuthbert through tightly gritted teeth. Show me you understand.'

The doge wriggled his eyebrows in a show of acceptance and Cuthbert slowly released his grip. Giovanni rubbed his neck with one hand as he clicked the fingers of the other. In a moment Cuthbert was wrapped up in the limbs of the two guards, their arms locking him in place and causing him to thrash his legs violently in a vain attempt at escape. Nicolo and Robert exchanged conspiratorial glances before vaulting to the rescue of their friend and acquaintance. Robert punched the first guard full on the nose while Nicolo manoeuvred his stance in such a way as to aim a kick squarely between the legs of the second. Both fell rubbing their respective body part.

Nicolo turned to the bald man. 'Now would be a good time to make up for lost time, father.'

Franco hesitated for a moment, then lunged for Jacques as Nicolo grabbed the priest's arms.

'Robert, the curtain ropes. Now!' called Nicolo.

In a few heartbeats Jacques and the guards were tied to their chairs with the most expensive fastener ever used by would-be kidnappers. Cuthbert motioned as if to attack the doge again but this time Giovanni was ready for him, mentally speaking at least. He raised his arms placatingly.

'Cuthbert, please' he called in a gentle shout. He may have considered it to have been skilfully delivered, had he more than a split second in which to assess his effort. 'I meant no offence. I was merely offering you an explanation of the message. I would not expect anybody outside of my network to understand the code within.'

'You don't even know you're doing it, do you?' said Cuthbert with a sudden confidence. He was getting a feel for his audience now and had learned how to manipulate this to his advantage over recent weeks, although usually with considerably more alcohol in his immediate past than was currently the case. 'You think you know exactly what to say to have people act the way you want but you can't read me, can you? You're guessing! You see me in pilgrim clothes with a note from my father and a worried look in my eye and you think you have me all worked out. You may even have heard stories about me from my father as you have Nicolo's. If that is the basis for your assessment then, by God, you have no idea what's coming. I am a much changed man from th...'

Cuthbert was interrupted by a bony fist swinging into his jaw from the end of the doge's arm, sending the Englishman through an expensive looking vase and on to the hard floor.

'He does go on, doesn't he?' said Giovanni to the room.

Robert, Nicolo and Franco closed in.

'I could just knock him out' said Franco helpfully. 'If this little rebellion goes squiffy at least I can say he must have remembered my part in it all wrong.'

'How gallant of you, father' said Nicolo. 'I can see how well you must fit in to the world of espionage.'

'Careful now, Nicolo. Where do you think you got it from? The orange doesn't fall far from the tree.'

'It's apple' said Robert. 'The apple doesn't fall far from the tree.'

'Don't compare me to you and your lifetime of duplicitousness' said Nicolo, ignoring Robert.

'Really?' said Franco. 'And at what age would you say you first showed a skill for covert misdirection and environmental manipulation?'

That was the last straw for Robert, he had heard enough. 'Well this is a lovely reunion, but I'd like to get back to the matter at hand if it's all the same with you. Pass me that crystal goblet, would you?'

'Let's cut out the middle man' said Franco, lifting the goblet and throwing it at the unprepared doge, hitting him square in the forehead. It reached its target with the precision of a man who could throw a fish into a basket from fifty paces. Giovanni went temporarily cross-eyed before falling gracelessly on top of the prone Cuthbert.

'Bravo!' said Robert. 'Now, does anybody have any suggestions as to how we're going to tidy this mess up?'

Nicolo, Robert, Franco and a recently revived Cuthbert stood in front of the restrained group. Giovanni was still unconscious, slumped unceremoniously on a chair. The two guards sat motionless next to him, unsure as to where they should place their loyalties just yet. Only Jacques moved, and he did so with commendable vigour, twice having tipped his chair right over and adding new pains to an ever increasing list. Nicolo lifted his arm to show a fine scroll held tightly in his hand, took a small step forward so he was just outside the thrashing range of Jacques' arms, and looked the priest dead in his eyes.

'You have read this, of course' he began. 'As have these two lackeys, I'm sure. It certainly explains their hasty initiation into your inner circle.' He unfurled the parchment and held it at arm's length. 'For the benefit of drama, and of Cuthbert here, I shall read out the message within. It begins:

"My dear friend JB. Your letters have been of little comfort to me, though I thank you for their existence. I find myself no longer able to remain a prisoner in my own lands while my people suffer at the whim of this infernal pestilence. I am to return to the Palais des Papes to fulfil my obligations as pontiff at the earliest opportunity. For now, you may remove your veil and stand before the people as yourself. I will announce you as cardinal of Marseilles for your efforts, should you be seeking such an honour. Tell the servants I am sick and will surely be back to full health in a few short days. I remain, Papa C VI."'

Nicolo watched the broken priest as he spoke.

'Well that is fabulous news!' said Jacques, moving on to his next charade even as the echoes of the first filled the air. 'We shall have our pope back and I can return to living the life of a faithful man.'

'You are in a room full of conmen, *JB*, so you may cease your pitiful scrabbling and show your true intentions' said Franco. 'Why are you passing yourself off as the pope? What is your ambition?'

'I am but the humble servant of the Holy Father. I move only at his orders.'

'Except when you're moving him to suit your agenda' said Franco. 'I am no fool, I have served one of the greatest political minds of our time for many years. A simple priest is no challenge. Speak the truth or suffer the same fate as the doge here.'

The priest was saved the ignominy of the truth by sounds of disorder from the other side of the dark doors. Robert ran to them and pulled at the handle, falling backwards as a stinking bundle of rags barged past him and into the centre of the room.

CHAPTER TWENTY FIVE

E dith reached a turn in the corridor with the effortless difficulty of one with so many years behind them. The voices were louder now.

'How gallant of you, father. I can see how well you must fit in to the world of espionage.'

'Careful now, Nicolo. Where do you think you got it from? The orange doesn't fall far from the tree.'

She scuttled round the corner, slowing herself again as a new voice spoke.

'You are in a room full of conmen, JB, so you may cease your pitiful scrabbling and show your true intentions.'

She crouched a little lower and hurried towards the noise. As she neared the room a servant appeared around a distant corner, shouting for her to stop as he began a sprint towards her. Edith lessened her hobble a little and moved as fast as she could to the doorway. She threw herself into the room with commendable drama.

'It is here! It is here!' cried the Bejewelled Hag. 'The time of reckoning is upon us. I have seen the rivers dry and the mountains of the dead crumble to ashes. Hear me now or pay an eternal price!'

'Oh here we go' said Robert, 'another lunatic comes to the table.'

The servant charged into the room after her, his eyes wild in panicked apology.

'I'm sorry holy fa...' the servant began, stopping suddenly when he saw Jacques' unveiled head. A look that spoke of an intense desire to be anywhere else as soon as possible showed on his face as he fell spectacularly short of finding reason in the scene.

The hag spread her arms wide and circled the room as if wiping it clean of any accidentally summoned demons. She manipulated the men into a circle, sweeping her fingers past each of their faces as she screamed her maddened proclamations.

She stopped suddenly, crouching lower in the centre of her circle, and pointed at Jacques.

'You!' she squealed. 'You are a shadow. The girl will be upon you and your protectors will fade like dew on the field.'

'The Jew on the field?' said Robert, trying to break the cycle of insanity.

'I think she said dew' said Nicolo. 'Duh. Dew.'

'Right, that makes more sense. I think.'

'Enough!' cried the hag. 'Your time is like the wind that escapes to the heavens. Hear me or suffer blindly through what is to come!'

'Quiet, hag!' called Franco. 'You know nothing of value to us. We travel in more enlightened circles than those who are easily manipulated by your cheap shows.' He turned to the servant. 'Throw her out!'

'And bring some wine on your way back' added Cuthbert, to the unabashed relief of Jacques.

'Then you know the face that searches for the heart of the pope' said the hag.

The wine induced smile on Jacques' face vanished. 'Tell me' he said, doing his best to impersonate Clement's voice once again.

'Oh but I am just a simple vagabond' said the hag. 'There is nothing I could possibly know that would help you.'

'Enough of your games, wench' snapped Jacques. Spit out that which brings you here or be sent to the dungeons. If you are as all-seeing as you would have us believe you will know I speak with the authority of one who can control the papal interrogators.'

The hag shuffled uncomfortably. 'If you are ready to hear that which controls your destiny, then I will speak. The one who craves murder leaves but a solitary place of safety in her plan. She intends to kill away from the altar of the great house of God. Stay there and stay alive.'

'Oh for God's sake!' cried Jacques. 'The one place I can't bear to be is where I must spend the rest of my days. I would be better to give in to her now.'

'I would counsel against such a course of inaction' said the hag. 'I will describe her to your men, they will find the assassin with all haste, freeing you from the shackles of the altar.'

'That's not a bad idea actually' said Robert. 'Saves you getting your hands dirty too.'

'Guards!' called Jacques. Edith braced. 'Find this woman and bring her to me. I will be on the altar, protecting the office of the pope once again. I want word as soon as you have it. Now, will someone get these damned ropes off me or am I going to have to seek divine intervention for this too?'

'There are two pressing matters to attend to before our conclave is complete' said the hag.

'Be gone, withered woman' said Jacques, authority returning to his voice. 'I am done with you and your mystical shenanigans.'

'Would it not be prudent to learn of the appearance of the one who stalks you?'

'Ah. Well, yes. Tell me all you know of her then you can *be gone*.'

'She said there were two matters' said Cuthbert, wondering to himself whether his recently concussed ears had misheard. 'Should we not hear them both?'

'Fine' said Jacques. 'Be quick about it before my mercy shrivels.'

The Hag wrapped her blanket around her more closely, as if protecting herself from the revelation. 'I will tell all I know, but first you must promise me safe passage from this place. There are many who need my help in these *troubling times*.'

'Tell me what you know of this woman and you can dance a jig on the graves of the saints for all I care' said Jacques impatiently. 'Now come on woman, there is important work to be done.'

'First, you must take this' she said, handing Jacques a crucifix. 'You must wear it on the altar to keep the devil from your soul.'

CHAPTER TWENTY SIX

'**D**ominus vobiscum' said Jacques for the fourth time since he woke.

'Et cum spirito tuo' said the congregation in the collective monotones reserved for those repeating well worn phrases in holy places.

Jacques wondered how some priests kept hold of their sanity without a deacon to delegate these brain numbing services to. He had been saying mass throughout the daylight hours for three days now and his mind had long since passed simple boredom. It was now firmly ensconced in a purgatory of mental catatonia and only the arrival of a messenger with news of the assassin's demise would free him. Anyone studying his behaviour would have noticed how his services were punctuated with repeated glances to the sacristy door at the side of the great altar. As he finished each mass he would rush to it in the hope that a servant was on the other side with a great announcement. No message had yet arrived and he had sunk into a deeper state of despair. It said a lot about his view on saying mass himself that he pictured the end game as one devoid of such a task, rather than a sharp improvement in his life expectancy.

He finished the mass and pointlessly bade the congregation leave to go about their day. As expected, they felt their day would be best *gone about* right where they were and not a soul moved. Jacques left them to it and headed for the sacristy. He opened the door to the room that he fully expected to be empty, which it was, aside from the figure of Pope Clement VI standing ominously in a dusty sunbeam.

'Your Holiness' exclaimed Jacques, falling to his knees with the gratitude of a man who has escaped a fate worse than death. 'You're back!'

'I am' said the pope flatly. 'And so is the justice of the Lord.'

Jacques hoped he was referring to the killer's justice rather than his own. Answering for his actions now would be a worrying turn of events indeed.

'We have much to discuss, Father Bricoler. Come.'

The pope led them out of the back of the sacristy and into the maze of hallways that connected it to the Palais des Papes. They walked in silence all the way to the papal office, something that Jacques was ambivalent about. It gave him time to formulate answers to potential lines of interrogation, but also allowed his mind to piece together several worst case scenarios.

They reached the ornate wooden door and entered a scene that had not been a part of Jacques' imaginings. Giovanni di Murta had been confined to a cell since the incident with the crystal goblet but was now standing freely. Nicolo, Franco, Robert and Cuthbert sat at the pine table, each with expressions on their faces that spoke of a recent learning of some astonishing revelation.

'Sit' ordered the real pope.

Jacques sat at the head of the table, his line of sight filled with pairs of stoic eyes that bored into his tainted soul.

'Listen now, Jacques Bricoler, and do not say a word until I am done. That is an order from the pope himself, so don't go thinking you can talk your way out of it. I will send you to the dungeon if you so much as unpurse your lips.'

Jacques had been worried before but was now scared. He had never seen Clement like this before and was sure that whatever happened in the coming moments would see him having to refer to him as his *former* friend. He braced himself.

'I have been involved in an enlightening discussion with these fine fellows here' began the pope, 'and it seems you have been rather liberal with papal rules. The purpose of my sabbatical was to guarantee the smooth continuation of the papacy, both in the immediate term as well as the long term. You were to complete the daily duties assigned to the Holy Father to ensure that the faithful saw no panic in the palace. My absence was designed only to encourage the greatest possibility that I might survive through these dark days; God's representative on earth cannot be seen to be as vulnerable as the peasant after all. It seems, however, that your intent was rather more ambitious than you led me to believe. In a matter of days you abandoned the sacrament of mass, leaving mere cardinals in your place and paving the way for their inevitable demise. It takes a man with a certain strength of wit to maintain an appropriate grip on the lives of the flock, a man who can remain in control while all about him are losing their minds with fear. You are not that man, Jacques Bricoler. You have brought a good friend of mine to his knees in front of simple servants who are now an unwelcome addition to my inner circle. Your vanity has allowed pilgrims and spies alike into my rooms, compromising the sanctity of the office and creating a situation that would have been avoided had I not left an ego in charge of proceedings.'

The pope picked up a pear and took a bite from it, causing each of the group to wonder at the timing. Only Giovanni saw the move for what it was, a crude but effective reinstatement of the pope's power. When all ears are bent to the will of the speaker, an unexpected pause reinforces their position in the immediate hierarchy. The pope swallowed, washing the fruit down with a delicate sip of wine.

'I understand that you have also banished an invited guest, hag though she may have been. What secrecy remains of our clandestine activity is now flooding the city, wreaking havoc in the minds of the very people we are trying to protect. You have devastated my legacy. Needless to say, my offer to induct you into the College of Cardinals is rescinded. I will find a post for you at the very edge of Christendom, some miserable place on the brink of the world. I know of a crumbling monastery in weather beaten England that would welcome a devout priest to sate their voracious appetite for the sacraments. I hear the climate there has created a nation of sombre acolytes.'

'Hey!' called Cuthbert. 'We're not all...'

A glare from the pope stopped him as he spoke.

'As I was saying' continued Clement, 'you have done incalculable damage in the short time given to you. May you never darken the doors of high office for as long as our Lord deems you worthy of a place on this earth. Guards, tie him up!'

For once Jacques gave no reply. He had a few good ones he could use, but any statement he made now, no matter how accurate, eloquent or justified it may be, would be trumped by the prejudicial power held by his former friend, for that was undoubtedly what he now was.

'Now, to the more pressing issue of my would-be assassin' said the pope, moving on to other matters with a dispassion that stabbed at Jacques' under exercised heart. 'We know of her appearance and her timing but are ignorant of the rest of her plan, other than to know where she will not strike. I propose that I remain in my offices under the protection of trusted guards while Jacques here is honoured with the task of maintaining a papal presence at the cathedral altar for as long as his bones will hold him straight. If this assassin wishes to avoid an attack in the cathedral then we should assume it is with good reason. Let us show that the pope will not abandon his station at the time of greatest need. We will force her to the altar and stack the cards in our favour. Giovanni, do you have anything to add?'

The doge of Genoa raised himself to his great, lanky height and glowered at Franco. 'As I have already said, I will show mercy in the presence of the Holy Father and forego my judgment for your traitorous behaviour. For the moment, at least. You may demonstrate your reinvigorated loyalty to me in the coming hours, Franco Anatra, and may your actions save you from a demise worthy of a tale for the scribes. We have much to accomplish and little room for deviation from our orders. The information we have leads us to a singular course of action. While Jacques remains our bait at the altar, those of us without a title will remain in the congregation, watching for the assassin and ready to take them down when the time comes. They plan to strike tomorrow, if we have read the signs correctly. I suggest we all rest until dawn, it will be a long day.'

'I will have rooms made ready for you' said the pope. 'In case there are any among you who feel escape is a preferred option there will be trusted guards posted in each of your rooms and you are not permitted to speak with them, nor each other, until we meet here at first light. I'm sure I don't need to explain my motivation for such impolite hospitality.'

He placed the core of his pear on a dark metal plate and clapped his hands twice. The two guards stood to perfect attention like stone pillars in a storm.

'Tell the chamberlain to ready four rooms, close to the dungeons and with two of our most loyal guards to join you in supervision duties. Have a cardinal's meal left in each room and double the blankets.' He turned to the four men. 'Let it not be said that I am an ungracious host.'

The four men were now feeling the pressure of spending too much time in the eye of a diplomatic tornado. They gave the polite nod performed by those in no position to show their true feelings and waited impatiently to be dismissed from the room. Each of them were glad of the chance to spend some time on their own, free to unfasten their minds from the wild horse of high politics for a few hours.

The pope raised his arm, freezing the scene for a moment as the door closed behind the guards.

'One more thing before we retire, gentlemen. I wish to put an end to the mystery surrounding this Cutler business. It is of no consequence now that we are entwined in our immediate fate and it is vital we begin tomorrow with minds free from questions.'

Nicolo's eyes widened as Pope Clement VI of Avignon tore at the shroud that had kept The Cutler hidden.

CHAPTER TWENTY SEVEN

'It is set' said Edith, pulling a wooden bowl of potage towards her. 'The pope will be in the cathedral with your token around his neck. You may travel without fear right to the very steps of the altar.'

'What if they see me?' asked Hildegund, determined to seal any holes in their plan before she set out. 'If they know my appearance then I will surely fall before the pope.'

'When I have finished my bowl we will go to my home. I have a special concoction that will disguise you from that which they seek.'

'Are you sure you're not a witch? You definitely sounded a bit like one there. What is this mystical concoction? If there are any amphibious eyes in it then you can find another way.'

'I am no witch, it is a simple mixture of milk and manure to mask the pale tones of your hair.'

'You will not rub anything of the sort into my scalp!' exclaimed Hildegund.

'Would you prefer to fall in the aisle of the cathedral, the guards of the Palais des Papes all around you with spears and an appetite for *protection*?'

'Well, no, of course not' muttered Hildegund.

'Then it's settled, we will rub excrement into your hair and send shockwaves to all corners of the empire.'

CHAPTER TWENTY EIGHT

Robert broke the stunned silence, turning to The Cutler and stating the obvious. 'You're not doing a great job of this reunion so far really, are you? First you reveal you could have saved your son weeks of turmoil at the Palazzo Pubblico and now it turns out you're the very man he's been trying to find all this time. No wonder he left you behind in Catania.'

'You know nothing of me or my son, Englishman! Concern yourself with your current predicament and leave me to mine' snapped Franco.

Nicolo looked Giovanni dead in the eye as he passed the doge's scroll to his father. 'I was told to give this to you' he said. 'May it be the end of my dealings with cutlers of all kinds.'

'That is no longer relevant' said the doge, a rare look of anxiety showing on his angular face. 'Our situation has evolved, pay no heed to the message. Here, give it to me.'

Franco ignored his former master, tearing at the seal and unfurling the scroll. The colour drained from his face before refilling with an angry crimson. He handed the parchment to Nicolo who digested the message without reaction.

It read:

"You are both dead men walking"

'Are we, indeed?' said Nicolo, readying himself for another sales pitch. 'I would counsel against such a course of action, *Giovanni*. I have three friends here who would be quite happy, I am sure, to assist me in the reversal of your poorly judged memorandum. I count yourself alone on the other side. Our Holy Father would not be so quick to cast such a violent edict, benevolent as he is, and Father Bricoler here is hanging on to his own mortality by his fingernails without meddling in the affairs of others. Your control of events is diminishing, even as we speak. If your wish for the pope's safety is to be fulfilled then you would do well to remember that it is we who have the numbers required to do so. If the pope should fall then you will surely fall with him, for you have been lax in the protection of your weakness. Your fates have become entwined into symbiosis like fleas on a rat. If we four were to walk out of the palace then all your scheming and positioning will be for nought.'

'You sound like the old hag' said Giovanni, unperturbed by the insolent Sicilian before him. 'Remember this, Anatra. I hold the power here, not you, not the guards, not the charlatan pope. I, and I alone.'

'You may hold the power' said Cuthbert from behind the doge, 'but I hold this.' He thrust a long shard from the broken vase deep into the chest of Giovanni di Murta, former doge of all Genoa. 'That should make up for the priest I didn't kill, wouldn't you say, Robert?'

Giovanni's eyes widened in shock before locking in place. He tilted slowly backwards until his head met the floor and would have been grateful for the deep rug that eased his landing, had he not expired during the journey.

There were a few moments of silent disbelief before Robert brought everyone back into the room. 'Cuthbert! What the hell have you done?'

'Done, Robert' said Cuthbert. 'It is done. He was getting delusions of grandeur.'

'*Delusions of grandeur!?* He's the leader of an empire!'

'Was, Robert. Was.'

'Stop correcting my grammar. There's a time and a place for that and shortly after committing a murder in the papal palace is not one of them.'

It was Nicolo's turn to come to. 'Jesus Christ, Cuthbert! If you didn't need to repent before you certainly do now. What have you done?'

'Can you all stop asking me what I've done? I would have thought it was rather obvious. He was getting in the way.'

'*In the way!?*' screamed Nicolo. 'He may be... may *have* been an ego on legs but he was the doge of Genoa. What do you think is going to happen to us now?'

Cuthbert scratched his shoulder and slumped on to a chair, as if the roof of the palace was weighing down on him. He took a deep breath. 'Nicolo. Robert. All of you' he began, in a sad voice that promised some great confession. 'You are all safe. Safe from the reaction to come for what has happened here. Safe from the spies that circle the man. I did it, not you. I will tell the world and face the consequences if that is what it will take. It is of no difference to me, for there is one thing I am not safe from.'

He ripped his grey cloak from a tear at the collar. They stared at his taut skin, at the small red boil that sat there like a pincerless crab on a beach. They looked at Cuthbert's eyes, at the sorrow that filled those sapphire rings.

Robert steadied himself with the table. 'Oh Cuthbert! How long have you known?'

'It started to itch this morning. I thought it may have been something else. Something less final. Alas, it seems I will lie in the pits of the dead for all eternity. Saves me going home to be a priest, I suppose. I was never too keen on the idea.'

'We need to dispose of his body' said Franco, his distilled pragmatism filling the room. 'I suggest we burn him in the dungeons.'

'I'm not dead yet!' cried Cuthbert.

'Not you, the doge' said Franco, his voice absent of emotion.

'Hang on a minute, Franco' said Robert. 'He hasn't finished twitching and you've got him bundled up and sent to the furnace. How about we digest events a little first?'

'You can digest all you want, but I'm keener to remove any evidence before another uninvited guest bursts through those doors.'

'He's got a point, Robert' said Nicolo. 'If we get caught with the body then we're all going to the dungeons, with or without Cuthbert's altruism.'

'Fine, but I'm not going near it. Corpses always give me the willies.'

'I, on the other hand, love carrying them to dungeons, the creepier the better' snapped Nicolo. 'We will roll him up in the rug and draw lots. Two of us can carry him down while another two distract any officials we may pass on the way. The rest of us will stay here and ensure no-one tries any funny business. '

'I say we all go' said Franco. 'There are none in this room who trust another completely and the stakes are too high to play chance with human nature.'

'You don't think eight people, including the doge's corpse here, escorting a rug to a dungeon will raise an eyebrow?' said the pope. 'You are fools of the highest order, gentlemen.'

'Then tell us your bright idea' said Cuthbert, showing insolence to the highest office of the religion he was formerly devoted to. 'Waiting for the rats to find him will have us making uncomfortable small talk for some considerable time.'

'You are in the papal office, peasant. Mind your tongue.'

'Why?' said Cuthbert.

'Well' said the pope, surprised. 'It's not the done thing, is it? I'm God's representative on earth and all that. You'll burn in hell.'

'Only if there is one' said Cuthbert flagrantly. 'What if there isn't a heaven or a hell? What then? Then we're simply two men standing in a room, one of whom has just shown a penchant for disposing of irritations.'

'If there is one? Of course there is one!'

'So you say, but I see no proof of such a fantastic claim. What I can see is a corpse on the floor. *Your* floor, pope, so you had better come up with a better idea than the dungeon if you wish to keep this scandal a secret.'

The pope caved. 'We could use the great fireplace here' he offered weakly.

'Perfect!' said Franco. 'We will leave him to burn and lock the door behind us. If anyone asks we'll say he is a victim of the pestilence and must burn to ashes before the doors can be reopened.'

'Then it's settled' said Jacques, clapping his hands in conclusion. 'What now?'

'We were stopping an assassin from murdering you' offered Robert.

'Ah yes. That' said the pope.

Franco rolled his eyes. 'This would be so much easier if any of you had the slightest experience dealing with corpses. I'm working with amateurs here.'

'I had to dig my grandmother's grave once' said Robert.

'Just the once?' said Franco. 'You must have done a good job then. Here, lift him up by the armpits.'

'I'm not going anywhere near his head' said Robert.

'Fine, I'll take the top half, you grab his feet.'

Robert crept to Giovanni's toes and tried to bend down. He failed to do so, looking back to Franco instead. 'Are you sure we have to...'

'Yes.'

'Right. Just wanted to be sure before I rolled the doge of Genoa inside a rug.'

Franco rubbed the bridge of his nose patiently. 'We're not rolling him in the rug, man. All that would achieve would be to burn a rather fetching piece of tapestry.'

'It's not tapestry, it's carpentry, or something like that' said Jacques.

'What is it with you and tapestries?' asked the pope.

'Gentlemen, please!' snapped Franco. 'Now, Robert. Please take the doge by his ankles and help me carry him to the fireplace.'

Robert crouched down, turned his head away from the dead feet and scrunched his eyes closed, just for good measure. He took a deep breath through his mouth and locked his fingers around Giovanni's ankles.

Franco hooked his arms under the armpits with the nonchalance of a man well used to cleaning up murderous actions. 'One... two... three... up!'

They wobbled and shuffled across the floor to the fireplace before swinging the body back and forth a few times to build some momentum. As they were about to let go Nicolo called out.

'Wait! Wait!'

Robert's grip failed, sending the cadaver to the floor with a damp thud.

'Jesus, Nicolo! We were almost done there. What are you playing at?'

'We should check his pockets first. There may be all kinds of valuable information in there.'

'He's got a point' said the pope. 'Cuthbert, you should be the one to check his pockets. You got us into this mess.'

'Fine' said Cuthbert flatly.

He stepped past the pope and knelt down beside Giovanni's still body. The dark green of his doublet was darker near the tear and glistened a little too much for Cuthbert's liking. He reached into the pocket and rummaged around with his fingers.

'Nothing' he declared.

'Can we get back to disposing of the body now?' asked Robert. 'As much as I'm enjoying it we do have other matters to attend to.'

They lifted the corpse again, swinging it back and forth and letting is drop onto the wide fire. Nothing happened for a few moments. Then there was a sizzle as the wetness of his clothes met the heat of the flame. It was a nauseous sound that caused the group to back away a few paces. Only Franco remained still, wiping his hands together as if dusting flour from his fingers.

'Now, to the next item on the agenda' he said.

The sizzle became louder.

'Let's go to a different room?' said the pope. 'I'm not standing here while a corpse burns beside us.'

'Where would you suggest?' said Franco. 'The kitchens perhaps? How about the altar in the cathedral?

Unless you can lock the doors from the inside and find us a secret tunnel to a private chamber then you will have to suffer the mild irritation as we plan the saving of your life. Is that agreeable to you?'

Pope Clement smirked as he crossed to a dark wooden cabinet on the far side of the room and opened a drawer. He pulled out a large iron key and locked the doors to the room.

'This way, gentlemen' he said, raising an eyebrow to Franco as if to say *like this?* 'A pope must have a means to hide safely from unwanted visitors.'

He leant on an unremarkable panel in the wall that swivelled as he did so, revealing a dark space behind. He gestured for them to follow as he climbed inside, feeling his way along the black corridor and stopping dead as his touch found what he was searching for. There was a click and a slow breeze of stale air. A dim light fell into the tunnel and one by one the group filed into a small room with a low ceiling, barely large enough to fit them all in.

One of the guards stopped outside and turned his back to them.

'Oi!' shouted Franco.

'Oh right sir, sorry sir' said the guard. 'Old habits die hard.'

'Well isn't this cosy?' said Robert. 'However, I feel it is a little unnecessary.'

'And what would make you say that?' asked Franco.

'Well, two things really' said Robert. 'Firstly, our plan is virtually complete. We go to the cathedral and wait while Jacques here says mass over and over. When the killer shows up we accost her and throw her in the dungeon. Am I missing something?'

'And your second point?' said Franco refusing to concede the slightest ground.

'Secondly, I would rather not spend much longer in such a small room with a plague victim. No offence, Cuthbert.'

'None taken.'

Jacques was the first to react, pushing past Robert and the two guards to the door and hurtling back down the dark passageway. The rest looked at each other briefly before trying to squeeze through the narrow door at the same time.

Cuthbert was the last of them to appear back in the papal office, stepping slowly over the threshold as he stared solemnly at the floor.

'I have only a few days left to me' he said. 'Let me be the last line of defence. Perhaps that will be enough to save me from the debauchery of my pilgrimage.'

'Then you should stay close to the altar' said Franco. 'Guards, you stay at the entrance to the cathedral. You know what needs to be done there. Check people for weapons too, if they lose their weapon they cease to be an assassin. The rest of us will spread out within the nave and watch for the woman.'

'We should have a signal for when we see her' said Nicolo.

'We could shout *there's the killer!*' offered Robert.

'And how would that help our discretion?' asked Franco seriously.

'It was a little joke' said Robert. 'You may not have encountered one before.'

'Perhaps it could work' said Franco, missing the sleight. 'It may cause a stampede, trapping her in a pile of the faithful.'

'I think it would be better if we remained in the shadows for as long as possible' said Jacques diplomatically. 'We can raise an arm if we think we have identified her. Left arm means they are to the left of the nave, right arm for the right side.'

'That could work too' said Franco, studying the ceiling of the room intensely as though the suggestion was written there.

'What if we're facing the entrance?' said one of the guards.

'Alright, forget about which way you're facing. Just raise an arm to show which direction they're in.'

'What then?' said one of the guards. 'Are we to leap onto the weapon ourselves?'

'If that's what it takes' said Cuthbert in the flat tones of a man who has resigned himself to his fate.

'It's alright for you, you'll be dead by the end of the week anyway' said the guard.

'Oh yes, I'm quite the lucky one' said Cuthbert.

'Gentlemen' said the pope. 'I think we are of one mind, despite the bickering. Jacques will be on the altar,

I will remain in the sacristy. We watch the cathedral until we are able to identify the woman. Once that is done you will raise an arm in signal and you all close in. If the six of you cannot take down a single woman then...' He cocked his head as if to suggest that wouldn't be a problem.

'Are we all agreed?' asked Franco.

There were varying degrees of enthusiasm in the nodding that followed.

'Wonderful, let's go.'

CHAPTER TWENTY NINE

The defenders spread out across the cathedral. Pope Clement lingered in the locked sacristy, peeking through a small crack where the door met the wall, while Jacques was at the pulpit preaching to the congregation on the merits of forgiveness. Cuthbert knelt piously in the front row of pews, acting out a role that would have required no effort just a few short weeks ago but now represented something of a challenge to him. Nicolo was standing against the outer wall a dozen rows behind him while Robert and Franco stood on the opposite side of the nave, all six of their eyes darting around the thronged space for signs of the killer. At the entrance were the two guards, struggling to stroll casually after years of patient immobility. To anyone with a mind to study them they appeared to be two men with leg stutters, twitching their way from one side of the doorway to another as if miming their way through invisible walls.

Jacques continued with his sermon, carefully setting a precautionary mood should events turn a little too visible. *'Come now, let us settle the matter, says the Lord. Though your sins are like scarlet, they shall be as white as snow; though they are red as crimson, they shall be like wool.'*

Hildegund strode up the steps to the cathedral entrance, the breeze flapping her brown hair against her face. She was approached by a guard who patted her down robustly before waving her on down the central aisle of the great nave. Her confident gait caught the attention of Franco and he moved down the edges of the pews to find a better line of sight. As she reached the front row she took a seat about a third of the way in, directly beside Cuthbert, and bowed her head in prayer. Franco retreated to his place, passing Robert as he did so.

'Not her. Wrong hair.'

'No need to tell me twice' said Robert, winking despite the gravity of the situation.

'Cease with your inanity' said Franco, impatience bubbling in his throat.

Nicolo didn't give her a second glance.

Jacques continued his performance. *'If you are willing and obedient, you shall eat the good of the land; but if you refuse and rebel, you shall be devoured by the sword, for the mouth of the Lord has spoken.'*

Hildegund muttered something under her breath. Cuthbert turned to her. 'Troubling times, aren't they?' he said.

She looked up, surprised to have conversation made with her so close to the cathedral altar.

'Times are always troubling' she said, noncommittally.

'Yet today we are all in danger, God's vengeance is gaining strength and we must do all we can to protect ourselves. Repentance is all that can save us now, wouldn't you say? I am glad to have a seat so close to the Holy Father in my time of greatest need.'

'Indeed.'

'If there is one place safe from trouble in all of Christendom it is surely here, in sight of His representative on earth.'

Hildegund's focus was wavering in the face of this wittering peasant. Her impatience bubbled to the surface. 'Then pray! That is what you are here to do, is it not? Our time here is finite and should not be wasted with chatter in such a sacred place.'

Irritation had diluted her concentration, uncloaking her accent a little and widening Cuthbert's eyes. He raised his left arm, then shouted with flustered excitement. 'Here! She is here!'

Hildegund punched Cuthbert hard in his cheek, sending his body to the floor and his mind to an instant sleep, albeit a brief one, for the second time in two days. She sprung from the pew and ran onto the altar, causing those still focused on Jacques' droning figure to scream in shock. Franco was already sprinting, cursing himself for letting their prey slip through his deductions with something as crass as a change in hair colour. He grabbed at Robert's cloak as he went, pulling the Englishman with him for a few paces before letting go. Robert followed, taking in the scene as he did so. People were beginning to react, strangers uninitiated

316 | *Cheating Death*

into this gang of papal protectors were getting in the way.

The crowd was descending on the altar.

Hildegund was only a few paces away from the false pope when something hit her on the back of the head. She turned around instinctively despite her desire to reach Jacques. The congregation had indeed risen up against her, but only as far as the step that defined the boundary of the altar. It was one thing to help protect a man of the cloth, but quite another to go so far as sacrilege in the process it seemed, especially when you were only there to reduce your net sinning quantum in the first place. A well aimed missal from the nave was better than a punch on the altar when the day of reckoning came.

She rubbed the back of her head and turned to Jacques, reaching him in a few long strides and pushing him over with an energetic shove. She pinned him down, using her knees to keep his shoulders flat against the cold floor and grabbed at the crucifix around his neck. She pulled hard, snapping the necklace and ripping the cap from the bottom to reveal a long, sharp point. She could hear someone arriving over her as she thrust the spike into Jacques' chest, calling out as she did so.

'For Steffen! Damnation for Heusch!'

Father Jacques Bricoler sagged, his muscles relaxing for the last time as Hildegund rolled off him to await her justice. Cuthbert landed on top of her, pulling her arms away from him and kneeling on her neck. He raised a fist to crash into the murderous face but as it reached its zenith it remained there, caught in the grip of Franco.

'No' he ordered. 'We still need her; she is in cahoots with the hag. There may be more surprises to come.'

Cuthbert relented, stepping off Hildegund and allowing Franco to restrain her. There was still a clear path to the sacristy, the power of the altar keeping the crowd at bay like magnetic poles. They headed straight for it, dragging Jacques and Hildegund with them, unaware that the pope was following their movements through the crack in the door. It opened just as Franco lunged for it, sending the group tumbling into the room in a manner that was considerably less dignified than they deserved.

Clement slammed the door shut, locking it behind him as he waved them towards another door. He led them through, into the passageways that were his route back to the palace.

They bustled into the papal office and were met with a rancid smell of burning flesh.

'Open a window someone!' ordered Franco.

'There must be somewhere else we can go' said Robert.

'There are ways to get to every part of the palace, from the dungeons to the roof. Some even I do not know. I do, however, know the way to my bedrooms. This way!' called Clement, ushering the befuddled group back out of the room.

'You have more than one?' said Robert.

To a man they ignored him, choosing instead to protect their immediate futures. Clement locked the door to his office and guided them through the labyrinth of corridors, stopping at last at a plain, narrow door. He unlocked it and stepped inside, allowing the group to follow him in before locking it behind him once more. The body of Jacques was laid on the floor and Cuthbert crossed the priest's arms over his chest. Pope Clement stood over him then, muttering words that Nicolo assumed were the last rites. They were a little late, but the thought was there. He tried to make out what he was saying in case he found himself in the presence of another expiring plague victim but the pope's voice was too quiet in the noisy room. Conversations were breaking out among them, the list of loose ends growing by the minute.

'Let's just throw him on top of Giovanni' said Robert.

'There is no need to hide his death, we didn't do this one' said Franco with a lucidity far exceeding that of anyone else present.

'Ah yes' said Robert. 'It's amazing how you can get used to murder really, isn't it?'

'Somebody tie this woman up' said Franco, trying his best to orchestrate the rabble. 'She is our only concern.

Father Bricoler will be given a proper funeral when the time comes. For now, all we must turn our minds to is what to do with her.'

'Am I the only one concerned at our dwindling numbers?' said Robert, searching for sanity in a cess pit of unpredictability. 'That's two of us now' he added.

'Is it really, pilgrim?' said the pope, condescension flowing from his voice. 'Thank you for the update. Since you are clearly the most astute among us you may also be aware that it is I who am most likely to make it three. There is an old woman out there with more information than we have. She may be acting out her great plan even as we stand here. We must deal with her before we can rest more easily in our beds.'

'I'm not sure I'd rest easy with a corpse listening to my snoring' said Robert.

'Are you quite finished?' said Franco. 'I appreciate that those inexperienced in such events are prone to reacting in different ways, but your constant search for a laugh from the crowd is beginning to get under my skin. I would advise caution before proclaiming your next great morsel of entertainment. The real men are busy trying to get us out of this predicament.'

Robert shrunk a little.

'We should take steps to find out what this woman knows' continued Franco. 'May I suggest a visit to the dungeons? There is an unusual air in those cavernous rooms that lends itself to honesty and openness.'

'Let us not delay' said the pope. 'We need information from her with all haste. Do it.'

'Hang on a minute' said Robert. He turned to Franco. 'This isn't a quip.'

Franco gave an impatient nod.

'We haven't even asked her what she knows yet. We should at least do that before we leap all the way to torture.'

'Who said anything about torture?' said the pope.

'Well, you know... dungeons? I would think it a reasonable assumption that a trip there isn't going to be for a private performance of *Madame Cribbins And Her Jolly Stockings*.'

'Go on then' said Franco, using his last drop of patience as he did so.

Robert turned to Hildegund. 'Tell us what you know about this old hag' he said.

'No' replied Hildegund.

Robert wasn't sure what his follow up question should be. 'Please?' he offered.

'No.'

Robert decided there and then to never get a job as an interrogator. 'Seems to me the dungeon might be the only way to get information from this one after all, she's a tough nut to crack.'

'Well you gave it a good go' said the pope. 'Now, if we could get back to business?'

'I'll take her downstairs and see what information can be liberated from her. Robert and Cuthbert, you go out onto the streets and search for the hag. If you find her, bring her back. If you are unsuccessful then I don't want to see either of you again. We live at different levels and I can't see any reason for us to pretend otherwise. If you cannot find a blind old woman then you are of no use to me.'

'You may have noticed we are, in fact, people' said Cuthbert, 'and not some merchant's goods to be used or discarded at the whim of an insignificant and amoral spy.'

'Oh *I* am the amoral one, am I? You may recall that it was not I who penetrated the heart of a doge with a dagger, Master Downey. If anyone here is to be tarred with an amoral reputation it is you and not I.'

'Quite the contrary' said Cuthbert, 'for I am acutely aware of the shamefulness of my actions, quite aware too of the fate that may now await me in the next life. Had it been you wielding the weapon I am not so sure you would have felt emotion of any kind. It is a man's reaction to events that determines their morality, Franco, not the deed itself.'

'We have no time for petty squabbles' interjected the pope. 'We must all play our part in our final act together. You will search for the hag and bring her back to the palace. Should you not find her then you will report what you have learnt back to us, even if that is nothing. Our acquaintance will then be at an end and you will be free to go about your business. Remember gentlemen, the doge may be dead but his eyes are not. Do not abandon your final post.'

'Or what?' said Cuthbert defiantly. 'Are you going to kill me? Because if you are I'd say you have about two days.'

'There are many different ways a man can leave this world' said Franco, 'and the pestilence should be your preferred method of departure, I can assure you of that.'

'Where are the guards?' said Nicolo to the room.

Several pairs of eyes roamed around their sockets as each member of the party scanned the room surreptitiously.

'I have sent them on another mission, one of great import' lied Franco, sure that they had taken their opportunity for escape rather more expediently than the others. 'Pay no heed to their movements. Now, what are we to do with you, Nicolo?'

'You will do nothing without my consent, let me be absolutely clear about that. My part in this is complete. I have delivered my message, after a fashion, and the one whose shackles restrained me is no longer the master of my fate. Plus he's dead, so either way, I'm off. It was nice catching up with you, old man. Perhaps one day I will find a way to reconcile your words with your actions. Until then, may you escape this pestilence and live a long and happy life. I will play no part in it, for that is the hand you have dealt.'

'You are wrong, Nicolo. On one point at least.'

'Do not try to justify yourself now, the wound you have opened is not one that can be closed with a few well placed words. Remember this; you may be a master of surveillance and diplomatic chicanery, but I am a master of words and deception. Do not try to sell to the salesman.'

'I do not doubt your talents, Nicolo, but you are aiming at the wrong target. You hope for me to live a long life, yet that will not be the case. I share a boat with your friend. Look.' He pulled up his tunic, revealing pustules in both armpits.

Nicolo felt an instant pang of loss, but not for the man standing before him. He felt for the father in Catania, the hard working fisherman he knew as a child. This man was a different person entirely, one who had diluted his memories and consigned the provenance of his upbringing to the flames. Had the father of his childhood spoken those words he would have buckled to the floor.

'My father died when he fell into the papal office and revealed himself as a charlatan. Do not seek to harvest pity when all you have sown is doubt.'

'Then I will commit my final effort to the search of this hag. May my last action be that of a good and honest man.'

'Then you should consider something a little more wholesome than torturing this woman. I can say with some confidence that violent interrogations are not on St Peter's *good deeds* list.'

Franco flinched uncomfortably. His son was right, but he had no choice. He had to go to the dungeons with Hildegund, for good or ill.

'Think better of me as my passing diminishes in the mists of your memory, Nicolo. There is much I would wish to tell you, but I have neither time nor authority to do so.'

'Your shortage of time negates a requirement for permission' said Nicolo. 'Do what you must, you are but a memory to me even now.'

He looked into his father's thawing eyes, turning then to the two Englishmen. 'Robert, I suggest we search for this wretched woman as best we can. It is the only way to untangle us from this sordid mess. Cuthbert, you should spend your last days in whatever way you see fit.'

'I will help you, if you will have me so close' said Cuthbert. 'A man must have something to live for if he is to extend his time on this earth. If I enter a tavern alone it would be a short cut to the grave.'

'Then it's settled. We will search for the woman until your health requires us to help make you comfortable.' He crossed over to the pope and gave a small genuflection. 'With your blessing we will leave you and the spy to make appropriate arrangements for Father Bricoler's last journey. It has been an enlightening experience, Holy Father. May your reign henceforth be less turbulent.'

'Go' said Pope Clement VI. 'I will deal with Father Bricoler and await your report.'

The three men wanted nothing more than to sprint down the corridors of the Palais des Papes and were to be commended for the restrained nature of their exit.

Robert shook the pope's hand awkwardly, unsure of the correct protocol to abide by when offering a goodbye to the Supreme Pontiff of the Universal Church. He blanked Franco and followed Nicolo to the door.

Cuthbert walked over to the pine table, picking up a small scroll with a broken red seal. He stepped up to the pope and held it out. 'My father asked I leave this within sight of the pope. I now doubt its importance, but here it is in any case. I have done what was asked of me, and may God judge whether my actions are worthy.'

The pope took the scroll and read it to himself. 'I will see to it that these petitions are made.' He turned to Franco. 'If you have the means to do so, send word to Cuthbert's father that his son fulfilled his last promise. Send something of value with it too, I will not have his family feel hunger while I have means to stave it.'

'You are generous indeed, Holy Father' said Cuthbert with more faithful conviction than he had felt since he left Calais. He was perilously close to his day of reckoning and it would do no harm to fudge his numbers a little. He turned away from the pope and followed his friends out of the papal office, ignoring Franco as he did so.

CHAPTER THIRTY

Franco closed the dungeon door behind him, fastening several locks and shuttering the small viewing window. His work often demanded privacy, this time more than ever. To the trained eye the room was divided into sections of ever increasing persuasiveness. There was a modest set of stocks near the door for those at the beginning of their tortuous journey. At the far end of the room was the dreadful rack, a device whose notable absence of spikes and blades belied its effectiveness. Quite astonishing results can often be garnered from the most basic of principles. Franco was an admirer of the rack; he had witnessed some of the most complex torture machines in the world but none compared to the fundamental eloquence of stretching a man's limbs with an oversized screw.

He ushered Hildegund to a bench at one end of the room and asked her to sit.

'Do you know why you are here?' he asked.

'If you think you hold the answer to such a seemingly innocuous question then we are going to be here a while' said Hildegund, stoic defiance roaring from her eyes.

'Oh, I don't believe we will be here too long' said Franco. 'I will learn all the information I require in a few short moments, then you will be free.'

'Death is not freedom, spy. For me, death is the end. I am long resigned to my fate, so you may have your fun and do what you will. There will be no revelation from my wracked body, no final submission to your will.'

'There is much for you to learn, woman, for I have but one simple question. Why does your resolve remain so ferrous in the face of certain doom?'

'Any fortitude I may exude is born of a desire to see justice for the life of my brother. That I failed is a wrong I cannot right. Have your tools test my integrity, for there is nothing of value in my mind. You will elicit nothing, spy, and may your imminent reckoning be a reflection of your actions.'

'Ah, but your mind holds information that is of value to some, *spy*' said Franco.

'I am no spy!' snapped Hildegund.

Franco knelt by a small grate in the wall, forcing its reluctant hinges to shriek as he opened it. 'You are now' he said. 'This leads to an opening beyond the palace grounds. It is not a pleasant journey, but there is life on the other side, at least. The old doge may be dead, but the network of his office remains and there is one cog in that great machine that is in need of replacement.'

'I have neither the skills nor the inclination for such a position' said Hildegund.

'You underestimate your talent, woman. There are few who can travel from so far to achieve something of such significance as the murder of the pope himself.'

'I failed. The pope remains in the palace and my brother's vengeance goes unfulfilled.'

'Yet you killed the visible pope. There are not many in this world who could have foreseen such an unprecedented turn of events. Take my place. Vengeance may be your only driving force as you sit here, but we all change. What seems vital to our existence in one moment may be but a trivial distraction in another. I see no reason why you should extinguish such a flickering chance at a new life.'

'I will not do it. I surrendered my life when I set out from my home in the east. I am no fool, I knew the consequences of my actions. Whether I succeeded in my mission or failed, the attempt alone was enough to ensure my days would end at the moment of truth. When one has acquiesced to one's fate there is little that can be said to alter your perspective. You will come to realise this in the coming hours.'

'You will be dead to the world, Hildegund. Free to live a new life with people who would see you as a stranger. Think of the power you would hold over them; their lives would be yours to control, for you will have the ear of the doge, whoever that may turn out to be. If I swear to your honour he will trust your judgment. Make a new life for yourself and do not waste your gift. Perhaps it will give you opportunity enough to avenge your brother, should fate allow it. I would counsel strongly against episcopicide, however.'

'There is much I would need to know before embarking' said Hildegund, sidestepping the inferred request. 'Are you prepared to pass on the knowledge of your great secrets to an uninitiated woman, one whose commitment to your crusade is not yet secure?'

'Then let us tether it to the great cause. All that is required is an oath to bind you to the Genoese empire. Once those words are spoken I will pass all I know on to you, including how to make it through the tunnels.'

'Does the oath include a faithful pledge to God?' said Hildegund.

'No. It is a pragmatic man's oath. Religion only serves to muddy the waters of truth and honesty.'

'Then we are agreed. I will be a fair and just spy.'

'That's what we all think at the start.'

CHAPTER THIRTY ONE

The three men sat at their table in the Greave Dunning and stared blankly into tankards of warm ale. They were at a crossroads and all were reluctant to open negotiations. It was Cuthbert who broke the silent impasse, his face beginning to glisten in the cold room.

'I should not be considered in your decision' he said. 'My time is surely measured in hours and my fall will be swift. I am now nought but a burden to you.'

'Cheer up, friend' said Robert. 'We will look after you until the end comes, then we will decide what to do. You need not concern yourself with our petty strife.'

'Would you grant a wish to a dying man?' said Cuthbert.

'Of course, anything' said Robert.

'Promise?'

'Of course I would. You too, Nicolo, right?'

Nicolo stirred from his daydream. 'Whuh?'

'Cuthbert has a final wish.'

'You have to promise' said Cuthbert.

'We do' said Robert, kicking out at Nicolo under the table.

'Yes, we do' said Nicolo.

'You have to say you promise. I need a full sentence from you, an oath.'

'Is your final wish a request to be a merciless pedant for a day or two?' said Robert. 'Because if it is, then I think you've aimed a little low. You can ask anything of us, as we would of you if our positions were reversed.'

'Full sentence. *Please.*'

Robert and Nicolo exchanged looks, breathed in deeply, and said together 'We promise to grant you your dying wish.'

Cuthbert nodded gently. 'Thank you.'

'Well?' asked Robert.

'My final wish is for you to climb with me to the roof of the palace and leave me there.'

'Then that is what we shall do' said Nicolo.

They sat in motionless silence again, none of them having a stomach for their ale.

'Are you ready?' asked Robert.

'No, but then who answers otherwise?' said Cuthbert.

Robert and Nicolo walked in a trance through the busy market square. Neither spoke of their journey to the roof of the palace, nor of the conversation that unfolded there. Their shared reflection required no words; it spoke for itself. They passed stallholders pleading for business without hearing them, they passed the raised victims of the pestilence as they were carried to carts without seeing them, and they were pushed out of the way by disconsolate family members without feeling them.

They did hear a thud from the floor close to the palace wall far behind them and the clamour that followed. They walked on in a deeper silence.

CHAPTER THIRTY TWO

Pope Clement VI knelt next to the lifeless body of his old friend. There had been many years of separation and they had both changed greatly during that time, but the man was a leading player in their symbiotic memories. They had shared their formative years as young men and nothing in the intervening period could alter that, other than to add nuance to the emotions that would be evoked whenever he reminisced on simpler times.

It had been a strange time since Jacques' arrival. His agenda, if indeed there was one, was still unclear to him. If he was the victim of a coup, then it was poorly executed; there seemed little that Jacques' actions would gain him in the long term. Perhaps this was only the opening act of an intricately planned conspiracy. Perhaps there was no ulterior motive at all. Time would not tell, nor conjecture resolve.

He poured oil from a crystal jug onto his fingers and made the sign of the cross on his friend's forehead, muttering again the prayer reserved for those on their way to the next life. He blessed himself and stood again, made his way out of the room and headed for the Cardinal's quarters. Jacques would be given a farewell fitting of a pope, whether he deserved one or not.

✝

Franco bustled through the throngs of the market place, feeling his aching body begin its long, slow sag as he went.

'Son!'

He scanned the faces of the crowd frantically, hoping to catch sight of Nicolo among the panicked expressions. Fear was everywhere, not least within himself.

'Son!'

Nothing.

He squeezed between the fountain and a group of gesticulating men without pausing, grazing his arm on the rough stone as he pushed his body through the gap. Without breaking stride he rolled up his sleeve and felt the raw graze that was already appearing just below his elbow. He rubbed it gently and winced a little at the pain before slamming to a dead stop beside a baker's stall.

'You alright, sir?' said the baker.

Franco stared through the wound and on towards his future.

'I said, are you alright? Can I help you?'

Franco looked up slowly. A passion filled his eyes, wild but euphoric.

'This wound will never heal. I must make amends' he said, and ran off towards the opposite end of the square.

'Right you are, sir' said the baker. 'Nice day for it.'

'Son!'

Franco had careered around the city for almost an hour now, calling out as his body struggled to keep up with the exertion. He stopped outside a tavern and leant against its wall, breathing heavily. He wondered how he was going to find him before the plague found his heart. A young boy scurried past him, eyes full of mischief. A short, thin woman followed him at an increasing distance, shouting as she moved.

'Claude, you damned nuisance, get back here now before I set your father on you!'

Franco looked between the boy and the woman. He straightened himself again, puffed out his chest and roared as loudly as he could muster.

'NICOLO!'

A horde of eyes turned to him and those closest to the tavern wall quickly moved away from the apparent drunkard. The sound of a falling bench came from within the tavern, following shortly after by that of old iron hinges creaking open more quickly than they would like.

'Father?' said Nicolo.

'Nicolo, my son!' said Franco, falling against his son's body as his cried enough. 'Thank the stars I have found you in time.'

'In time for what?' asked Nicolo, still sceptical despite the poor man's condition.

'Inside. We both need a drink.'

'Three' said the barman.

Robert placed three coins on the table and set two of the mugs in front of Nicolo and his father. 'I'll be over there getting drunk' he said, pointing to an empty table in the corner of the room. 'Take all the time you need.'

Nicolo turned his mug so the handle was facing away from him, took a large draught of the ale and looked his father in the eye.

'So tell me, what is so important that you feel the need to spend your last precious moments on this earth with the very person you betrayed so emphatically?'

'I did not betray you, Nicolo. I protected you.'

'Did you protect me in the doge's palace? Did you protect me in Piombino? In Livorno? Marseilles?'

'Yes.'

'No. You abandoned me to the whims of fate that herded me towards the rising plague. That is not protection, that is desertion.'

'And are you so sure that I deserted you? Do you know for certain that that is the course of action I took? Remember, Nicolo, there is a difference between protection and interference.'

'I don't remember you doing either while I flirted with the pestilence in Bassifondi. You may be here in the hope that I will relent and forgive you as you expire, but I have said goodbye to the Franco who raised me, the Franco who taught me how to gut a fish and tie a knot with one hand behind my back. He became a memory in the papal palace when I saw Franco the spy for the first time. My father died in the Palazzo Pubblico of Genoa the day he gave me up to di Murta.'

'And yet I saw fit to travel to Piombino and live like a vagrant while you slept in the warmth of the Keystones tavern.'

Nicolo's eyes narrowed.

'Having knowledge of a scene does not place you there, *Franco*. The network you live in is vast and there are, I am sure, many who would relinquish such information for the right price. What your spy did not tell you, it seems, is that I spoke to the tramp and it was not you. You may be a more deceptive man than I thought possible but I know the sound of my own father's voice.'

Franco took a sip of his ale and cleared his throat. 'I wouldn't go in there if I were you, sir. There is something hanging in the air.'

Had Nicolo's eyes not already narrowed they would have done so. He was taken back to the door of the Keystones tavern at the Piombino docks, to the smell of the air and the vision of hell he had witnessed above the tannery. The memory stretched out until it met his childhood coming the other way. He thought of simpler times; of certainty and predictability. He felt an unexpected urge to return to those days in Catania and navigate the course of his life again. Would he travel a different path, or would the winds of fate sail him to the gates of the Palazzo Pubblico once more.

'Now do you believe me?' asked Franco.

Nicolo's thoughts came back to the room. 'I believe that you were there, but I am yet to be convinced you travelled with my protection in mind. You were Giovanni's man, father; to follow me was to do his bidding and you have shown me nothing that proves your intentions to be anything other than that. You may have convinced me of your location but that proves nothing.'

'Then there is no more I can say. I had hoped to hear my son forgive me as my days ticked down, but I see that I have caused more hurt than I had imagined.'

Franco pushed his seat backwards and stood to his full height.

'I am going to the cathedral to die in our Lord's house. You may forgive me now or when I am in the earth, but please forgive me Nicolo, my son.'

He walked out of the tavern, the creak from the hinges echoing in Nicolo's mind. He would always remember their noise as the last action of his father's that he would experience.

✝

'What are we to do?' said Robert as they sat quietly at the fountain.

Nicolo tried to stoke his pragmatism amid the storm of emotions that clouded his thoughts. 'We have but two options, to stay or to leave' he said at last. 'If we leave we cannot go south, as much as I yearn to see Catania again. The pestilence has ravaged the people there.'

'So we can go north or search for the hag' said Robert.

'I am in no mood for decisions. Let us take the path of least resistance for once. We can spend a short while looking for the blind woman, then head north when we have failed, for that is surely what will come of any attempt.'

'Agreed. We can go north to my home in England. It is a plain life there but likely to be free from this disaster. If it is not, then we will continue north to the ends of the earth.'

'There is one thing I must do before we leave the city. It won't take long.'

The crowd in front of them parted and a tall, dark haired woman holding a rag over her face approached them, tossing them a scrap of parchment before slinking away into the throng once more. Robert picked it up and read the scrawled writing, then handed it to Nicolo. It read:

"I am gone. The twilight of my life will not be determined by those with more power than compassion. Do not look for clues, there are none you can use to follow or find me, for I do not yet know in which direction I will head. Wherever I choose to end my days will be a place ignorant of the events here. Leave me to my peace and my reckoning."

Nicolo crossed the threshold of the cathedral once more. The scene inside was chaotic, the faithful contorted in collective fear after the day's events. Some were showing their repentance energetically, throwing themselves to the floor repeatedly at the feet of the stone saints. Others knelt piously amid the hubbub and prayed silently for an escape, be it from the claws of the pestilence or the diminishingly iron grip of this world.

He ignored those in the open, instead searching the dark alcoves where he would surely be hiding. In front of him now was the altar with the transept stretching the walls away from him on either side. He turned to his left, just as he had done as a young boy in the church of St Augustine the Meek, and saw the unmistakable shadow. He approached it and knelt down until his mouth was almost touching the man's ear. He could see the chest rising and falling weakly in a shallow rhythm.

'I forgive you.'

CHAPTER THIRTY THREE

'Not you two again' said the first guard at the entrance to the Palais des Papes. 'Don't think you can get past us so easily this time. Once beaten, twice tried.'

'It's once bitten, twice shy' said Robert.

'No it's not' said the first guard. 'That doesn't make any sense at all, and who said anything about biting anyway? You've tried to get past us twice now, and we were beaten the first time.'

'And don't call us shy' said the second guard. 'Nobody calls us shy and gets away with it.'

Nicolo's parchment thin patience ripped. He punched the second guard square in the jaw and walked on into the palace.

The first guard aimed a fist towards Robert but stopped at the look in the Englishman's eyes. There was something immovable there, a resolution that warned against provocation.

'I'm sure his holiness will be pleased to see you again' said the first guard, opening his body to let Robert through.

'I wouldn't count on it.'

The two men made their way through the corridors to the papal office. The great doors were still locked and a subtle odour lingered in the air. It promised an olfactory experience altogether more physical should they be inclined to open the doors. They weren't, so they moved on to the bedrooms, the place where they last saw the pope and where they hoped they would see him for the final time.

They entered without knocking, a sign of how accustomed they had become in mingling with the Avignon elite. The pope lay on his bed with a pillow placed deliberately over his face to block out the world.

'We have news' announced Nicolo. He had prepared his speech well, planning to keep the details ambiguous and the opportunity for cross examination minimal. He continued without waiting for a response. 'The hag is not long for this world and has left the city, never to return. She had this message delivered to us.' He handed the parchment to the pope. 'Our bargain is fulfilled. We will leave the city today, your holiness, and may the pestilence spare your papacy.'

The pope did not speak, instead removing the pillow from his face and hoisting himself up onto his elbows. He drew in a great breath and lifted his chin to take in the visitors.

'Leave us' he ordered.

Robert and Nicolo looked about them for signs of another person in the room. Their gazes landed on the body of Jacques, then on each other.

'He's losing it' said Robert. 'Let's go.'

They nodded respectfully and backed slowly out of the room, their involvement in high politics finally drawing to a close.

As they walked the corridors of the Palais des Papes for the last time, Nicolo turned to Robert, his mind rekindling a mischief that had been dormant for longer than he cared to admit.

'That was terribly nice of him to offer all the food and drink we can carry, don't you think? We have a long journey ahead of us, no harm in making the most of the papal kitchen before we start.'

Robert's eyes glinted. 'Don't forget his offer of horses. Heroes like us should ride off into the sunset on jet black steeds, it's only proper.'

'Come on then' said Nicolo, grabbing Robert's arm and pulling him down the stairs. 'The papal kitchens won't pilfer themselves.'

EPILOGUE

The plague had rescinded at last, but not before it had shepherded them to the far north of Scotland, home of hills and little else. They had settled down in a small fishing community with another dozen or so souls and opened the villagers' first tavern. Quite how the locals had survived until then was a mystery to both of them. Nicolo insisted on naming it, arguing that his first sighting of the pestilence should be remembered, for all that it was a symbol of doom for so many. Robert had agreed and together they were making a success of the Keystones tavern.

Robert filled a wooden tankard with ale and delivered it to his customer. 'The usual, Fingal.'

Fingal nodded in thanks without looking up from his drunken study of the table.

'You're welcome' said Robert.

He passed through the tight doorway that led to the kitchen. Inside were his three children, now in their teenage years and each busy with their daily tasks. Dishes were being washed, floors were being scrubbed and vegetables were being chopped. He passed them and climbed the precarious staircase to their living quarters.

His wife sat in the small room, ignoring him effortlessly as he entered.

'Evening, wife' he said.

'Is it?' she asked bitterly. 'I wouldn't say there was anything good about it in this godforsaken ice box.'

'I simply said it was evening, I never suggested it was...' He trailed off, choosing to avoid the inevitable argument that would follow. 'Watch the tavern tonight, I'm going out in the boat with Nicolo.'

He walked out of the room with the confident gait of a man who knew he was the boss of his little kingdom, then slunk back in like a child when he realised he had forgotten his hat.

'Don't let Fingal get too drunk. I don't want the girls cleaning potage from the walls again.'

Nicolo wrapped the holy blanket around his shoulders. He would have to buy a new one before the winter set in again, one with fewer gaps for the wind to find as he sat in their small fishing boat. Robert passed him a hunk of mutton.

'This is the life, eh?' said Nicolo.

'I should have left the wife behind' said Robert, ignoring his friend's remark. 'I could have gone straight by Aldridge-on-the-Grange and been a happier man for it.'

'Ah, but you'd miss the children no matter what you might say. Living with your wife is a price you must pay I'm afraid.'

'Perhaps I could get her a job in the town. She'd make a great housekeeper for someone.'

'Forget it, if the pestilence couldn't separate you then a few miles of heather certainly won't. Anyway, we have this boat. Think of it as a mini pilgrimage every couple of days. Plus, we have as much ale as we can quaff now. No need to put on a show every time we want a drink.'

'There is that, I suppose' said Robert. 'Maybe this is as good as it gets.'

'Until the next life. There is always the promise of eternity in heaven.'

'I can't drink a promise, Nicolo. I'd rather have a happy life now than the promise of something intangible.'

'You sound like my father.'

'At least he's living the high life in heaven now.'

'Quite so.'

Nicolo watched the floats on his fishing net bob gently in the water. This *is* the life, he thought. Now that the chaos of Avignon was behind him it was safe for him to allow his mind to linger on the events there. At the time he was caught up in the whirlwind of high politics and of helping to prevent episcopicide, but here on the still loch in high summer he found the mental space to process all that had happened and ruminate on the fates of those he left behind. He had heard no news on the whereabouts of the Germanic woman, nor the hag, and he could only assume they had returned to their lives, such as remained of them. The pope was still the pope, as far as he knew, and Jacques and Giovanni were most definitely still dead. Cuthbert, however, lived on in the memories he shared with Robert, and Nicolo could think of no better testament to the man. Their acquaintance may have been brief, but Cuthbert's impact on his approach to life was incalculable. The conman that set out from Catania so long ago was lost somewhere in the travels that brought him to this quiet Scottish waterside, and he was all the more contented for it.

Robert turned to his friend and nudged him from his daydreaming. He raised a piece of mutton in salute. 'Here's to the quiet life, Nicolo.'

'Amen to that.'

THE END

HISTORICAL NOTE

I have always enjoyed historical notes. To me, the accuracy of the book's content comes second to the enjoyment of the story but it is always nice to learn which parts were real and which imagined. By now you may have noticed that Cheating Death is a satirical take on this dark period in human history, and as such I was less concerned about historical accuracy than the story. That said, I would like to calibrate a few points on the off chance that any reader has chosen to take any of the preceding information as gospel.

Firstly, a few of the characters are real historical figures, in name at least. Pope Clement VI was the pope, based in Avignon, when the Black Death reached the city. His papacy was defined by a lavish lifestyle and a vigorous reduction of the papal coffers. Coincidentally, he died twenty years to the day from the opening of this story, on the 6th December 1352.

Giovanni di Murta was the doge of Genoa in 1347. Though he must surely have nurtured some level of espionage during his reign, there is nothing to suggest it was as omnipresent as I have made it out to be.

The plague had been rife in Asia for a number of years before it reached Europe. An estimated twenty five million people are said to have died there. While there were several landings of the plague in Europe, it is considered a truth that it first reached Europe from the Crimea, with Genoese galleys landing in Sicily in October 1347, shortly before Nicolo's initial meeting with Giovanni.

The Flagellant movement was rife in areas similar to Darmstadt in what is now Germany, though the timeline is a little skewed. The plague reached there after it hit Avignon, and the Flagellants rose up once the disease had ravaged a significant portion of the population. It was a reaction to the hypothesis that God was punishing his people for their errant ways. I moved the timing of its arrival there to allow Hildegund to make the journey in time to meet Nicolo coming the other way.

If you're now at a loose end, I recommend translating some of the incidental characters' names.

Mrs Cabbage was not a famed baker of special apple buns in Umbridge. As far as I can tell it was her currant buns that were her most cherished creation.

www.ingramcontent.com/pod-product-compliance
Lightning Source LLC
Chambersburg PA
CBHW030402180626
46812CB00005B/1893